Wolf

Also by Jim Harrison

FICTION

CHILDREN'S LITERATURE

POETRY

ESSAYS

MEMOIR

JIM HARRISON

Wolf

Grove Press
New York

First published by Simon&Schuster in 1971

Published simultaneously in Canada
Printed in the United States of America

This Grove Atlantic edition: December 2018

This book was set in 12 pt Cochin by Alpha Design & Composition of Pittsfield, NH

Library of Congress Cataloging-in-Publication data is available for this title.

ISBN 978-0-8021-2887-4
eISBN 978-0-8021-9006-2

Grove Press
an imprint of Grove Atlantic
154 West 14th Street
New York, NY 10011

Distributed by Publishers Group West

groveatlantic.com

18 19 20 21   10 9 8 7 6 5 4 3 2 1

TO
TOM McGUANE
and
In Memoriam, MISSY 1966-1971

When you wake up, with the remains of a paradise half-seen in dreams hanging down over you like the hair on someone who's been drowned . . .
—JULIO CORTAZAR, *Hopscotch*

Author's Note

When the dog barks or growls her warning in the night I question whether it will be a stray cat, a skunk, a killer or a ghost. It occurred to me the other morning that people don't talk about death because even to the simplest of them death isn't very interesting. Of course this all changes when it draws near to the particular individual but until then death has the probability, the actuality of our moon shot to a zebra. There must be reasons why I seem to closet funerals and weddings and love affairs together: mortal accidents, simply the *given* on which a shabby structure may be subtracted or added. Even now the challenge of having risked a pomposity and perhaps won its opprobrium is a signal that a new shower of lint and sulphur should fall to further laminate the human condition in its habitual shield of filth. An obtuse paragraph is always toxic. But to get on with the story— I'm not going to talk about death. This is a memoir dealing mostly with the years 1956-1960 written from the vantage of the present—it is a false memoir at that and not even chronological and its author is a self-antiqued thirty-three, a juncture when literary souls always turn around and look backward. Most of the poisons have been injected, some self-inflicted; how does one weigh mental scar tissue? I'm sure a device will finally be invented but at this point in history we must settle for prose, and no matter how many fans they have, nature, love and bourbon have been proven failures as cancer cures. My name happens to be Swanson, neither a very true nor honorable name — not true because the name had been given my grandfather, a Swede, on Ellis Island: immigration officials had decided that too many Nordic immigrants possessed the same or similar names and it would be much simpler if they were changed totally or new ones found somewhere in the ancestry. Each entering soul was given a polite three minutes to think it over. Swanson it became though hardly the grandson or son of swan; my first is Carol, to be avoided as feminine, the second, Severin, is too arch and foreign, so I am insistently Swanson to myself and to anyone who cares to call me anything. And not honorable because no one in the short, rather known, history of my family has done anything worth taking note of — the births mostly took place in the home and the marriages were hurried private affairs often with the question of the legitimacy of a child imminent. My one grandfather was a failed farmer with over a half century given to a nearly arid sixty acres. He died without having managed the price of a tractor and left an unpaid mortgage to his heirs. The other grandfather was a retired lumberjack, troublemaker, farmer, lout, drunk. An aunt given to fripperies claims that a distant relative had graduated from Yale early in the nineteenth century but nobody believes her. My father was the first on either side of the familial fence to graduate from college; he became a government agriculturist during the Great Depression and died in a violent accident, by any fair estimation an unhappy man. In deference to the cult of star buffs, I was born a Sagittarian deep in the unusually nasty winter of 1937; my childhood was pleasant and completely unremarkable and will barely be touched upon again.

Anyway, here is the story, the fiction, the romance — "My frame was wrenched by a woeful agony which forced me to tell my tale," someone said a long time ago. I've never seen a wolf — zoo beasts are not to be counted; they are ultimately no more interesting than dead carp, sullen, furtive, morose. Perhaps I'll never see a wolf. And I don't offer this little problem as central to anyone but myself.

Wolf

Chapter 1

Huron Mountains

You could travel west out of Reed City, a small county seat in an unfertile valley with a small yellow brick courthouse and a plugged cannon on its lawn next to a marble slab with the names of the World War One and Two dead inscribed in gold and the not dead plainly inscribed with the suspicious neatness of cemetery script, *those who served*, farther west through fifty miles of pine barrens dotted with small farm settlements often of less than thirty people, or merely a grocery store and gas station adjoined by a shabby aluminum trailer or a basement house with the first and perhaps second stories awaiting more prosperous times, the stores themselves with little and aged stock — lunch meat, bologna pickled in a jar, Polish sausage, tinned foods covered with dust, plaquettes of fish lures, mosquito repellent in aerosol cans, live bait and a pop cooler outside the door — but not many of these — a narrow road through mixed conifers,

cedar and jack pine, some stunted scrub oak, birch, and
the short-lived poplar, a pulp tree usually living less than
twenty years and clotting the woods floor with its rotting
trunks and branches, and west through the low pelvic mysteries of swamps divided invisibly from the air by interlock-
ing creeks and small rivers, made unbearable in spring and
summer by mosquitoes and black flies, swamps dank with
brackish water and pools of green slime, small knolls of
fern, bog marshes of sphagnum, spongelike and tortuous
to the human foot and bordered by impenetrable tamarack
thickets: in short a land with no appreciable history and
a continuously vile climate, lumbered off for a hundred
years with few traces of the grand white pine which once
covered it, an occasional charred almost petrified stump
four feet in diameter, evidence of trees which rose nearly
two hundred feet and covered the northern half of the
state and the Upper Peninsula, razed with truly insolent
completeness by the lumber barons after the Civil War with
all the money going to the cities of the south—Saginaw,
Lansing, Detroit—and east to Boston and New York; and
the houses, even the large farmhouses on reasonably good
land, sloppily built, ramshackle and craftless compared to
Massachusetts or Vermont; west to Lake Michigan then to
turn north along its coast to the Straits of Mackinac, cross
the mammoth bridge, travel west another three hundred
miles through the sparsely populated Upper Peninsula and
then north again into the comparatively vast, the peopleless Huron Mountains.

❊   ❊   ❊

I crawled out of the sleeping bag and dipped a cup of water from a small tin pail but the water had warmed and a breeze during the night had blown some ashes into it and they mixed there in the surface film with dead mosquitoes. I drew on my pants and boots and walked to the creek. Dew had soaked the grass and ferns, made the leaves limp under my feet; earth was pale green a half hour before the sun would come up and over and through the ridge of trees to the east. I knelt and drank from the creek, the water so cold the teeth ached. I closed the tent flaps, gathered my binoculars (which I would quickly lose) and a worthless .30-30 rifle with bad sights my father had owned, and took a compass reading which I knew would be inaccurate and pointless as the ground in the area was full of varying amounts of iron ore. But I fixed on a knoll a mile or so away and then on the supposed direction of the car several miles directly south by southwest and set out for a hike. Two hours later I was unfathomably lost.

There is a brief time when first lost that you are sure you will be lost forever. Your heart flutters and you become winded with little walking and everything you know or think you know about the woods is forgotten, or you aren't sure you ever knew enough in the beginning. The compass reads an impossible direction. The view from the treetop you reach with effort reveals only the tops of other trees, or if you follow a stream you know you are walking at least three times further than necessary as the stream winds and twists, makes heavy-growthed flats with hairpin bends and builds swampy areas that make walking very wet and the footing unsure, the mosquitoes clouding around your head as you move. It is first of all embarrassment mixed with a little terror; when the frantic pumping ceases and you regain your breath it is easy enough to turn around and retrace the path you've thrashed through the brush. The rare deaths that do occur are simply a matter of the lost waiting too long to turn around.

I lay along a tree trunk fallen half across the stream, its roots weakened by the undercut bank. I dozed for a while in the sun, then upon waking sighted the rifle from this prone position at a leaf, then at a large cropping of rocks downstream from the tree.

I had wanted to move farther upstream and set up camp on higher ground to get some breeze and to be less vulnerable to the bugs but I only found the tent in the middle of the evening. It was ten o'clock and still not quite dark when I ate my supper of boiled pinto beans and onions. I doused the entire plateful with red pepper sauce and lay back against a tree thinking how much I wanted a drink, a large water glass filled with warm whiskey, or a succession of doubles with beer used as a chaser. I thought back to the Kettle of Fish bar on Macdougal Street where I first began drinking in earnest. Everyone there seemed twice my age (I was eighteen) and I could get dizzy on four glasses of ale. Eighty cents. But habits are of interest only to the habitual-fat men talk about their diets for hours without boredom, shedding imaginary pounds. I took a long drink of water to wash the fire from my throat and looked at my watch in the firelight. Stopped again; I slipped the watch off noticing the strip of white skin beneath it on the wrist somehow not related to the rest of my body. A friend had a *pachuco* cross carved beneath his watchband. I flipped this seven-dollar special into the fire thinking idly that in the heat the hands might whirl backwards or in reverse of those old movie montages where a calendar's pages are flipped and trains crisscross the nation from corner of screen to corner of screen, from triumph to triumph with a star's name growing ever larger on the billboards and marquees. I rubbed mosquito dope onto my hands and face and neck and crawled into the sleeping bag.

We drove down a gravel road bordered on both sides with Lombardy poplars which had begun to die with leaves gone on the topmost branches. My father fiddled with the radio then said no ballgame today it's Monday. We turned into a driveway and moved jouncing over ruts to a farmhouse which from the road had been concealed in a grove of elm and maple trees. When we stopped two dogs rushed out from under the porch as if to devour the car to get at us. My father got out and said come along but I stayed in the car, in part not to get my new shoes dirty which since we left town I had been rubbing busily against the back of my pantleg for a shine. He left and the dogs didn't bother him. They looked like they were from the same litter—half collie and half shepherd—I had had a similar dog a few years before, Penny, but she had bitten the mailman and we had to give her to a farmer who I learned later shot her for killing chickens. I heard laughter and turned in the car to see in the far corner of the shaded yard three girls playing with a swing. There was an elm tree and from a lower branch a rope was suspended with a tire attached to it; they were taking turns swinging, and the oldest had to lift the smallest who was about five up into the tire which she straddled, a leg on either side. The little one had lost three fingers on one hand and had some lilacs between the thumb and fore-finger, holding the swing with the other hand. The lilacs were growing along a ditch on the far side of the house. It was May and they were blooming white and purple in great clumps and their heavy scent mixed with the smell of wild mint from the ditch. The house was covered with brown imitation brick siding, nearly a trademark for the poor, with a cement porch darkened with tall honeysuckle bushes. The oldest girl who looked about twelve got into the swing and pulled herself higher and higher, the little one holding her ears as if something were going to explode. She straddled the swing and her dress fluttered higher with each pass. I looked down at my shoes again then played with the radio dial. I looked back at her and I could see her legs and hips all the way up to her panties and waist. I felt cloudy and giggly and had an urge to go over and talk to them. But then my father returned from the barn and shook hands with a man and we left.

I awoke no later than midnight and the fire was out what with only pine to burn, a nearly heatless wood compared to beech or maple. I thought I heard something and I reached for the rifle which lay along the sleeping bag. I got up and started a fire and decided to make coffee and stay up all night rather than be attacked by nameless beasts all of which were in my head and were due, I'm sure, to my brain drying out. "There stands the glass that will ease all my pain," sang Webb Pierce. It would begin to get light before four A.M. I've always been immoderately clock-oriented. But that was part of what seemed wrong with my infrequent periods of actual labor: the deadly predictability of jobs everyone sighs about, a glut of clocks and my thin neck twisting to their perfect circles, around and around and around. I remembered working in an office in Boston and during the second week there I looked up at the clock on the wall and it was two-thirty instead of the expected four-thirty. I began weeping real salt tears (partly the five doubles for lunch no doubt). A clock-torn child of twenty-seven with tears rolling down his plump cheeks onto his shirt collar, the shirt unbuttoned because it was too small, taken from a dead father's dresser drawer.

The creek roared and tumbled past boulders where I dipped the coffeepot, the noise concealing the movements of the gryphon on the verge of leaping and tearing out my throat. The pink-elephant bit for d.t.'s is bullshit. I was thinking of sauterne and California. It took almost a month to hitch home and I had gone there for no reason anyway, or as Tom Joad had said, "There's something going on out there in the West." Certainly is. In San Francisco in a deserted building called the Hanging Gardens by those who slept there we had split a hundred peyote buttons four ways, small cacti which after peeling remind one of gelatinous rotten green peppers. I chewed up an overdose of twenty buttons raw, one after another as if they were some sort of miraculous food then vomited out a window repeatedly for hours. When my mind finally refocused my bedroll was gone. And I walked for what seemed like a year down to Hosmer to catch the labor bus for the bean fields outside of San Jose. A strange form of poison. Not to be recommended, at least not in such large doses. The experience isn't verbally transferable — I've never read a record that came close. Years afterward a small part of my brain still felt the effects.

I drank several cups of coffee looking off into the moonless cloudy dark beyond the fire. As long as you have to die anyway it may as well be between a grizzly's jaws but they're a thousand miles farther west. In the peyote trance the naked chorus girls foolishly summoned up were peeled and beet-red with snatches an inky and oily black, hard as basalt. The old joke of a woman strangling a rat between her legs. In bars all over the country they are beaver pie poontang pussy quiff cunt shag clam and so on. That thirty-eight-year-old woman in Detroit with violently teased hair and a beer-fed roll of fat around her middle, red mouth like a war wound winks at you in the mirror above the bottles and you wink back with your blind eye and buy her a drink, schnapps on the rocks, and you light her cigarette and look at her fingers which have claws that remind you of a leopard. She has an ankle bracelet announcing BOB in silver. She pouts and babytalks about the movies and whatever happened to Randolph Scott and she says she is a cosmotologist. She knows the cosmos. A home permanent. A Toni. Dressing hair & girl talk. You go into the toilet and look at yourself in the mirror and think that if you were a real American, maybe a marine or a paratrooper or a truckdriver, you would screw her. But you're not so you hover over the urinal and by now your cock has almost shrunk back in your body in reverse lust and you think of excuses. She probably has syph! Or she hasn't showered in a week, she's an old lizard skin, or if she had as many pricks sticking out of her as she's had stuck in her she would look like a porcupine, or she's simply too fat. But it doesn't work so you come out of the toilet and she's following your movement in the mirror as you bolt through the door and into the street, feeling somehow not very virile but safe, thinking it would have been like fucking a vacuum cleaner, thinking of cool monasteries in the country with birds singing sweetly outside the windows and the Mother Superior kneeling before you after vespers. No nuns in monasteries. Or at least a cheerleader after a high school football game sincere about love with a cedar hope chest begun, some homemade bleached muslin pillow cases folded in the bottom with *his* and *hers* needleworked in mauve. And as she makes love with no interest she talks of the funny experiment in chemistry class that was *so* stinky. Naked from waist to bobbysocks.

I checked my trotlines, a simple device to catch fish without fishing. You bait the small hook and tie the line to a tree or low-hanging branch. The first line held nothing but a bare hook but the second had a small brook trout, the stupidest of trout, about nine inches long. I cleaned it and let the guts wash away in the creek not wanting to attract raccoons who seem able to smell fish guts from miles away. I put the trout in foil and let it steam with a slice of onion then ate it with bread and salt. For dessert I stuck my finger in a small jar of honey and licked it off. The sky was barely beginning to lighten and invisible birds sang, rather as we are told now, to warn other birds away.

I slept a few hours after the sun came up; strange about night fears and how my courage strengthens by noon. I had hummed my soaked brain to sleep with "The Old Rugged Cross," the equivalent for me of a trench confession. A woman sang it at the funeral in a clear tremulous whine, a wet wind coming through barn slats. But the grandmother had insisted on this anachronism and it was her oldest son. I sang many hymns during a summer in New York City in a room on Grove Street that looked out onto a six-by-six air vent the bottom of which was covered with newspapers, bottles and old mopheads. Rats crawled there in daylight. I couldn't handle the city; it seemed consistently malefic and I wanted to be elsewhere but I couldn't go home, having announced I had left forever. Old songs learned as a fifteen-year-old Baptist convert: "There's a Fountain Filled with Blood" (drawn from Emmanuel's veins), or "Safe Am I" (in the hollow of His hand), or the best one, "Wonderful the Matchless Grace of Jesus." I simply had no business there in Sodom but refused at nineteen to accept the fact. Sally salved me, Grace greased me home. No control over my cheap sense of such words as destiny and time. I wrote lists of things I wanted or missed for want of the ability to complete a sentence; always half drunk in airless heat as if the words were squeezed out through the knuckles:

sun bug dirt soil lilac leaf leaves hair spirea maple thigh teeth eyes grass tree fish pine bluegill bass wood dock shore sand lilypads sea reeds perch water weeds clouds horses goldenrod road sparrows rock deer chicken-hawk stump ravine blackberry bush cabin pump hill night sleep juice whiskey cards slate rock bird dusk dawn hay boat loon door girl barn straw wheat canary bridge falcon asphalt fern cow bees dragonfly violets beard farm stall window wind rain waves spider snake ant river beer sweat oak birch creek swamp bud rabbit turtle worms beef stars milk sunfish rock-bass ears tent cock mud buckwheat pepper gravel ass crickets grasshopper elm barbed-wire tomatoes bible cucumber melon spinach bacon ham potatoes flesh death fence oriole corn robin apple manure thresher pickles basement brush dog-wood bread cheese wine cove moss porch gulley trout fish-pole spaniel mow rope reins nose leek onion feet

When finished I had a choking sensation and walked around with it for days. I would start on West Forty-second and walk along the docks under the highways, always as close to the water as possible, around the tip of the island and the Battery then up to East Forty-second, scarcely noticing or remembering anything. I couldn't return home as a failure, having sold my graduation suit and pawned my graduation watch. The salutatorian's speech was "Youth,

Awake." A busboy, then washing the inside windshields at a carwash, then a bookstore clerk for a dollar twenty an hour. I always was as stealthy as possible on Tenth Avenue, having seen *Slaughter on Tenth Avenue* years before.

By noon the air had become warm and still though far above great dark stratocumulus clouds rolled along from the northwest, across Lake Superior from Canada. There would be a bad storm and I wasn't ready for it; I jogged the three or four miles back to the tent, the first raindrops beginning to fall on the leaves and the wind gray and chilling. I gathered as much kindling as possible and threw it in the tent, then began digging a ditch around the tent with a hatchet, scooping the dirt and roots with my hands for want of a shovel. By the time I was finished my clothes and skin were soaked and I crawled into the tent and stripped, shivering while the storm roared along, a cloudburst that bent trees and broke limbs, made creeks through the woods. I slept in exhaustion and awoke about evening and saw through the flaps a puddle where my fire had been. It was still raining, though now softly, and very cold. I wanted suddenly to be in a hotel in New York or Boston, to be warm after sleeping off lunch and to take the cellophane off a glass in a yellow bathroom and pour whiskey in the glass then add a half inch or so of chlorinated water and plan the evening.

When Marcia went to California I followed a week later but missed her in Sacramento from which she traveled south to Santa Fe, New Mexico. I was broke by Sacramento and had in any event lost interest in her; seeing new country or a new city has always wiped the immediate past clean. I didn't have a picture of her and when I tried to envision her, the features would change vaguely and then I would have to start over as if dressing a bald mannequin, but then an eye would drop to the floor or the mouth would enlarge or the ears would disappear. When I tried to imagine her with someone else I felt nothing; she had mentioned several times that she wanted to make love to an Indian someday, not, of course, ever having met one; a Cheyenne brave with full war regalia blasting her. Then he takes her scalp and she lookes like a shaved bloody collaborator after World War Two in France, in black and white in *Life* magazine. Nothing, no feeling. Perhaps it could have been different had we stayed together but I didn't want to marry; I wanted to save money and go to Sweden where I would see if any distant relatives looked like me and when I discovered that they didn't, I would go to a small island in the Stockholm archipelago and learn to be a fisherman, and spend my life on a boat catching cod. The Baltic would always be cold and the beaches covered with black stones. After a decade or so I would write a note home in broken, misspelled Swedish which my family would take to a local college to get trans-lated. I would announce that I had decided to follow the trade of my great-grandfather and had already fathered a brood of towheaded idiots by a fat woman who ate nothing but butter and fried salt herring.

The last evening I spent with Marcia was melancholy and sweet. We sat on the porch swing at her house until it began to get dark; then we walked across the lawn and down the driveway to my old Plymouth. It was still very warm, a dry August evening when darkness does nothing to freshen the air. We drove the ten miles to the cabin in silence and when we pulled up in front of the cabin I missed his motorcycle by inches. I thought Victor must have walked to the tavern down the road. She got out before I could open the door for her. The lights weren't on but I found the switch near the door with no difficulty. The cabin had been cleaned, though hastily. The walls halfway to the ceiling were paneled in cheap knotty pine and above that a bright yellow paint on uneven plaster. There were no curtains on the windows. The linoleum was florid red and worn bare in front of the sink. I poured her a glass of beer and drank the rest from the bottle as there was only one clean glass. She seemed quite comfortable despite the ugliness of the room, walking around rather gracefully, looking at Victor's photos of his women and sipping the beer. I asked her if she wanted some more beer and she said she didn't care. Then she walked into the bathroom and said that there were bugs in the sink. I went in and we stood looking down at the cold whiteness of the sink and the moths and dead mosquitoes around the drain. We looked up simultaneously—the mirror looked back at us with a terrifying clarity—her face, less tanned in the bright light, damp brow, her long hair caught up in a bun. I stood behind her with a look of such patent absurdity that she laughed. I felt that I had attained consciousness for the first time in weeks, that her beauty had previously been only an idea. She slipped off her blouse and then let her skirt drop to the floor. I felt light, airy as if I were watching the scene from a distance or in a dream. She turned to me and put her face against my neck. I kissed her briefly and looked into the mirror. In the bottom of the mirror the cheeks of her buttocks were pressed tightly by our weight against the sink, then her back, smooth but surprisingly well muscled, and my hands darker against her white skin. Then I saw my face poised over her shoulder and I smiled and stuck out my tongue.

Much later, after I had taken her home and returned to the cabin, I thought that I had never had such great pleasure with so little thought, that all of what occurred had done so in a sensual haze interrupted only by drinks of cold water and a few cigarettes. Even the trip back to her house had been diffuse, hypnotic. It is strange to know a girl you can love without words, with whom language is only an interference. It was always so with Marcia. We talked and laughed and walked around a great deal but when we began caressing it became an utterly wordless rite. The first time we made love there had been blood but she apparently had not thought her virginity worth mentioning.

Now with the kindling from the tent I made a dim sputtering fire, barely enough to boil the coffee. My breath rose from the tent mouth, the air not much less than freezing in June. In New York the people with money would have that spavined look of being on the verge of summer vacation whether for two weeks or a month or the whole summer for some wives. Barbara would be leaving for Georgia with the child, perhaps leaving the child there on her way to Europe. She had seemed so hopelessly corrupt when I first met her, strangely lamblike but with an aggressive decadence that confessed real planning, as a few girls of a particular sort of literary bent plotted their lives on the bases of novels they had read. I met her at Romero's, a mixed race bar in the Village where she had come with a lanky Negro from her painting class. She had been loudly and hysterically drunk within an hour and her friend had left in embarrassment.

—Are you part Mexican? she had asked.

—No, I had said, nearly immobilized by shyness.

—Well, you look it. Are you sure?

—Maybe ever so little bit, I lied. I wanted to please her. She looked like a fashion model, easily the most beautiful creature I had ever met.

We talked senselessly for a few minutes and I ordered her another drink but the bartender refused. She left abruptly and I followed, very sure that I would trip between the stool and the door. The bartender grinned. I felt old and sophisticated but still clumsy. We walked a few blocks, she in wobbling silence, to a luncheonette where we had coffee and where the counter waitress told me to get the girl out of there before she puked. When we got to my room she quickly stripped and put on a T-shirt of mine for lack of pajamas then threw herself into bed. Asleep before I could focus my eyes on her body or say anything. I got naked into bed and touched her belly but she was already snoring. I felt curiously numb and giddy as I had a year or so before when I put my equipment on before a football game knowing I would spend the next few hours getting the shit kicked out of me. I lay there for a while touching her legs and breasts and sex, where I left my hand, thinking that this was actually the first time I had slept all night with a girl and that it was unmanly to take advantage of a drunk woman. Her stomach growled beneath my hand and I hoped she wouldn't throw up as it was four days before I was due for clean sheets. Then I got up and turned on the light and looked at her, first from a distance then very closely, an inch or two away to be exact. I thought my heart would explode, I got back in bed and hovered over her trying to enter but I finished at touch.

I awoke at dawn feeling very depressed and guilty and watched her from a chair by the window. Her breathing was deep and steady in the shadows, the sheet drawn back far enough to show a smooth hip and white buttock, the remnant of a suntan on her back. I got up early out of habit but disliked doing so in the city, the clank and hiss of the garbage truck on empty Houston Street, the soiled light, even in the summer the sun never quite clear, the air smelling as if it had been sprayed with some oily chemical. She moved slightly then turned over on her belly, the sheet twisting about her, pulling farther down until it encircled her thighs. Like a picture in a dirty magazine. No excitement but an unexpected deadness. She seemed to radiate heat and sleep with her had been suffocating — the strange sweet odor of her, the perfume wearing thin, the room shrinking in bitter sleeplessness with first light. I dozed in the chair for an hour or two, waking to the full noise of the street.

She still slept though covered now. I went out in the hall
and took a shower and when I returned she stood in front
of the hotplate on the dresser making coffee.

— Those niggers tried to get me drunk, she said smiling.

— I don't remember it that way.

She cooled her coffee with water, drank it hurriedly.
Then she wrapped herself in the loosened sheet.

— I want a shower.

I told her where it was and to be careful as the hot
water, when there was any at all, was scalding. A girl naked
or practically, the important part naked anyway, drinking
coffee in my room. I almost wanted to go back home and
tell an old friend. I got into the bed which was warm and
smelled beery.

I lay there in my trousers breathing deeply to quiet
my nervousness. When she returned in what seemed an
hour she stood completely naked beside the bed combing
her hair with short nervous strokes, looking down at me. I
reached out and touched her. She turned, dropped the comb,
and got in bed beside me, reaching her one hand down and
unzipping my pants. I took them off quickly and we kissed. I
entered her without pausing though she wasn't nearly ready.

Early that evening I walked her down to the corner of
Macdougal so she could hail a taxi. We watched some children playing basketball in a small park behind a high fence.
She gave me her phone number and address. I felt different
and wondered if anyone would notice. We had alternately
screwed and slept and smoked throughout the day with a
short trip out to a delicatessen. She put my prick in her mouth
which had only happened once before with a whore in Grand

Rapids, and I went down on her which I had never done before, though I had read about it with my friends back home. We all assumed that everyone had eaten a woman and when some poor freak admitted he hadn't we all laughed knowingly whether in the locker room or on the farm. I felt sore and raw. At nineteen one day's worth of screwing had nearly equaled all that had occurred in my life up to that date. Every curiosity was settled for the moment and I could still smell her on my hands and lips. And nose. I walked into the Kettle of Fish bar and loudly ordered an ale which was a definite change as I usually mumbled in bars with a sort of hick Herb Shriner accent that New Yorkers had difficulty understanding.

I used the rest of the kindling and dried a small log into burning. I fried some potatoes and onions and ate them out of the pan. It was barely light but clear and the first shafts of sunlight caught the mist rising up through the brush and trees. As it did in the Black Forest in 1267 with peasants rising early, drawing on their boots in the wet dawn. I wiped the rifle with my shirt, the beads of moisture that had formed on its cold steel barrel, and began walking upstream again to continue where the rain had interrupted me the day before. By the look of the conservation map it was the deepest part of the forest unmarked even by log roads, and with the un-named creek I camped beside running from the closest of two small lakes in a thin crooked trickle, widening gradually as it poured northward to Lake Superior.

About a mile from the tent I came upon a conical pile of fresh bear crap. Eating thimbleberries, must be. It took

a few moments to recover from the shock but then I knew
black bears scarcely ever bothered anyone. I walked quietly
through the wet ferns which had soaked me to the waist,
then saw perhaps a hundred yards ahead on a hummock
on the edge of a small marsh the bear. He suddenly turned
to me, catching my scent, then with an almost indiscernible
speed crashed and whuffed off into the marsh.

*All of them were the same. Convinced of this, they revolved
their particularities around a single head, the body's parts
too were interchangeable. When young there was the breath-
lessness of looking up the word "sin" in the dictionary after
a morning spent in Bible school. Jezebel, Mary Magdalene,
Ruth at my feet, Lot's daughters, Solomon's concubines. They
caused the frenzy at Gadara when the madman, who broke his
bonds over and over, was healed and the spirits went into a herd
of swine, three thousand of them, and they cast themselves into
the sea and drowned. Froth and waves from pigs drowning. I
multiplied the pigs in the pen next to the corncrib. There were
eight of them and it was difficult to imagine thousands each
with the spirit of an evil woman. When you have changed
and cleansed yourself of all vileness the dozen or so women
around the country you have mistreated will know this and
cast themselves into the Red Sea or into the pigpen. They could
be pinpointed on a map of the United States and Canada. I
would that you were either hot or cold in Laodicea. Underpants
drawn down the thighs behind a chicken coop. She said at
twelve see my ass. In front of your eyes and no one to confess
it to. The dead woman who played the piano for Wednesday
night prayer meeting is in heaven now and can see what you*

do to yourself at night and what you do to others at home or work or play. Nothing can be hidden from the dead and they can't help us though they must weep for us. You could hear the chickens clucking, the ground scratched bare underfoot. You have no hair I have some. I will get mine after my next birthday I'm told. Uncles at war in Guadalcanal might die. You touched her thing. At the Nazarene Revival the preacher said in the circus tent the young couple's little daughter fell into the pigpen and was eaten by the pigs in punishment. He turned to drink and women. She turned to drink and other men. Then they heard a hymn on the radio and many had prayed for them especially their mothers and they wept by the radio and asked for forgiveness. Soon they had a new child. God works in many ways His wonders. I'll go to Africa and be a missionary and save the heathen Negro savages though fraught with dangerous lions and snakes. Her ass is bare, the chickens clucking in circles thinking we're going to feed them. The missionary played the accordion and sang a hymn in the African language and showed slides of the Dark Continent. And of a leper with a giant jaw and one ear missing who had been brought to Christ at the mission. The girls were forced to marry at ten, in the fourth grade only. I found a book of Flash Gordon in my cousin's desk where in the rocket ship Flash Gordon put his thing all the way through the woman and out the other side where a man had it in his mouth. In one place and out the other. Joe Palooka too with boxing gloves on, trunks around his knees before the fight with famous people at ringside. A friend of mine had given their Negro maid five dollars of Christmas money to raise her dress way up. What did she look like I don't know her underpants were on underneath the dress. Five dollars. In summer rowing down the lake at night we looked in the window and she had no clothes on at all. I'm not sure they are all like that, if their hair is a different color they are certain to be built differently. But when I came up through the waters in my white flannel pants everything was new and the Holy Ghost was in the baptismal font felt in my chest which was at bursting. Maybe held the breath too long. It lasted, the ghost, for a week or so even if my father said you wont have to take a bath joking. Or am I a heathen? Billy Sunday saved my father for two days but he got drunk on the third. Backsliding they call it.

Now at noon a breeze blew up from the southwest and the day became warm and humid. I sat against a stump and watched the small lake rippling. When I reached the lake I shot a turtle off a distant log in disgust and fatigue, the sweat dripping down into eyes and in the swamp I passed through, clouds of black flies and mosquitoes, an eye nearly swollen shut with bites. The turtle had exploded with the force of the 180-grain bullet. Pointless cruelty. In the family, or the choking I felt was not consistent with the past. Hounds in the dark leaping against the tree and in the beam of the flashlight a raccoon looks down, is blasted from the tree and torn in pieces by the hounds. Whets their appetite to let them eat one once in a while.

I shot five times into a bee swarm once, hanging clotted in a tree, a huge cluster of small moving grapes and the queen deep in the center being fed and protected by them all. They closed around the shots, the dead falling to the ground. The cheapness in my family, to spend your first fourteen years in the nineteenth century, and then be swept into the twentieth; and at shock point to become a Baptist and study to be a preacher. Many are called but few are chosen, they said. Two years in a church the soul swollen and bitten by it. The black woman sang, "I'm going to tell God how you treat me." In Philippians or Ephesians. Paul taught us. Purify my thoughts O Christ. Better to burn than to perish, holding the unloaded shotgun across the lap in despair of becoming pure. We didn't come from apes to act like gods, the world was born six thousand years ago Bishop Ussher proved and only Satan would have us think otherwise. Our Country had gone wrong and when the Hoover Dam was built eight or nine men died and were buried in its cement from our lust for money. Christ don't let these pictures tempt me. Brains rot with self-abuse. Euclidean it was and an absorbed millennium of cruelty; the shame for my family and relatives, only my father had been to college and he studied agriculture and had bad grammar. How could anything come to this, rather from it, with years spent on milking cows, cutting down trees or eating herring. A whole stretch of them quit school at sixteen out of religious conviction, wanting no more than the law required; Mennonites, ignorant and harmless, they kept to themselves and refused to seek the law with one another. They invented crop rotation and the women wore black and black skull caps. That is all that could be said about them.

It was warm and breezy enough for the mosquitoes and flies to disappear. I shed my clothes and walked into the water, gingerly stepping on the lake's soft bottom; at chest depth I began swimming, the water icy and clear, toward the log. There were a few pieces of the turtle flesh and then one large chunk of turtle shell I could see on the bottom by shading my eyes. Put it back together. My heart was in the egg and it dropped to the floor. I floated on my back and saw one still cloud. Where would the turtle have died otherwise? In winter deep in the mud. As bears do, dying in their sleep from age. There were thousands of undiscovered bodies in America, on railroad sidings and in rented rooms, in culverts, in the woods.

When I got back to the tent I dozed in the late afternoon sun. I wanted one place. Lost all character in travel; in one thousand miles, even less, one could become something because there was nothing to displace. Stay here. The streets of Laredo, Texas, festered and kept to themselves. You were sure that everyone would start shooting if they could do so with impunity. But maybe that was true of any state. A sailor on the sidewalk in a circle of the curious on Saturday night in Scollay Square in Boston, the handle of a screwdriver sticking out of his cheek. They tore it down, Scollay Square. In the West Forties near Ninth Avenue the policeman clubbed the Puerto Rican on the felt hat. The hat dropped bloody in front of a $1.19 steak house. Another policeman stood by the squad car watching the Puerto Rican on his hands and knees dripping gore. Then they took him off in the car. The small crowd left and I looked at the hat for a moment. What happened to it? A friend who had been shot said it felt like being slugged though not too hard. A safe place in Utah, where I worked for a farmer for a week. Ate with the family. They were impressed that I had been to college. I said my wife had died and they were very nice to me. This will to lie gratuitously is handy.

The night was liquid and warm. I threw a handful of green ferns on the fire to smoke away the mosquitoes and the smoke curled and hovered over the fire and the tent and finally sought out the roof of boughs above me. A moonless night. In Spain where I had never been I slept under a lemon tree with a viper nestled in my lap for warmth. Smelled like a muskmelon I broke over a tractor fender, the juice and seeds dripping on the ground. I took off all my clothes and walked around the fire in my boots, staring past the perimeter of darkness. A thin dog bark in the distance. Coyote. Might be quite close as the creek's steady rush hid noises. I shivered and moved closer to the fire, standing in the plume of smoke until my eyes watered. If there was fire in the middle of earth why wasn't the ground warm. No brain for science or perhaps anything else, only what stuck like a burr to clothes. Or was sufficiently bizarre. I ran my hands over my body as a doctor might looking for something awry. In the new world muscles would be freakish. Nothing for bulges to do, no mindless labor but something of another kind. Work. Helping my dad and grandfather get in the hay. Pitch it with forks onto the wagon until the pile looked huge and unsteady, then the horses would pull the wagon to the barn where the hay would be pitched into the mow. So young the fork felt heavy to lift. After supper I would follow my grandfather to the barn and watch the cows be milked. Four tits. Milk

would never come for my own fingers, though I had secretly
tried. My grandfather would aim the tit and squirt me in the
face or squirt a stream of milk into the mouth of a barn cat
which would always be waiting. Throw some hay down,
spread it in the long trough in front of the stanchions, and
some for the horses. I hated to walk behind the horses but
the one hoof cocked was to rest. There were stories of the
killed and maimed, one kick did it, knocked through the side
of the barn. The bull tethered, led by the ring in its nose was
safe. Work dulled the brain, left the brain elsewhere seek-
ing a sweet place to forget tiredness. Had to fill in around
the foundation by hand as the bulldozer might buckle the
wall, a week's worth of shoveling. The well pit kept caving
in until we dug a hole ten feet by ten by ten. No timbers to
shore it. Laying a thousand feet of irrigation pipe when it
was brutally hot, a dollar per hour and no overtime, or unloading a fertilizer truck in the metal Quonset shed with a
gas mask on as the bags sometimes broke. And the hardest
work, handling twelve-inch cement blocks, seventy pounds
apiece, for a house that would have brick facing, perhaps
a thousand of them in the walls. Unloaded in a day thirty-
five tons by hand. Too tired to screw or go fishing or to the
movies, the hands numb and raw. Someone has to do it. Not
me again. Near Stockton the bean field stretched out past
seeing. We picked in rows for two cents a pound. I made
seven dollars in a twelve-hour day while the Mexican girl I
met in Salinas averaged fourteen dollars a day. Found a job
running a forklift in a cannery in San Jose.

❅ ❅ ❅

In the sleeping bag the smell of smoke on my body was overpowering. Asleep on the skin and awake at center I thought of the drive up past Toledo and Detroit and Lansing, finally reaching the country I liked north of Mount Pleasant and Clare where I turned left to drive the eighty miles through Evart to Reed City. Past the road that led to the cabin. Where a witch, a true one, lived in a shack in the woods and lived on berries and boiled opossum or any animal found freshly run over by a car on the road. Three hundred and fifty million animals dead on roads each year. I counted eighty once on a summer night on a stretch of road west of Clare. They could not learn the world wasn't theirs. Over the earth perhaps a billion a year struck down. I hit a fox years before in Massachusetts, swerved to a halt and saw it scrambling in a tight circle on the shoulder of the road. And beat its skull in with a tire iron because its back was broken and one hind leg dragged askew. The fox snarled then whimpered trying to retreat. Couldn't let it take days to die — they ran about freely, less wary than usual, in February and March when they mated.

Reed City where I had spent my best years seemed crabbed and ugly and small and I drove quickly through it. Nothing more tiresome than the idyll of someone's youth. The world from three or four feet high with all things remembered in unique wonderment, pored over in late years, confessed, hugged, wrung of their residue in disgust with the present. How hopeless to live it over and over again, to savor only the good parts, forgetting the countless wounds which seemed to lie deeper and were kept masked with force. Though the one clinical psychologist I had been to persuaded me I lived like a child. That was why I didn't need my childhood to assuage or heal present griefs. I was still a child with small chance of being anything else, perhaps. Fine. Always quitting, schools, jobs, hunting or fishing or walking, as a child gorges on candy or new games. On occasion I even climbed trees when I was sure I wasn't watched. Novelty they called it, a victim of change, a new street to walk down in a new city to a new bar or new river with a new bridge to look off and a new author to read late at night in a new room. In Waltham by the Charles it had been Dostoevsky for weeks on end after I finished work as a busboy in an Italian restaurant. Boston became St. Petersburg with two feet of snow in a single night. I moved to St. Botolph street and quit my job after saving a hundred dollars. The room was so ill-heated I wore my father's cast-off overcoat the entire month, even to bed, and when the heat came on intermittently I would take it off and hang it out the window to air. The wino in the next room pissed out the window to avoid walking downstairs to the toilet. I wrote down my thoughts on two pages of a yellow law tablet and moved again to New York City in the spring where I hoped to leave for Sweden when enough money had been saved. After five months of unemployment and Tokay in New York I left for Michigan where in another four months I was able to save seventy dollars and hitchhike to California. All drifters dream of mountains of gold hidden in the greenery of Peru, Lafitte's treasure in some coral reef off the Tortugas, finding a thick billfold in a gutter or becoming an overnight movie star after someone had discovered their interesting face or becoming a rich woman's lover. She was beautiful but until she had him no man had been able to satisfy her whimsical tastes. Then he saw the world by sheer cock power—Biarritz, Marrakesh, Saipan, Hong Kong. Through the draperies he looked out on the Avenue des Cochons, his body pillaged but happy. Behind him on a Louis Quatorze bed she held the now dead duck to her breast. Then she plucked the feathers from the duck with her teeth as a falcon would, in quick jerking motions. He only endured such perversities for the thousand dollars a week allowance she gave him and sometimes the small pleasures which she offered in return. He would sell her to some Bedouins when they reached Somaliland for the fall shooting, first taking her jewels and as much cash as possible. Back in my room I felt drugged with fantasy. I wanted to find a real muddy billfold in a real gutter. Flushed with sauterne I felt my life about to change. You will cross an ocean or a body of water and find love with a woman who speaks a strange tongue, said a girl who read my horoscope. Or as the president of a giant corporation I would institute fair employment practices. Widows of those accidentally killed by being sucked into the blast furnaces of my steel mills would blush at my generosity, often bend over the desk for a quick one. All fantasies ruined by the errant detail. Early in high school I entered a UAW (United Auto Workers) essay contest on labor history: "Eugene Debs sat mutely in his jail cell. Whither labor? he queried himself." My brother had won the American Legion contest for the "best essay on a theme of patriotism" and had read it from a stage in a school assembly, the setting symmetrical with two uniformed men on each side of the podium and two flags. I thought success at writing might run in the family and had waited anxiously for the mail to bring news of my trip to Washington (first prize) and then my predestined rise through the ranks until I was an equal, then a successor to Walter Reuther. Reuther would say, "Glad to have you aboard," or something like that with misty eyes. No one could see the scars the shotgun blast had left, fired by goons through the kitchen window. Goons would stop at nothing, not even murder. The Ford, Dodge and Mott families and others lived in porcine splendor on unpaid wages while the Leader lay bleeding on the linoleum. Years later at a socialist meeting in New York City short, homely people read from *L'Humanité* and laughed. I didn't know French and the poster said it was supposed to be a social occasion. Orange drink and doughnuts. It was to be my only political meeting though I signed petitions and protest statements around Washington Square daily. I heard rumors about Eisenhower and Madame Chiang and how the oil depletion allowance financed private Texan armies which would eventually take over the country. Or that the Rosenbergs were framed and that serious people, especially young men, should try to join Fidel Castro in the Oriente Province. I believed everything and even attended a secret meeting of Castro sympathizers in Spanish Harlem, though the plotting was in Spanish and I understood no Spanish save *vaya con Dios, gracias,* and in my *adobe hacienda.* After five months of New York I weighed thirty pounds less and after four months of California, ten pounds further down the scale. Ideally I would have weighed nothing in a few more years.

❀   ❀   ❀

There were scars along the creek bank from the spring runoff, scattered driftwood and uprooted yellow beech in piles and clots, and watermarks on trees. Late winter here would be strange, the local record was close to three hundred inches of snow, with temperatures running if rarely to forty below zero. The deer would yard up deep in cedar swamps and scour the limited browse and often if there were a spring blizzard, starve to death by the thousands. Even the bobcats would deplete the supply of snowshoe hares; a few years back an estimated fifty thousand deer died, driven into submission by a March blizzard when they were at their weakest. In spring all creeks would become torrents, heaving and turbulent, fed by melting snow and ice and rain. I wanted to see it but the country would be impenetrable in winter, except by snowmobile, a machine that horrified me and seemed to accelerate the ruin of all places not normally reached. There were no inviolate places, only outposts that were less visited than others. The Arctic was drilled for oil, great pools of waste oil seeping through glaciers. The continent was becoming Europe in my own lifetime and I felt desperate. The merest smell of profit would lead us to gut any beauty left, there was no sentimentality involved. We had been doing so since we got off the boat and nothing would stop us now. Even our instincts to save were perverse; we made parks which in fact were "nature zoos" crossed by superhighways, and in the future large areas would be surrounded by narrow gauge fence so that the animals wouldn't be harried and stared to death. It was almost a comfort to think of how many people the grizzlies with their sense of property might take with them in their plummet to extinction. I had read a story about a woman who proudly told of shooting one while it slept. Small pocket of fur flew, a .375 Magnum slug tearing through the beast in a split second. Odd how they know when they're being hunted, even as a fox does when he doubles back to watch his pursuers draw close. They run fox to exhaustion with snowmobiles then club them to death. Moose in Ontario killed at close range floundering in the snow, also run to fatigue by machines. Elephants know that they're being shot at as the Indian women did at Cripple Creek and whales are familiar with the fatal accuracy of the modern harpoon. And the wolf was destroyed because it killed game animals from hunger, perhaps fifty left in the Upper Peninsula, rarely seen as they had the wit to recognize their enemy. The feral dogs living in swamps returning to their ancient home in a single generation understood when they were shot for killing deer. But there were a few places like this one that would yield up little profit and was at least temporarily safe since the rivers had recovered from the widespread mining fifty years before and the cutting of pulp fed deer with new growth.

Of what use was a mountainside blotched with chalets, and ski people, certainly the most insensate group of chichi morons I'd ever met. They had their "right" as did the lumber and mining and oil interests. But I did not have to like them for it. There was an amusing irony in the fact that the land would be fucked up before the blacks would have the leisure to enjoy it, one more piece of subtle genocide.

My brain felt cold and weak from this war with everyone; I found most of those who agreed even less palatable than the destroyers. No matter how deeply one went into the

forest or into the mountains a jet contrail would somehow
appear as a wound across the sky. But I had no talent for
reform and could not stop pouring whiskey into my face
unless it was miles away, flatly unreachable. Those born in
big cities, some of them, tried to save cities. I could not dry
out my brain long enough to regard any day with total focus.
Others in my generation took drugs and perhaps expanded
their consciousness, that was open to question, and I drank
and contracted my brain into halts and stutters, a gray fist
of bitterness.

The woods were warm and lovely again with the sun on
the ground mottled by the small leaves of the birch waving
slightly above the tent in the light breeze. I drowsed and
dozed. Once on the grass I saw the moon between Marcia's
thighs, ear against leg and one cloud beneath it. May, and
the cherry tree beyond my feet had lost all but a few of its
blossoms, the petals were a cushion on the ground. Her tame
pigeons croaked in the cage behind the garage and the noise
purled in the warm air. Grass sweet eat some, face wet with
her warmth. Car passes on the gravel road, its headlights
sweeping above our bodies. The stains of green on my knees
and back from the wheatfield across the road where we went
to hide when it was still daylight. Soil was damp and I was
the blanket. She sat there and one might think there was
a girl over there sitting in the wheatfield. On me. Glut of
aimless splendid fucking in the car, on couches, in a shower,
in locked bathrooms at parties, in the clump of lilacs and
beneath the cherry tree. It is so far away and makes my brain

ache. And in the spring when I felt melancholy for weeks, faintly insane with pockets bulging with picked flowers. We never talked very much and I wish that I could remember more now. And only that spring of fog and sleep with her as if we were living under warm flowing water. She waited on the ground while I sat in the crotch of a tree and drank the wine, the whole bottle in two or three gulps. So it would work quickly and well. Even then.

Waking from a nap in middle evening and the light almost gone. A new moon and the wood was dry enough to burn. I ate three trout not much larger than smelt and the last of the bread. Two tins of meat left and I'd have to hike back to the car for food if I could find it. Perhaps I would shoot something or diet or walk north to the Huron River and try to catch some larger trout. That is, if I could find the river; maps made terrain so simple but four or five miles through the woods with no visible landmarks was a different matter. I dipped three fingers into the honey jar noticing that my hand was filthy. Fools drank water from a stream going through a cedar swamp and often were violently ill far from help. Unless the stream is big, has a strong current, is far from civilization, you should boil all water. Found a cool spring coming through rock on the Escanaba. I once drew water fifty yards downstream from a deer carcass half in the stream and stinking. I admired the easy competency of my older brother and father in the woods, or what had been my father before the accident. Filth, smoke and disorder everywhere. Bah bah black sheep. Fuckup. Sweat and bug repellent stinging in scratches. I almost savored my pigginess which I viewed as central to my character. Where were the pig hocks and sauerkraut and black beer? And tripe and calves' brains and liver? Lydia, Lydia my sweet, bring me your gland. Night falleth with long hair. No soap could be found for my hands anyhow. Ashes work or fine wet sand. When we used to get weed stains from pulling weeds we broke open tomatoes and they cleaned the stains away.

Chapter 2

Boston

I'm not very interested in my opinion of Boston. I've lived there twice and both times quite miserably. At nineteen I lived for a month on the Charles in Waltham thinking it was all somehow Boston. I heated Campbell's soup in the sink in my room and opened it only when I presumed the hot water had melted its jelled substance. I even tried the alphabet type but the can was incomplete, lacking the letters that would enable me to eat my name and be whisked to Lapland where I might consult the final shaman. I also dwelled on a prominent local suicide which had taken place three decades before. What local bridge did Quentin Compson use?

Then I moved to St. Botolph Street, the area is torn down now, and felt much better. Here would be my true hot center of anguish — January at its coldest, a hunchback for a landlady, an immediate neighbor with a cleft palate who as an unemployed merchant seaman told me that "drinking doesn't pay dividends." But there was such warmth in Tokay or sauterne, Thunderbird as they called it, fortified sherry with the maximal alcohol, hence warmth, at a minimal price. I worked as a busboy in an Italian restaurant and ate food off the plates of others, once in famished greed getting a filter tip cigarette butt caught in my throat. Hidden in a chicken wing. The money was good when you added the portion stolen from the waiter's tips. The waiter whose area I serviced was a homosexual Arab with less than totally clean immigration papers. He suspected me of stealing but I told him I would either kick his face in or make an anonymous call to certain high-placed authorities at which point he would be returned to whatever filthy little country he came from. The jig was up as they don't say any more when his day-off replacement, an Italian housewife with hair on her ankles, caught me and I was fired by the manager. He talked to me in his office the walls of which were covered with autographed pictures of show business personalities, minor ones (Jerry Vale, Dorothy Collins, Snooky Lanson, Gisele Mac-Kenzie, Julius LaRosa) who rarely make the late night TV shows. He wrote a check for twelve dollars, the amount owed me, and told me I was through as a busboy in Boston. He had connections. Everyone in Boston has connections down to the crummiest night porter who bets fifty cents a week on the numbers. They think about their connections on the subway to Dorchester.

I had by this time saved two hundred dollars which I intended as a stake for New York City but instead blew it in three days on a young Armenian belly dancer who was closely watched by two enormous hairy brothers. She let me have her for thirty dollars in the back of a taxicab after my face had become familiar enough in the club. She had to be sure I wasn't a freak, that my love for her and the Levantine music she undulated to didn't conceal some dangerous fetish. I understood her precautions. Boston is the sort of city where much of the population strangles cats. Or it is easy to imagine Bostonians lashing their own feet with coat hangers, screwing holes in cabbages, having nightly dreams of back-scuttling Magdalene or some poor nun spied upon on the street. On the Common one morning I watched a priest crazily eating daffodils on his hands and knees and then throwing up a stream of yellow petals in the swan pond. A passing cop only said, "Good morning, father," as if this were normal behavior. Much later in my life I got the same sensation walking around Dublin; a chill in my body knowing that if these dark energies were ever released the power would equal that of an unpunctured baked potato exploding in an oven.

Three days here now and I had begun to think I'd have enough to eat. My confidence in my ability to find the car with ease is nil. Touch my shrinking belly but I'm anyway thirty pounds overweight—the creeping fat started back in Boston where I drank all those numberless cases of ale. Delicious. Wish I had a case cooling in the creek, a TV commercial. And I wanted to stay at the very least seven days for the sake of numerology. Maybe I'll shoot a deer and eat it all, eyes, rumen. Make hoof soup out of hoofs.

❁   ❁   ❁

It was uncomfortable stretched out along the top of the radiator in her apartment with each cast-iron ridge making a painful but warm indentation in my back. So warm, unlike my Botolph room. And dreaming of the Yucatan, Merida, Cozumel, which even though infested with vipers and tarantulas would be warm and steamy. I would suspend myself in a hammock to be safe from snakes and construct metal rat catchers like they do with ships to keep the scorpions and tarantulas away. Can tarantulas crawl up smooth-metal? Do they have gluey feet? I once went sixty-nine with a beautiful girl in a hammock and we became too preoccupied and violent and the hammock tipped us over onto the floor, at least a four-foot drop. She landed on top of me which made the etiquette of the accident proper but my shoulder was painfully wrenched. She thought it was very funny and was still juiced up but the pain in my bruised lips and nose and shoulder had unsexed me: full mast half mast no mast. O storm and all of that. I took a hot bath and put a heating pad over my face up to my nose. She cooked some bratwurst for dinner but it was difficult to chew so I drank two bottles of wine with a straw and let her soothe me by her bobbing head which I scratched alternately in lust, diffidence and pain.

Off Newbury Street again and up the stairs where she waited. All faint and pink as a quartz mine. No aquacities here. Corn shucks. Tamales.
    —Don't do that, she said.

—What?

—That.

—Why?

—Because. Just because.

Really too hot for fuckery. Room livid and airless. We lay there sweating as animals apparently don't. I heard only through their mouths: running dogs pink tongue. I ached as metal might.

—It's still hard, she said.

—A mistake.

Her buttocks were squishy but still somehow appealing. Needed rigorous exercise, less pasta and cream in the coffee.

—Your ass is like grape jelly. Did anyone ever, tell you that?

—Fuck you. I've seen dozens bigger than yours.

—No doubt. You've looked at so many. The Army Corps of Engineers said I'm high average.

Waitresses smelling of lamb stew. I dressed quickly and went down the stairs and into the street. I went into the first bar and drank two glasses of beer then a shot of bourbon dropped into the third glass as they do in Detroit. A time bomb. For hygiene. In the toilet I aimed at the shrinking deodorant puck then a cigarette butt. In youth they were Jap airplanes to be shot at. A witticism at eye level on the wall: "Boston College eats shit." No doubt about that, Jesuits with plateful. The cook ladled seconds. Lurid goo us, they say, gimme all the luv ya got.

And more: she raises herself on an elbow. Her eyes narrow and focus in the dim light of the room.

—Why aren't you up yet? she asks.

—It would disappoint you. You come in here, take off your clothes and ask me why I'm not up. I'm nothing more than a flange banger for old lizard skins.

—Can't you be a little bit nicer?

Thirty-third repeat. She is active in ward politics in a serene way being a Smith graduate with a sensible wardrobe. She is an ardent feminist, divorced from a "phony" in advertising. She believes we are not making love but relating physically. She sees an analyst and says the analyst advises against our relationship. I tell her often that she only comes around in hopes of collecting the four hundred I owe her.

—What did you do last night? she asks, patting my shoulder.

—Buggered a beautiful high school sophomore I met weeping on the Common. She was a virgin and was afraid it would hurt.

—I don't know why I put up with you. I know a lot of men that would like to be in your shoes.

Still more and I wanted romance. I unlocked the door; there was no question about it, she was on her hands and knees with the lax look of a depraved Confederate officer, all blond stringy hair, a bit of a mustache, skin blotches, a coat of sweat on which a name could be written.

—Why didn't you come when you called? I've been waiting.

—Obviously.

I walked around behind her. She had fixed this surprise at least an hour before and perhaps resumed the posture with each step on the stairway.

—Can you fix me something to eat first?

—What's wrong with you? she choked, rising to her feet clumsily. From the bathroom her boo-hoos were crisp and defined as good smoke rings.

I fried some eggs and ate them in silence while she looked out the window at the snow-covered parking lot three floors below.

I dreamed of whiskey again and when I awoke it was cold and raining steadily. I sank farther into my sleeping bag warming myself with moist breath. So cold and it is summer; better check trotlines, run in circles, dig with hatchet near a pine stump for pitch to start a fire. I dressed awkwardly in the tent then jogged to the creek; the first line was weightless, the bait gone, but the second held a brook trout close to a foot long. Breakfast. The rain slackened and the wind began to change directions, a vague warming from the southwest.

A diversion or digression here: loving openly and nearly the beloved. Anyone's rum-soaked brain might own such a thing in his past. It scarcely matters if the loved one is an aunt with the incipient threat of incest, or the druggist's daughter behind the soda counter, or as in my own case a cheerleader in the tenth grade. And another, this one. A girl at a summer cottage on a lake up near West Boylston, Massachusetts. She was fifteen and I was seventeen. Later on, not even much later on in life, one misses this sense of life horribly.

So absent when we are merely glands with small brutish brains attached. Loving as if we were fictional creatures, geometrical, pure, diamonds to be looked at through many clear and open facets, but still human; the throat constricts, the tear glands overwhelm, the world is tactile and fresh again and we return to it over and over, willfully recapturing a beautiful but senseless dream:

I awoke shortly after dawn to a ring tapping the window. I saw her framed in the darkened parlor window — I was sleeping on a cot on the porch — motioning for me to get up. I regretted my promise. I didn't ride well and was sure I would look foolish, perhaps fall off and dash my brains out against a rock or tree. It was delicious to lie on the porch at dawn with the chattering of birds coming up from the lake, and the raindrops falling lightly off the still leaves. I remembered vaguely a brief thunderstorm during the night: the lightning illumined the leaves of the sugar maple tossed by the breeze and the tree looked white and ghostly. She tapped again and I got up, dressing slowly as my clothes were cool and damp. The morning was darkly overcast and through the pearls of raindrops on the screen I could see mist move in coils across the lake.

She waited impatiently while I drank some instant coffee, made before the water had come to full boil. I had to explain in a whisper that it was inconceivable to leave the house without coffee. We paused to listen to her father snore then someone turn in a creaking bed then back to silence. She was dressed in a loose-fitting pullover sweater, the sort Irish peasants knit to earn their mashed potatoes, and light tan riding breeches. When she stood at the stove trying to scrape a teaspoonful of coffee out of the jar she dropped the spoon and I was brought out of my drowsiness by the sight of her stooping figure, the breeches pulled tightly across her buttocks, and the lines where the panties pressed into the flesh. Only fifteen years old.

I closed the door softly and followed her up the driveway to the gravel road. Still a light sprinkle of rain but mostly off the trees and the mist drifting now across the marsh and into the woods. The dampness entered my bones and I shivered.

She bent to pick up a stone, the breeches drawn tightly again. Let's play dog or doctor or something, I thought.

—Here. Throw this at the birds, she said, handing me the stone.

I threw at a blackbird sitting on a mailbox some fifty yards away.

—Why didn't you dance with me last night? I said, watching the stone sail into a thicket.

—Because you were drunk and disgusting and I'm going steady.

—You're a bitch.

She turned to me, shocked. —You swore at me.

We took a shortcut, crossing a field and wetting ourselves to the knees with rain-soaked grass and weeds. I began to feel lightheaded, loony, with a hangover but still somehow exhilarated.

I stopped to light a cigarette and she turned and paused looking at her wet boots.

—If we don't hurry you'll get a bad horse.

—All horses are bad.

God protect me from large animals that cause pain. I
could already feel the inevitable shock waves of pain up my
spine, my head joggling or my neck snapping like a snake's
if the horse jumped over anything higher than a footprint.
Riding wasn't totally unpleasant if the saddles had horns
but this was to be "English" and I thought of them and why
they hadn't won the war by themselves. No saddlehorns of
course. Bad food and teeth though I had never met one.
Back home they were more sensible and rode "Western"
and had no pretensions and had things to hold on to when
they were up in the air.

Later in the afternoon after we returned I put on my
bathing suit and walked down to the dock. My hangover had
gone to my stomach, rather my stomach shared in it, both
head and trunk queasy and faintly ringing. The goddamn
horse had run to keep up with hers no matter how hard I
jerked at the reins. In fact the first time I jerked, the horse
had moved sideways with startling speed and I thought I
might return to the church and not drink any more beer or
smoke if God would get me off the horse and home safely
and in my own bed without pain. My mother would call me
for breakfast and I would say an invisible grace over the
bacon and my brain would be as pure as the moon.

She was sitting at the end of the dock and I walked
past her without a word, my legs unsteady and aching, and
let myself off backwards into the water. She said nothing so
I swam head down out toward the raft watching the light
sandy bottom disappear, the water growing darker. When
I got to the raft I let my feet trail downward into the colder
water while the warm encircled and glistened around my

chest. I imagined a water of perfect coldness that would be
solid ice near bottom in reverse of illogical nature. I saw that
she wasn't watching so I swam idly back to shore, partly on
my back, looking directly at the sun. In grade school there
had been an albino who could stare at the sun longer than
anyone else. This trick was his only token of respect and he
bored everyone with his "Come watch me stare at the sun I
bet you can't." He disappeared in the sixth grade, some said
to the school for freaks in Lapeer, others said to the school
for the blind in Lansing.

When I reached the dock she was still sitting with
her elbows propped on her knees with the book close to
her chest. I stood in the shallow water, leaned a bit and
impulsively put my head against the inside of her knee. She
squirmed from the water trickling down her thigh then suddenly grasped my head between her knees.

—I've caught a sea serpent.

My ears hurt but I forgot them looking down her thighs
to the small pubic bunch where they met in her swimsuit.
At the moment I didn't even desire her. The antipathy of
the horseback ride and the dance the night before was too
fresh. And her apparent scorn or distance was difficult to
understand, the way she mimicked my midwestern drawl.
And the dance smelling of the polished hardwood floor and
my awkward beery drunk self watching the others dance so
gracefully. Later the decision to drive two hundred miles to
New York City, sobriety setting in when someone puked in
the back seat. The car seemed cold and it began to rain. One
of the droplets trickled into her crotch. Then she released
my head and I pulled myself up on the dock and let myself

dry in the sun alongside of her with my eyes shielded by my forearm.

—Do you sleep with that guy?

—Where?

—I mean do you make love?

—It's none of your business.

I looked at her back, the gentle way her butt met the dock. She was fairly tall and wasp-waisted but otherwise seemed so ample for her age.

—I just wondered. Nothing personal.

—We're going to wait until I'm sixteen.

She turned and put the book down on my legs and took off her sunglasses.

—Do you have many girls?

—Quite a few, I lied.

—Do you respect them?

—Of course. What do you think they're for?

She turned back to the lake and lifted the book from my thighs. I quivered and felt my cock begin to enlarge, like her or not. She glanced at my bathing suit then put her hand directly on me.

—Men are made so funny.

She gathered her towel and book and walked up the dock to the path to the cottage.

After dinner we sat around, seven of us including her parents and brother and sister and my friend, and listened to Berlioz' Requiem. I was bored and tired and said I had a headache and was going to get some fresh air. I walked down to the lake feeling strange about her. She seemed too young, unfinished; her charm was girlish and at seventeen

I had only dreams and visions of plump heavy-breasted women that supposedly would shriek and moan with plea- sure. Earth seemed so quiet and expectant that night. It was the summer the H-bomb was announced and I remember how the idea fascinated me, the speculation in my naïve New Testament brain that the earth would burn like a tuft of cot- ton soaked in kerosene, the universe would split apart and Jesus would appear for the Second Coming, self-brilliant with the light of His head which was like the sun. Our own sun would be a charred disc and the cold moon blood-red reflecting the fire in the universe. On the dock though I had not connected myself in anyway with this disaster. I would live on with my own particular expectancies and ambitions intact. My senses were those of a child, my ears flooded with frogs croaking, and there was still the smell of bathing suits drying. Someone far out in the lake was trolling for bass in the full moon. Their voices were inaudible but I could hear the creaking of the oarlocks. They lit a match and the small flare made them briefly visible in a small circle of light.

I heard steps behind me but didn't turn. I thought it was only my friend and didn't want to encourage conver- sation. But then there was a smooth hand on my neck and she asked me for a cigarette which surprised me. In my hometown it would have been scandalous for a girl of fifteen to smoke. She smoked the entire cigarette before saying anything then she said that they had been talking about me up in the cottage and how utterly rude I was. How I didn't wash in the morning and I bit my fork when I ate and said "huh" and "yah" and so on. And didn't help out. I told her that as a future great poet I was obligated to leave civilities

to the civilized. She said I didn't look like a poet—my skin
was the color of cocoa from working on construction and
my hair close-cropped as a burdock. Her tone indicated that
in her own mind my destiny was settled—I was a yokel, a
clyde, as we teased those in high school who showed up
with manure still on their boots.

—I think you're all a bunch of fuckheaded phony
creeps.

—Why be impolite? I just said what they said.

—What do you think?

—I don't know.

I drew in my breath and felt as angry as I had ever been.
The sort of anger that precedes a fist fight when your eyes
tinge all outlines in red. I had felt the same way in football
when a halfback had gotten past me on a quick-opener. The
next time whether he had the ball or was simply blocking I
would necktie him from my middle linebacker position out
of simple generalized anger at being fooled. Or in Colorado
when another busboy who turned out to be a NCAA boxer
jabbed me fifty times before I could raise my hands and I
grabbed him and ran his face along a stucco-walled building until much of the skin came off and he looked peeled.

—I'm leaving in the morning.

—Why?

I put my hand on her shoulder and turned her toward
me and kissed her. She was stiff and didn't open her lips.
Then we kissed again lying back on the dock, this time with
her mouth open. We necked and embraced for about an
hour until my lips felt bruised but she wouldn't let me take
off her underpants. I rubbed my cock against them with

her legs wrapped around me until I came off against her
stomach. We separated then and I gave her my handkerchief
and lit a cigarette for her and one for myself.

—I love you, I said.

—No you don't.

End of idyll. I could not continue to live without them.
The three or four in my life have maintained my balance.
We left at dawn the next morning. I slid a note under her
bedroom door telling her again that I loved her. The door
abruptly opened and she came into my arms in her pale
blue summer nightie. We embraced and I let my hands slide
under and across her bare back and lower to her thighs then
in front to her sex and breasts not ceasing the kiss. Then
I walked away through the screen door without looking
back and got into the car. My friend drove a steady ninety
miles an hour to New York City where we checked into a
shabby hotel and wandered around the Village for two days
until we had only enough money to drive home. The first
night the elevator operator said he would bring us a whore.
When she knocked we were a bit frightened but then we
were eased by drinking most of a bottle of brandy. "French
for five, full screw for ten." The two of us reconnoitered in
the bathroom while she chugged the brandy. We decided
a combined twenty would cut too deeply into our funds so
that we would have to settle for a blowjob. We flipped and
I was to be first. I walked back into the bedroom and took
off all my clothes except my socks and handed her five dollars. She said that I had a nice tan and that she often took
a few days off and went out to Jones Beach. I lay back and
imagined it was the girl, that each sliding and collapse of the

lips was hers rather than the whore's which only accelerated the bargain. I felt mildly weepy and melancholy and dressed and went for a walk while my friend took his pleasure.

I walked over to Washington Square where a large crowd had gathered for a chamber music concert. I listened to a Telemann then a Monteverdi piece which only accentuated my melancholy. When I got back home to Michigan we wrote to each other for a year or so and when I moved to New York City at nineteen she came for a visit but never found me as I changed rooms often to avoid back rent. When a long letter from her was finally forwarded to me I wept. She said that she had taken a suitcase and wanted to stay with me a week or so before going off to school, that she had covered her activities through a friend and her parents wouldn't have known. On violet stationery with small flowers in the upper corner and scented with lavender. I read it dozens of times until it was stained with ale and coffee and sweat, rumpled from being stuffed in my billfold. I read it in bars, near fountains, in Central Park, in museums, in the grass on the bank of the Hudson near George Washington Bridge, and most often in my room, over and over in my room. There was a terrible finality to it, something missed permanently. She would begin seeing her old friend and I was to have been some sort of interim, like sleeping with a gypsy. I didn't care. At nineteen a body is so total. What else is there? The gift of the body and aimless nights of love. I sent her my prized Gallimard Rimbaud as a parting gift, leather-bound, onionskin paper with a crabbed love note on the flyleaf. "Should you change your mind . . ." Final end of idyll.

A half dozen years later I heard she was married. Nine years later I passed her home in Worcester, Massachusetts. I went into a neighborhood grocery store for cigarettes hoping to meet her by mistake even if she was pushing a baby carriage with quadruplets in it. I was amazed at the trembling sensation I felt at being so close to her after so many years, a mere block away. But she didn't appear and I finally drove away.

The cheap pup tent had begun to leak where I had scraped against it on the inside. Canvas does this. I was thinking of the expensive nylon tent I would buy someday, one piece with a floor, weighing only five pounds instead of twenty pounds of molding canvas. But the weather had turned warmer and the breeze had become soft and slight. Through the flaps I watched a doe, perhaps a hundred yards away, approach the creek for a drink in the twilight. Diurnal. Why no faun? She was plump and her summer coat was a deep reddish brown. Then she scented me and bounded soundlessly off into the brush the white underside of her tail flagging into the greenery. I got up when the rain stopped and boiled some pinto beans and chopped onion into which I dumped a tin of unhealthy-looking Argentine beef. Probably have to be shot for hoof and mouth disease. Buried by a bulldozer driven by God wearing bronzed sunglasses as in the movie *Hud*. Destroy this animal.

In the morning the sun was shining and it was warm so I decided to find the car and pack in the rest of my food. And resist driving fifty miles, one hundred miles round trip,

for four fifths of whiskey, or five fifths, or even more. With
whiskey I would become weeping and incompetent, perhaps
chop off a toe with the hatchet or roll in some poison oak or
get cramps and drown in the lake. I wanted to go back to
the lake; on the other side, in the distance, I thought I saw
what must be an osprey nest rising above the reeds on a gray
pine stump. There are very few osprey left and I wanted to
watch one at close range.

My second session in Boston came after an unsuccessful
college career and two years of unemployment. Between
jobs, you know. Looking for something better from a base
of zero. Nowadays education is the ticket to the future. I
don't scorn these clichés which express our fondest hopes
and dreams. I've long realized that if in addition to a thousand or so song lyrics they composed my sole continuous
vocabulary I would be famous and rich, rich and famous.
Rather than being turned away at the Ritz for having bucked
teeth, a single eye, and a butter-smeared face and lapel,
I would be welcomed with cymbals and snare drum and
Benny Goodman's clarinet. The butter was of course not real
butter or even margarine, but a badge of identity. As long
as I lived within the pages of a white-on-white comic book
I needed some sort of identification. Butter it would be. Or
a suspicious approximation gotten, the accusation goes, on
muff-diving expeditions on Memorial Drive. Radcliffe girls
were narcissistic and less than totally hygienic. Thus my
other notorious badge. A galvanized pail of hot water laced
with Duz or Fab and a sponge and Brillo Pads. Difficult

but worthwhile to carry. I'm sure you'll understand. This was before the days of Raspberry or Champagne douche, before the halcyon days when mice were transfigured into ultra-violet pom-poms. So I was an unlicensed scrubwoman far from home on my knees without portfolio, a sponge in one hand, in the other an angry red fist holding the apple of uncontrollable peace.

Anyway, on this second trip when I was trying to make a new start, collect myself, get my head above water, I would sit every morning in a Hayes-Bickford cafeteria reading the want ads in the *Globe*. This situation is too familiar to be amusing. Bank teller trainee $333 per month. I read an article in the Boston *Globe* on how while the locally unemployed were "miserable" they were not "desperate" and made a notation on the back of an application blank to check the difference in the Oxford Unabridged when I passed the library again. I always had at least ten of these blanks on my person. They tended to get frayed after a while and when I discarded them, a great deal of time had to be spent transferring my notes. I admit that I spent more time making notes than filling out applications. I could write my name with a great flourish at the top, but then begin to hedge at the address, home and local, and by the time I reached the social security line my energy would be sapped. All before reaching previous job experience, spouse, mother-in-law's maiden name, references. I waited for a time somewhere in the future when in a gratuitous burst of energy I would fill them out by the dozens, get a job, and move to the top. Once I was twelve stories above ground in a personnel office waiting to be interviewed for a creative opening in direct mail advertising. I sat reading business magazines for an hour, secretively licking my hand in order to brush down my cowlick. My stealth was unnecessary, the receptionist seemed to have forgotten my presence. I noticed that my lapel bulged unattractively from all the blanks stuffed in the pocket. I looked for a wastebasket but realized that it must be on the other side of the receptionist's desk or concealed in the room as furniture. Beside me was a window and I stood feigning interest in the street below. I took the sheaf of application blanks out and nudged them off the sill letting them slide as a group to death in the streets. They clung together for several stories but then a gust of wind caught them and they spread, floating gently as paper airplanes. If only an astronaut had been passing in parade. Several people looked up including a policeman on the other side of the street. I hastily backed away from the window.

—I saw you do that, the receptionist said.

I thought of shooting myself when the food ran out but immediately recognized the thought as literary. I would stick around until 2000 if only to tell my grandchildren I was right in 1970. The country by then totally denatured, lacking even the warmth of a pigpen, the humanity of a cow stanchion. Barns would be shrines and their gray leatherish boards would be licked and prayed to. I'm signing my body over to a medical school and using the cash, I think a hundred dollars, for dynamite. I can't though redress that grizzly shot while taking a nap or the Cripple Creek or the Sand Creek massacre. I dreamed of the latter once but the Sioux women

had become flour-white and danced around a fire with black
and green flames. For punishment the country of course has
become Germany with the Mississippi our Ruhr, the Ohio
the Rhine. My father who was a conservationist told me so
twenty years back but that was his profession. It is good that
he died in '63 before the extremity of the damage became apparent, before the bandwagon would appear with its load of
politicians farting and bleating out slogans and obtusities. A
sonic boom crushes a baby mink's skull. We know that. Isn't
it enough? If I were to shoot myself I would be obligated to
burn or bury my clothes and equipment, perhaps dig a deep
hole like a garbage pit in which to fall or a hole in which,
naked, I could drop the rifle with my last movement. Flesh
is reasonably good fertilizer, or even better, predator food. A
family of coyotes would live off the carcass for a few days.
Then the grass and ferns would grow up through the skeleton
until the porcupines had gnawed it away for its salt content.
That is why you find few deer antlers in the woods. But this
is largely romance. I like French restaurants. This is reason
enough not to kill myself; a mousse of pike, noisettes de veau,
Alsatian snails, fish soups. Or my own Mexican cooking,
crepes stuffed with chicken with a hot chilli sauce and sour
cream to assuage the bite of the red peppers. Or wine. Or
gallons of amber whiskey. Or my old remedy for colds used
in New York, Boston, San Francisco and home: first a quart
of freshly squeezed grapefruit juice, then a half gallon of lukewarm water to further cleanse the system. After two hours'
rest in a dark room broil a two-to-three-pound porterhouse
rare and eat it with your hands with no salt. After this with
your stomach swollen, distended, an extremely hot bath in

the dark in which you slowly sip the best bourbon you can
afford, at least a fifth, until the bottle is empty. This might
take four hours depending on your capacity. Then you sleep
for twenty-four hours and when you awake the world will
be new and you won't have a cold. Some people with weak
systems will have hangovers but that is not my fault. I'm not
a doctor. Go to your own doctor. You can go through this
whole process even if you don't have a cold and it's equally
pleasurable. I sometimes add a Havana cigar to the bath section but they are very expensive now and hard to come by.
This prescription also cures melancholy and makes you a mad
fucker for days afterwards. Oysters don't. When flush I once
ate four dozen oysters in a Union Oyster House in Boston and
then went over to Edward's Western Bar and was unable to
drink anything because I knew some of the oysters were still
alive, if vaguely, swishing around in my stomach with every
movement. Made for a bad evening at a nudie movie with my
Bostonian neighbors jacking off under newspapers. Rattle
rattle crinkle went the newspapers in the dark theater. Besides
I've had bad shellfish and vomited in complete, gymnastically
exact somersaults on the streets of Gloucester. A moderately
large crowd gathered. And I held a friend's hand in a hospital
as he died from hepatitis and complications. He kept whis-
pering, "Spread the word to artists everywhere, even on the
Continent and South America. No shellfish and dirty needles.
Take your speed orally. No oysters if they're peeking and no
clams in months without an *r*." His hand loosened in mine.
Our tears had fallen with metronomic steadiness but now his
stopped. I wailed while he grew to stone within his body, his
liver yellow and bald, an encephalitic head spewing poison

even after death. I drew the sheet over his face and buzzed
for a nurse. The protuberance of his liver under the muslin
made it appear that he died with a football on his stomach,
appropriate, as he used to love touch football in Central Park.
Then the nurse entered.

—The poet is morte.

—What?

—This guy is dead.

She looked at his face, drawing back the sheet.

—Right you are. Are you his doctor?

—In a very real way, yes. I practice only in special
cases.

She took two twenty-dollar gold pieces and placed
them over his sightless eyes and left the room. I pocketed
the gold pieces immediately and tried to pull down his eye-
lids but they snapped back like rubber bands or a condom
rolled down backwards. Finally I settled for a nickel and a
rabbit's foot I had been carrying for years. The rabbit's foot
looked a bit strange; it was from a snowshoe rabbit rather
than a cottontail and was long enough to stretch down to
his nose tip. I replaced the sheet.

Goodbye dearest friend, you till the farthest field now.
Say hello to Villon and Yeats. I'm sure you would want me to
have the gold pieces. These snazzbo hospitals go over-board.

A wordless yes to the gold piece question seemed to
fill the hallowed room as I left.

I once years back had an older but much unwiser profes-
sorial friend who told me after his seventh bloody mary:

—All you have to do is tell it like it is.

—But nothing is like anything, I replied with a very precise Oriental smile.

My compass wasn't in my pack or jacket pocket. I dragged out my sleeping bag and found it wedged in the ferns I had put down to absorb moisture. The dial was steamed up like a cheap watch often gets. It was a very expensive German compass given to me for Christmas. Not very subtle sabotage. The krauts are losing the touch, I thought, staring through the glass-encased fog, the red needle wavering. When I finally got a reading I didn't believe it and had known four days before that I wouldn't. But I put a package of raisins in my pocket, filled my World War Two canteen at the creek and set out for my car which I estimated to be about seven miles south-southwest. When I would reach the log road there'd be the question of which way to turn, left or right. Or maybe a Finn pulp cutter had broken a window and hot wired the car. A strange people, the Finns in the Upper Peninsula. They feed entirely on pasties — meat and rutabaga and potatoes wrapped in pie dough. They drink a great deal and when angry fight with axes and deer rifles. They aren't very inventive — even the pastie recipe was brought over from Cornwall during the copper boom in the last century. The Finns were imported as coolie labor and stuck to the area because of the snow and cold and short summers. It reminded them of another uninhabitable planet, their homeland. I met one in a bar who had chewed down a small cedar tree on a bet the year before and had pictures to prove it. He was virtually toothless having left his teeth in the wood to win his case of beer. I also had danced with a Finnish woman who showed me where her left tit had been shot off in a deer-hunting accident. The scar was an exact, a mirror image replica of the extinct Lassen volcano crater. I asked her if she would be willing to be shipped to the Smithsonian for verification.

What would happen to me if there were no woods to travel far back into — or when there is no more "backcountry" what will I do. Not that I am competent at it or feel truly comfortable. It is after all an alien world still existing, though truncated, in many places but its language largely forgotten. Someone has suggested that the will toward this world might be genetic. One of my grandfathers was a lumberjack, the other a farmer, ergo, when I am in New York seven or fifteen floors above ground I get vertigo. I simply can't adjust to layers and layers of people below and above me. I suffer excruciatingly in airplanes though I'm scarcely unique in this; but I crashed in a small plane at Meggs Field in Chicago when I was twelve or so. A strong cross wind off Lake Michigan caught us, tipped the plane and it cartwheeled down the runway shearing off the wings and settling finally a few feet from the breakwater upside down. A fire truck covered us with foam. I was hanging by my seatbelt, my shoes torn off by the impact and my brain pinwheeling in technicolor. We got our picture in the Chicago *Tribune* for surviving.

There is no romance in the woods in opposition to what fools insist. The romance is in progress, change, the

removing of the face of earth to install another face. Our
Indians were and still are great anti-romantics. Anyone
who disagrees should be parachuted or landed by float
plane in the Northwest Territory for a dose of romance.
I'm not talking about Wordsworth's Lake Country which
is beautiful, cute, cuddly, winsome, entirely housebroken.
On Whitsun a hundred thousand Englishmen trip around
those hills bumping into one another and pissing on one
another's boots.

If I were an arrogant heartless billionaire it would be
amusing to "plant" a hundred or so grizzlies or Kodiak bears
between Windermere and Penrith. But we don't have many
left ourselves, at least not enough to spare on a nation that
gobbles horsemeat, lets dogs get fat on candy and subject
to coronary attack.

I was especially desperate and lonely one week in April.
Boston was swimming under three feet of rain in two days
so I called an acquaintance in Vermont, a teacher at one of
those small colleges in New England that turn out a dis-
tinctive brand of adult by the cultivation of a certain style
of inclusive discipline. The point is not like the Marines,
to make "a man out of you," but to make a gentleman with
isolatable characteristics. Later, after they graduate, these
young men recognize each other, without previously meeting, as "Tulipberg Men." They avert their eyes and blush,
then slam together in an arcane embrace yelling secret words
and exchanging earlicks. Harvard, Yale, Princeton, Dartmouth are less obvious about such things. The superiority

is assumed and they are "old school" until they die, even if in secret while masquerading as radicals or poor people. A Dartmouth junior on a United flight to San Francisco told me that "Rocky" had been a Dartmouth "man." It is this splendid, worthless sort of camaraderie, Teutonic in origin, that lets these jerks mentally clusterfuck in the State Department while the world dies somewhere in the distance. Anyway I took the bus up to see Stuart and his wife. He told me on the phone, happily, that he was already an assistant professor with tenure. I said I was happy for you and yours and that I was currently living in Boston to straighten out the psychic knots in my life. I knew this would get me an invitation—Stuart is one of those people who like to talk things over with people and help them get up on their feet so they can meet the shit monsoon face to face. I bought a ticket with the last of my money at the bus station, telling the agent that there certainly seemed to be a long, long road winding to the land of my dreams.

I slept all the way up to Vermont forgetting to look at the heraldic, storied countryside. We stopped in each little village to pick up auto bumpers which the driver would slam into the baggage compartment and perhaps a single passenger. The streets of each village would be lined entirely with antique shops and the people, the few I could see through the blue-tinted window, reminded me of Georgians or Kentuckians. If you fuck your cousins for three hundred years something goes awry. This is true in parts of Lancaster County in Pennsylvania too where couples have been known to breed a half dozen albino dwarfs. When we finally reached Tulipberg I asked the driver how to get to

the college and he pointed over my left shoulder and said,
"Depends on how you want to go." These smartasses have
read about themselves in magazines and like to affect the
sort of taciturn dignity that they imagine their pilgrim forefathers had. I thanked him in a slow Texas drawl and said
something to the effect that you Yankees "shore are chuckle-
bait." And that down home even a greaser would have the
sense to kick the shit out of you for a stupid, impolite answer.
His hazel eyes flickered like a mink's at knifepoint.

I began to walk up the long hill to the college after
rechecking my billfold for the address. It was hard to imagine the school existed; the buildings were so covered with ivy
that they formed a single huge green mound if one squinted.
I asked a student for further directions and he called me sir.
A boy with a future.

I rang the doorbell and Mona answered saying you look
so skinny while pecking my nose. She said he's teaching now
but will be home for lunch and that there was a couch in
his study where I could rest from my trip. I lay back on the
couch and had a long, exhaustively boring fantasy about what
it would be like to screw Mona while the papa bear was off
teaching English 304. The worm failed to stir. The prospect
was lard. I got up and went over to the desk delighted with
the idea of snooping through the business with an ear toward
the door in case Mona should check on me. Perhaps she had
thoughts of using my poor body for a morning hog wallow.

Stuart's really the same as before, I thought. The desk
was covered with check stubs and dental bills, a colorful ad
for a socially reliable reading plan, and under that in a red
manila folder what looked like a play but turned out to be a

movie scenario written by the assistant prof himself. Visions
of spreading out into the "media" I bet. Told to no one at the
faculty club of course because tenure had been gained on an
unfinished manuscript dealing with William Dean Howells'
boyhood days. I began reading the script with forced interest.
There was to be a close-up of children trampling snow behind
a billboard, then a young man locked in a kitchen and asking
plaintively for his mother. I read with insufficient attention
to keep the story organized, remembering parts of the script
as one remembers a collage looked at hastily. Outside the
window a forsythia hummed with bees, the curtain billowed
in the warm spring air. Through the door small-craft warnings could be heard on the radio. "Thunder rolls over Lake
Winnipesaukee" as a Harvard poet once said. I read on until
a shot "rang out" and I had to turn back several pages to find
out who was in the room other than the leading man. No
one. Suicide. Curtain, rather "pan" to the dead man's nostrils
which will never again flare in anger. It all fitted back into the
folder, packed full of modish grief and academic surrealism.
I grabbed a men's magazine off the file cabinet. There was a
three-page foldout of an emetic, extremely top-heavy blonde.
Gargantuan tits. The girl-next-door look on her face assuming
next door were a sideshow or whorehouse. An accompanying
statement said the girl loved music, both classical and Dixie-
land, pizza, Kahlil Gibran, cheeseburgers with extra pickles,
and intellectuals who wore Continental clothing and drove
MGs. Startling contrasts. An evening with her beginning with
Cozy Cole and a cheese-burger pizza, then in the cramped
MG, flubbering and mooing between the huge udders. But
then on a hot afternoon the week before in Cambridge I had

seen a girl in engineer boots and a mu-mu fixing her Triumph
650-cc. motorcycle.

The radio now blared a hip version of "Greensleeves"
and then the phone rang and she turned it down. It seemed
strange that such a song would persist through the ages,
coming into the twentieth century with its full weight of
melancholy intact. The melody was muted by the walls of
the study but with the odor of forsythia and sea rose and
blooming fruit trees in the yard I saw feudal England with
her forests of primary green and a woman, her finery faintly
soiled by the smoke of war and the dust of carriages but still
lovely. Irrelevant along this seaboard glutted with people,
not an acre of free soil between Boston and Washington. I
cautioned myself about such thoughts, their weight of utter
pointlessness. The humor in the new bridge that collapsed,
seen on television. The bridge writhed and bucked like a
rattlesnake with its head freshly cut off, then collapsed into
the river. Small engineering error. The stress of the times.
Struts akimbo, cable whipping.

She came to the door of the study and told me that Stuart would be another hour. It was preregistration week at
the college and his advisees had to be counseled. Take four
courses of flummery then take it in the ass. I could smell her
motherhood through the door—baby food, piss, Pablum, the
pail of diapers in the potty. Takes so much less time to house-
break a dog. She had modeled for a large department store
in Milwaukee before marrying Stuart. She deftly brought
up her "modeling days" in conversation again and again as
if it ameliorated the horror with which she regarded her two
children and the shabby rented house. She was still attractive

in a retired show girl way, but the floozy in the future was clearly visible in the fat she was putting on.

The evening's dinner terminated the weekend. After Stuart returned from school hours late and I had had a nap ruined by his little daughter poking a dirty finger in my eye, we launched into a long cocktail hour. At least six martinis apiece and she mixed herself doubles. She blabbered on about her lineage, Estonian nobility, who had flown the coop as always on the eve of the Great War. She was hurt when I giggled at the idea. You know all the phrasing, refugees of high birth trotting across the Carpathians through Transylvania, past the ruins of the Baron von Frankenstein's castle, always with their pockets stuffed with jewelry and Sèvres eggs, and alabaster dildos polished with use. She became angry at me and asked about my ancestors. I said that I had none who had ever set eyes on so much as a crypto-duchess. My ancestors were pig thieves and herring eaters who worked as little as possible and burned cow dung in their pot-bellied stoves because wood chopping was too onerous a chore. They often sat in barrels of potato and raisin wine, drawing the liquid osmotically up through their asses when they were too drunk to lift a glass.

She wasn't amused. Through all of this Stuart continued talking about his students and his progress on the Howells book. Some truly little-known facts about the boyhood of this fabulous author would be revealed. The book would "shake" to its foundations Howells scholarship in this country and abroad.

—Do you really give a fuck about him?

Stuart blanched and took a long drink.

—Somebody has to set the record straight.

Then porky chimed in in defense of her husband. How could a bum question an ambitious man? And in his own home. I apologized. My years since college were fraught with mental problems, anxieties that made me forget the grandness in our traditions of scholarship. We then sat down and ate Bengal curry which was tepid and a chocolate cake covered with stale grated coconut on the butterscotch frosting. She looked at my plate.

—Aren't you hungry?

—Sure but that curry was a belly packer and I've never been a dessert man.

Then a protracted argument about ghosts began over brandy. And astrology. She believed and he didn't. As the brandy bottle emptied, they were drinking it in gulps, the argument grew heated.

—You're a stupid cunt, Stuart said.

—That word! she screamed leaping at him and slapping his face.

He grabbed a wet diaper beside his chair and snapped it at her knocking off her glasses. Then they slapped at each other with a general windmill effect until she yanked his hair backwards over the couch and his mouth opened wide in a voiceless scream. She released her grip and they cried and embraced. I went to bed on the studio couch to the noise of their lovemaking on the dining-room floor.

From a promontory in a grove of birch trees I took another compass reading: by my own reckoning I should have covered a little over half the distance to the car. I had not stopped for even a short rest because a small cloud of deer flies were following me and I had forgotten to apply any bug dope before I left. These little mistakes can cause great pain—a deer fly looks like a rather large common house fly but their sting draws blood. I understand that only the female has a stinger and that the male wanders around sucking on leaves mutely hoping for a mid-air collision with the female. After their little fun in the sky the female eats the male, rather draws out his small quantity of blood through his soft underbelly. I've invented the latter bit of information to substantiate the old Hollywood "kiss of death" idea. If Lana or Faith Domergue kisses you there's no chance for survival. My compass reading gave my position as thirty degrees or so in the wrong direction. But it was easier walking that way. I aimed my tired body again, the empty pack flapping on my back, the day unpleasantly warm. My down-hill imaginary path would, I knew, lead me to a swamp or a marsh. There are hundreds of them in the area, at one time they were lakes but over the years they have gradually silted, become weed-choked, and the cedars took hold of the spongy soil and some tamarack also grew. I wanted to find a small creek and walk parallel to it on higher ground until it led me inevitably to the headwaters of the Huron River where my car was parked off a log road under a mammoth white pine tree.

It occurred to me that all my miseries in Boston were invented and geographical—a simple move to New York City would change everything. I would meet a *Vogue* model (a

trifle fleshier than the usual) and she would take me into
her very pleasant though modest three-room apartment
on East Seventy-seventh Street and keep me forever safe.
Daily rubdowns with coconut butter and drone bee ex-
crement would keep me young and attractive, and a diet
of steak crawling with wheat and other vegetable germs
would assure my health and consistent potency. She might
be a few inches taller than my five ten so after a hard day's
work splayed before Avedon she would let herself in with
her own key and I would jump up and down to kiss her
much like a toy poodle greets its master. After she had a
snack of poached broccoli lashed with native crude oil
her large eyes would darken, dart to my silk bell bottoms
wondering if I were ready to administer the hot beef injec-
tion. Sometimes I would prove kittenish and she would
have to chase me, her long legs and big feet flapping over
the carpet in pursuit.

Too homely to be a kept man. The last time I had been
in New York I had worked for a small building demolition
company at non-union wages. Sledging plaster.

I walked across the Charles Street bridge with a thirty-
cent box of caramel corn. If you drank from that river death
would come convulsively within the hour. The caramel corn
was a little stale. Last night's. Don't buy caramel corn in the
morning or you'll get some from yesterday's last batch. Too
chewy having absorbed some Bostonian moisture during its
night alone. I was headed for the Oxford Grill and a budget
lunch with five glasses of ale. I would read the New York
Times want ads to see if my future was waiting for me in
Manhattan.

Up the avenue past MIT where secret very important killing machines were being invented almost daily by
unscrupulous but very honest scientists. They commute
daily from Lexington and Concord, Weston and Lincoln,
where they live in colonial exactness. We've been told so
often what their wives conceal under the skin. And I don't
mean the PTA though that's part of it. A tear shed for the
grocery boy. Cantaloupe with ice cream at mid-morning
coffee and a heavy use of the telephone to exchange chit-
chat with soul sisters. Past the Necco plant with many
wafers for a nickel. Then the dangerous streets where young
wop thugs beat up students. Often deservedly I think.
If you're unemployed and your head is weighted down
with hair grease you resent those slumming fops with five-
hundred-dollar watches, long hair, five-dollar trousers and
hundred-dollar sport coats who call the subway station
a "kiosk." Lucky I was dressed anonymously in a Mari-
mekko jump suit. Really stinking Levi's and a black T-shirt
with cigarettes rolled up in one short sleeve and hair cut
close to the scalp. Looked like an unemployed busboy
which I was.

At the Grill I exchanged pleasantries with a bartender
who hated the "frigging" students and commuted from
Somerville where he lived with his mother. He gave me
daily unasked-for tips on the horses. Back across the river
in my local Allston bar there were five pay phones for those
timely calls. Sharkskin suits drinking "Cutty" and ginger
ale. Or scotch and cream. Social mobility I suppose but
now the upper classes drink cheap bourbon with tap water
and a sprig of ragweed. The poor are always fooled. Even

when they become rich. I had my first two ales and ordered scrod with parsley butter and mashed potatoes that inevitably came with chicken or beef gravy in most places, ham or fish notwithstanding. Two girls entered and took a seat in the booth behind me. I swiveled and took a look; one was painfully thin and would remain so until her light casket was lowered, the other smiled at me attractively with bucky beaver teeth like my own. A pendulum of gold around her neck which banker dad gave her for being good. Could she cover those teeth at important moments? I smiled back and approved of her with all of my weak, starved heart—her knee-high boots could support me for two weeks. The meal came and I covered the plate with catsup which is very nutritional besides being a family habit. I cleaned my plate quickly merging the fish with the caramel corn. I swiveled again and flashed another harmless smile at beaver girl but she had turned and was putting on her coat having finished her crème de menthe frappé. The making of the drink had sent my friend the bartender into a fit of spite; I told him to put bitters in it and next time she would order something civilized. Out the door. Will we meet again preferably down by the riverside. A tea-head friend entered and ordered sandwich and pop. He was halfway up in the air and needed no alcohol. He called me baby and invited me to a party to be held that night. I said that I'd come, then broke my promises and slid my single hidden five out of my billfold and had three double bourbons in quick succession. Then I walked down Boylston, crossed Memorial Drive and fell woozily asleep in the dirty grass near the crew boathouse.

I woke up in time to catch dinner at my brother's, Cornish game hens basted with peach brandy. Goody. He is a librarian and has repressed his lowlife instincts for a good marriage, reading, fine food and hard work. I admire him without reservation and never forget that back home he had been an Eagle Scout whereas I had been ousted from the troop as a chronic malcontent. He'd been kind to take me in for a while on various past occasions so I could keep my head above water and look for a job, loaning me a suit for imaginary interviews and other niceties I didn't deserve. Such grief I've caused everyone with nervous breakdowns during three successive Februaries. I simply can't get through the month without a brush with the booby hatch; I'm sure it's climatic, seasonal. The ice is breaking up so I can live again. Meanwhile a litter of weeping wife and mom and all of that which I don't take callously. Then I'd be driven to the bus station, given a pittance in addition to the ticket and urged in family conferences to try to make my way at something. My brother though enjoys hearing stories that I tell about the subterranean layers of drugs and sodomy that exist in his adopted city. Instance: I was offered the chance for five dollars to watch two lesbians couple. The bar was closing and a wizened little Greek had thus far collected an audience of five sailors. I was curious but didn't have five dollars. However I tell my brother I went and watched two rather frail girls on a couch while the sailors cheered them on which they no doubt did. And the secret Radcliffe rooming house for ultrarich girls where they have five Dobermans and a housemother who wears patent leather hip boots.

✿   ✿   ✿

Near the edge of the marsh among the cattails there was a flock of redwing blackbirds: the vermilion cusp under their wings brilliant against the green whenever they flew from stalk to stalk. I want to be decorated, a ridge along my back with fur on it, hackle of orange under my ears, long pointed molars, rooster comb of aquamarine down the center of my head and the whole body feathered in burnt sienna. That would show them, the frightening toast of the nation.

I stopped after encircling half the marsh and found with another compass reading that I was heading radically left from my mark. I turned in a march right and sighted on the tip of a dead tree perhaps a mile away then sat down and ate some raisins and dried beef and a swig from my canteen. The water was warmish, tasting of tin. The canteen had no doubt been left out in the sun at Guadalcanal or Bataan and perhaps a baby viper had nested in it when it was left capless. Or a family of spiders that specialized in eating insects off cobras' backs. My calculations were leaving me two hours behind, at least four by the time I reached the car; the sun looked high noon and heated my scalp around which flies buzzed landing momentarily until I would brush them off. There is a local miniscule bug wittily called "no-see-ums" which also tormented me with small red dots on my flesh. I itched everything until I had counted the night before in fire-light one hundred thirty-three scabs, large and small, both actively suppurating and lightly irritating. I felt at the time that nature should build me a sidewalk to the car and a pair of moderately expensive roller skates should appear by my side and a beautiful girl to lace them up tightly. I would say how about the next dance and we would Skater's Waltz to the car where even though hot and tired I would bang at her unmercifully in the back seat. One of her legs would be draped over the front seat with the rollers continuing to roll and the music going on as if she had a stereo cassette in the crack of her ass.

I got up painfully. O lord how long? Around the tree and in serpentine curl in the distance the green was a bit darker. Perhaps the creek I was looking for. The map anyway was inaccurate and I planned a stop at the conservation head-quarters where I had gotten the map: This is a piece of inaccurate shit, I would say, balling it up and throwing it in his face. There would be no retaliation—the forty pounds of chromium steel flamethrower would be so clearly visible on my back. I wanted a polite "we're sorry sir" then a promise for a massive effort to rectify the inaccuracies no matter the cost. I'll ship you lazy assholes a helicopter f.o.b. so you can look at your territory. Get your boots muddy, son, your hands are bleached and have paper burns. Then I would tear the patch off the shoulder of his uniform, kiss his neck and slide off into the dark leaving behind a changed officer.

I finally reached the tree and as I had suspected a small creek did burble by it; I walked along its bank, thrashing through the brush with an eye out for wolf tracks on any sand bars. There were supposedly a dozen or so in the area and I wanted to see one desperately. I met a hunter in Ishpeming who had once heard a wolf howling in the area, and an answering howl from another hill. But this was on the Yellow Dog plains some twenty miles to my east. There are only three or four hundred native wolves left in the United States. They are rarely heard and even more rarely seen, except in unnatural circumstances as on Isle Royale during the winter from a plane. I felt that if I could see one all my luck would change. Maybe I would track it until it stopped and greeted me and we would embrace and I would become a wolf.

I estimated that it was nearly five o'clock when I stumbled onto the rutted log road and saw my car blue and innocent sitting under the tree. Ten hours to walk seven miles. An ignorant maze path through the woods. I would have to sleep in the car rather than chancing the walk back before dark.

I got to the party very late having napped again after dinner. My sister-in-law is a light feeder so I had two game hens to myself, and even though they weren't cooked quite long enough for my taste I ate them down to their little pink bones and gristle. Even chewing the "pope's nose" which was what we always called the knobby bung bud. The walk to the party was close to fifty blocks of sweet drowsiness, my head just drunken enough to not quite perceive my feet. A half gallon of cheap rosé. A polite glass for the others then a ten-ounce water glass for me. Many of them. How well rosé goes with the spring, I had quipped, drenching my third napkin with sauce and fowl fat, my mustache stiff with it. Smelling of peach brandy now as I walked crushing fallen maple buds. So happy I could kiss a fireplug if there were no dogs on earth. A mustache enables one on waking to scent last night's sins. On a dark corner near the

Cambridge-Somerville line I pissed on a fireplug. Will puzzle
the neighborhood dogs for weeks no doubt. They'll trans-
mit questions through Morse code type barks and whines.
Where is this new creature?

The party was obviously descending from its apex when
I arrived. Dozens of people sprawled on the floor or sat
limply. Absolutely stoned. Who wrote about the frangipanic
clock? An eager undergraduate type said to me, I'm Bob
who are you? I'm Swanson, prince d'Allston. OK. A bookish
vulgar type he was with Bass Weejuns customized to allow a
Kennedy half dollar. Air very heavy with cannabis. I found
my friend sitting in a bedroom with eyes so dull and rheumy
they looked like they were painted with snot. His right hand
held a bomber which I lifted and lit, inhaling three enormous
drags and choking. A girl sitting at a dresser said that there
was hash in there too. Good for me, I'll catch up I thought.
She was a little too round-faced to be attractive and talked
out of the corner of her mouth, a characteristic the eastern
upper class shares with gangsters and pimps.

—A lovely night, I said.

—Is it? she replied smartly.

—It would be if you stuck your fat face out the window.

I cased the living room for female probabilities. None.
Either soiled, ugly or taken. I returned to the bedroom
changing my tune and exchanged pleasantries with moon-
face. She had evidently forgotten I had been with her a few
minutes before.

—You guys must have had a wonderful time, I said
over the deafening sound of the Beatles singing "Michelle."
I bet your name is Michelle.

—I wish it was. She looked down at her very distant feet tapping and swinging.

I suggested a little walk for fresh air and she followed me listlessly down the back stairs and out the door. No grass of any kind here. An alley with seventy-seven garbage cans stretched out. Hash now in my eyeballs. Better get to work. We necked and I looked around for a comfortable spot but there wasn't any. Boobies bare to street lamp at alley's end. I turned her around and lifted her skirt, no panties only the nest. I reached down to see if my prick was there. The drug made my zipper sound like a machine gun. My prick was there but further away than usual. I bent her over and entered working in a tireless slow motion. She said wow once or twice and hummed a little. Smack smack. When I came I stumbled backwards falling on my ass and felt no pain. She turned and looked at me idly, straightened her skirt and went back up to the party. I got up slowly nearly tripping on my pants which were strangling my ankles. The corrugated edges of a bottle cap stuck in the cheek of my ass. I pulled up my pants very dizzily and then walked out the alley and turned toward Harvard Square.

The inside of the car was very hot and stale-smelling. There was a choice of keeping the windows closed and dying of asphyxiation or opening them and being bitten to death. Bugs are God's creatures too, only less so than we are we have to assume if we have any sense. I opened a tin of Vienna sausages, teeny weenies in a brackish warm sauce. Flies buzzed in the open door and one malevolent wasp with a howtizer stinger hanging from its tail. I walked down to the creek which was wider in this location having been fed by springs in smaller creeks in the higher country. There was a small waterfall and a deep pool where the water plunged with a fine steady roar. Nice to sleep to. No night noises, the bear or leviathan to slide its paw in the car window. I rinsed out a piece of cheesecloth I had used to wipe the windshield and intended to wrap around my head as a bug protector. Then I quickly shed my clothes and dove into the eddy, swimming under the turbulent water of the falls. I opened my eyes in the white oxygenated icy water and then let its force carry me downstream a hundred feet or so. Numb, I'll float to the ocean. Lake Superior first, though. But snags, deadfalls would catch me, or a slippery boulder would receive my head and put the lights out. Floater dies in downward trip to sea. Remains were not found by anyone. No one was looking except a single angry kingfisher. I got out and walked back upstream on a bed of pine needles, cold to the bones. I stood naked on the log road for a moment lighting a cigarette in the sun. Still four hours or so before absolute dark which falls up here at about ten o'clock. I would go to sleep early and leave at dawn for my camp.

Curled at twilight in the back seat of the car and trying to breathe through the musty cheesecloth. Smell of lint and cleaning fluid, chalk dust, Spanish rice in high schools throughout the nation. Siss boom bah siss boom bahhh they yell at basketball games. Walking way out Boylston in Boston until it turned into Route 9. A right at Chestnut Hill Road and watching a beautiful tanned girl at Longwood Cricket Club bounce a tennis ball off the far cement wall.

Hair drawn back to keep it out of her eyes during the up-
coming match with Bryce Porker, depraved but handsome
coupon clipper. Sing of injustice all ober dis land, especially
here where I am behind the fence watching her long smooth
brown legs and how they aim upwards to her ass. Sleeveless
blouse and graceful arms. Fairly tall and high-waisted with
a startling face. Like Lauren Hutton's the *Vogue* model. I
read *Seventeen* in drugstores a little furtively. She glanced at
me and scowled. Private club with a waiting list of 66,333. I
have twelve cents exactly and will buy you a lemon Coke. I
held on to the fence with my fingers, a prisoner of war and
poverty, and, of course, hunger. She turned again with a
cool stare, not thirty-three feet away then walked toward the
distant clubhouse without a backward glance. I flopped in
the car seat nose pointed downward to the seat back, a single
mosquito now inside the cloth searching for my eyeball. She
doesn't evidently want my wordless lemon Coke. Come back
Bonnie. Right now. I wouldn't stare, I'll look up in the sky
at no birds. Probably is a sophomore at Sarah Lawrence
and is interested in the urban crisis. Fucks a fifty-five-year-
old political science professor, dodo Mr. Chips with a gray
goatee and he plied her at afternoon coffee with a vial of
cantharides. In the future I'll meet her by accident at a party
in New York. I'll shun her. Maybe slap her face with just the
tips of my fingers. She'll ask for forgiveness and say I wish
I had had that lemon Coke now that I know you're famous.
Precisely. After a week of discipline and endless strategic
caresses I'd give her to a barnstorming soccer team from
Africa. Or maybe to the Harlem Globetrotters. She had her
chance and didn't blow it. Walking through Chestnut Hill,

gardeners eyed me suspiciously and mastiffs were released
to chase me back to my own pitiful neighborhood. Dear
girl if you read this you'll recognize yourself. Remember
me and how I pressed my face against the Cyclone fence
until it was covered with red trapezoids. Remember? I wish
you a colostomy, piles, pyuria, and a short-peckered lisping
husband. May you rot between Dover and Dedham. May
you fall off your horse. Don't try to approach me. I have an
unlisted number and no phone and it's much, much too late.

I couldn't sleep in the car. I sat up and lit a cigarette
blowing smoke at the nearest mosquitoes. I got out of the
car and walked up the road until I was out of reach of the
pounding sound of the waterfall. A full moon, wolfbane
blooms tonight. I imagined, or was the figure real, that I
saw a large dog cross the road in the distance. A coyote or
a wolf. But my scent had to drive wolves away. No dogs
here. A coyote or a hallucination. The wolf to count had to
be seen clearly in daylight.

At dawn I packed the food and filled the canteen in the
creek after only an hour's restless sleep. My tracks on the
log road were covered here and there by those of a small
bear. Smelled the food. I locked the car and set out for my
tent and made the site before noon, less than half the time it
had taken me to find the car. My shoulders were sore from
the straps of my cheap pack and my body dead from the
night's nightmarish lack of sleep.

Boston. The night before I intended to leave I got horribly
drunk at Jake Wirth's and ate a half dozen frankfurters

and a blue cheese and Bermuda onion sandwich on dark
bread. That in addition to twelve double Jim Beams and a
few steins of beer put quite a dent in my savings. But there
were nutritional benefits I'm sure. I slept on the floor of
my room having arrived there by the grace of some strange
power; perhaps it was . . . but no it couldn't be. Sometime
before dawn I awoke suddenly, thinking someone was in the
room with me. The door was open. I felt that either something horrible was happening to me or would happen that
day. I got up from the floor and slammed the door shut and
then tried to sleep again. But I couldn't sleep so I sat naked
before the open window facing the roofs of the apartments
across the street. Perhaps this meant that I was going to
die today—the bus would carom across the median and roll
over. But I quickly forgot about death. I've had hundreds
of intuitions of death and none of them, fortunately, were
accurate.

A sea breeze began. The room had been stuffy and
damp but the breeze was stiff, cool and strong in the darkness and flooded me with fresh air. I heard a crow and saw it
dimly against the sky which owned a thin pale line of red in
the east. Then the other birds started but the crow's cawing
was first. I remembered that when you see a single crow he
is a scout but then none followed. A lone crow.

I got up from the chair and walked to the stove, stepping over my suitcase. I had inherited the suitcase from my
dad and it was fake leather with many cracks showing the
cardboard beneath. Linoleum cracks and shows the black
pitch beneath where crows are born and dwell. I wanted
some coffee and when I lit the gas my belly and genitals and

thighs turned blue. What color are the dead? A blue crow now with the price of a ticket to New York. A bus ticket. No tribe or fellow crows. Then I turned on the lamp out of fright and looked at my arms, the veins in the forearms thick and knotted and blue. Blood ready to clot without warning. A blue lump will float upward and around the shoulder to the heart's bull's-eye. Biliously drank the instant coffee and put on my clothes. The sun was now an orange oblong of light on the far wall. Rattle of milk bottles below. I was way back in my youth hiding in the reeds and lily pads with only my scalp and nose and eyes above the water line. My friend, the girl in the next cabin, was entering the water hesitantly. She was twelve, nearly hairless below the neck, plump, pink, very pretty with long black hair in pigtails. We greeted each other underwater and when we came up for air holding each other there were crows above the swamp across the lake.

A foul unseasonable cold was hanging in the air, rain which was almost sleet falling steadily. Boston lying out there, a dead wet cod with buggy eyes. The suitcase was heavy and cumbersome to carry; I shouldered it, then tried holding it in front of me as a buffer against the wet wind. Full of dirty clothes and too many books. I felt like pitching it in the gutter and starting clean. I caught the trolley for Park Street and was happy when it descended out of the ugliness into the dark hole at Kenmore Square. I got out at Copley impulsively and glanced up Huntington at Storyville which had gone out of business, a club where all the jazz greats had given their drugged and frantic hearts to the sybarites, sets so grand that hearts should have broken openly and blood poured to the floor. I crossed Copley

Square against the traffic — everyone beeped but I somehow
didn't care whether I was hit or not. Giant lawsuit frees man
forever from financial grief headlined the *Globe*. An airport
limousine pulling up before the Plaza barely missed me. I
had been in there only once, proposing marriage to a girl
while we sat at an ornately canopied bar that revolved like
a merry-go-round. I'd too much to drink and had asked
the bartender if he couldn't pull the plug and stop the god-
damned thing. And we were asked to leave and she cried
not because we were kicked out but that my proposal had
been so flip. I shifted the suitcase to my shoulder again
and stared at the public library where I had spent so much
time reading magazines and writing my history of rain and
grief. So many freaks in libraries. Same in New York and
Frisco. They shit on the toilet floor and blabber incoher-
ently, pestering everyone. Once I saw a young man yell
"look" in the lobby and let his prick hang out; he closed his
overcoat then and tried to run out the door, rather swirled
clumsily in the revolving door. One woman screamed but
most people shrugged. Depressing. He needed help. A lock
on his zipper for beginners.

Down Park Street to the bus station where I sat on a
bench and waited for the hourly New York shuttle. No spiff
here. Those most likely to spit or vomit ride buses; inmates
of any institution, freshly released, crisscross the country
in buses, all stations with the stink and mumbling woven
in, the smell of diesel exhaust and free exchange of terminal
viruses at the lunch counters, drinking fountains and rest
rooms. I sat next to a black soldier and we talked about the
Bruins and Patriots; sports are a common harmless interest

in waiting rooms. And all the pointy loafers cruising past with eyes on crotch bulge, hanging around to find a friend in need. Pop goes the weasel.

I had a cup of wretched acidic coffee, then finally boarded. A lovely girl got on at the Newton stop but there was no way to get near her so I looked at her neck until we reached the Connecticut border and I fell asleep. Then, further on, at a lunch stop near Hartford I got a closer look and saw that her face was covered with an even sheen of pimple hider. On certain days it seems that all loveliness has fled the earth. Upper lip over her teeth but one protruded with a suspicion of fang and vampire far in the past, a predisposition not to be changed by the sociology text she read in half-sentence snatches before looking up again. The poor are broke, they say. The upper class tends toward tennis and expensive water sports. And air travel while the poor ride buses. Immigrants tend to learn the language. Finally down Ninth Avenue to the beige colonic Port Authority. New York. I intended to stay for only a few days; see some people, and there was a very wan hope that I might collect a debt from an old friend. Then I would go home to Michigan, work up a grubstake, and perhaps head out for San Francisco where I would start another new life.

Chapter 3

The West

If you look at a map of the American West closely (I mean by West all land on the far side of Kansas City) you'll find an unequivocal resemblance to the topography of Siberia or the Urals. But television of course has proven this notion untrue—those thin blue and black and red lines on maps indicating rivers, roads and boundaries tell less than the whole story as we say. I'm not talking about the grandness of the Louisiana Purchase, the trek of Lewis and Clark, the endless string of wagon trains, the Donner party (quite a party) or the TV program *Low Cheapwhorehole*. Or even that dead bird *Route 66*, not the road but the program. And I'm not dealing here with the vicious average, the West as the result of a genocidal march, or the Turner Thesis with the West rolling up finally into a ball of tinsel glued with the blood of Chicanos and Indians. This is all the job of historians. Universities are littered with them and their

disputes over what area belongs to which prof; there are the
usual mimsy slap and molasses quarrels about who is going
to teach Louisiana Territory 503. But then they deserve their
own trifling smegma quarrels. We will wait until one of them
tells the true story in a monumental ten-volume study, *The
Drek Trek: The Westward Surge of Pigshit to the Pacific's Watery
Lip.* You must note that academic book and paper titles uniformly own full colons. This fact can be considered a key to
what they are teaching our children. Inflation is eating up
our savings. The colon is both full and empty. An implosion
rather than explosion is due. Perhaps deep in the bowels of
Montana in a vast cavern the absence of buffalo prepares a
non-stampede. Crazy Horse watches over them, still digest-
ing Cluster's heart.

Hard to be bitter with the warm evening sun dappling down
through the birches, mottling tent and ground with yellow. I
would shoot a doe and eat fresh meat but much of it would
rot. Better to eat roots and leave deer for the necessary
sportsman. A sweet story of how one booster type, rich,
owned a small herd of buffalo, raising them as a hobby and
culling (selective killing) when there were too many. Buffalo
steaks for sale and not bad tasting, somewhat like old moose,
better for pot roast than steak. Anyway an archer bought
an animal "on the hoof" to kill a trophy. After shooting
over thirty arrows into the beast from fairly close range the
buffalo failed to die and resembled a giant sparsely quilled
porcupine. The state police were called and a trooper fanned
his .38 into the slumping body, down on the front knees. The

buffalo then rolled over in its death throes crushing many valuable arrows. End of anecdote. Suggested punishment? Devise your own. Anyway the great outdoors must have shrunk visibly and if you were an astronaut looking down from a half thousand miles some sort of tremor or shudder must have been apparent. This is dead-end romanticism of course. Nothing happened. The trooper trooped home after work and told his wife. The owner shook his head and said "golly." The archer told his friends that buffalo were tough, dangerous ole hombres and hard to bring down.

When I first reached Laramie I bought a cowboy shirt and a high-crowned hat. My boots were still stiff, bought back in Fort Morgan, Colorado, where I got off the bus. End of the line—with my money low I thought I could hitch-hike from there to California, only fourteen hundred miles down the road and this was my second trip. Seasoned. On the first trip I had taken a bus to the Michigan border and spent all day getting to Terre Haute. I had to walk across most of Indianapolis; the roads confused me and when I finally got them straightened out a young couple picked me up and gave me a ride to Terre Haute. I stood about three hours before anyone stopped. This time it was a mechanic from Pittsburgh who said he was going to L.A. They never say Los Angeles—they say L.A. I intended to go to San Francisco, or I had the day before, but the long ride was tempting. By Joplin we knew each other well and he admitted the car was "hot" and that he was a bigamist and would disappear in L.A. Maybe go to Mexico until things cooled

off. He shared his cache of little white pills and we stayed
awake from Indiana to California, losing control of the car
only once in the Panhandle and then it was a harmless short
screaming trip out through the mesquite and back onto the
road without stopping.

I put all my food that wasn't tinned in an onion sack and
tied the opening with a rope which I threw over a tree limb
and secured. When I had gotten back to the tent there were
raccoon tracks all over and I didn't want all my remaining
food hauled away while I hiked back to the lake. I thought
of my wife for a few moments. Fine girl who strangely didn't
want to be married to a drunk. She wasn't, however, jeal-
ous of tents. I had been by now four and one half full days
without a drink—certainly my most extended sequence in
ten years. It wasn't so bad as long as there weren't people
around. I put some fishing line, hooks, sinkers in the pouch
I carried at my waist. No need for the canteen.

   The hike to the lake was easy and familiar. I saw my
tracks on the sand bar from which I had shot the turtle.
Hadn't carried the gun lately, useless heavy baggage.
Smarter to carry it in Oakland. I shaded my eyes and looked
at the far shore toward where I thought I had spotted an
osprey nest; the nest was there and I wondered what would
be the shortest, easiest way around the lake. If I had been
smart enough to bring binoculars I could have glassed both
shores and found out but then I had left in a hurry. Crazy
guy flees. I chose left, walking along the lake's edge with a
wary eye cocked for water snakes. I can bear almost any sort

of snake except rattlers and water snakes though I'm not partial to blue racers either because of their agility. Often while trout fishing I've seen them fat and thick and blue ten feet up in a cedar tree. I came to where a swamp abutted the lake and sat down and took off my boots, tying their laces together and slinging them around my neck. I waded gingerly at first but the bottom was solid though my feet were numbing from the cold water. I came around a point of firs jutting out into the water, by this time thigh deep in a patch of lily pads with their huge white flowers and smaller yellow flowers. On the far side of the point a creek emptied into the lake and even next to shore it was too deep to wade. Probably good fishing here but I wanted to reach the nest before noon. I pulled myself up into a thicket and sat down on a fallen tamarack and put on my boots. It was hot and I was sweating and the sweat washed the mosquito dope into my eyes which felt red and stung.

I stayed over night in Laramie in a fleabag hotel down near the railroad yards. Cowshit in the air and switching diesels all night. The hotel apparently doubled as the local cut-rate whorehouse. The room clerk, as usual tubercular and middle-aged, had looked at me inquiringly. Then there was laughter and drunken shouting throughout the night. I was going to go back to Cheyenne the next day to see the big rodeo I had heard about in a bar that evening. When I got into bed I slid my billfold down into my shorts. Then I got up and propped a chair under the doorknob kicking at the rungs until the wedge was solid. I smoked for a while and then got up again and looked out the window and watched the switching engines with their single headlights bobbing and the cars banging together, "Route of the Eagles" and "Route of the Phoebe Snow" and "Lackawanna" were my favorite car names. I took the pint of whiskey from my bedroll and drew heavily on it. Only half left and no chaser. I drank again until it was gone then slept peacefully to the varied noises, only discomfited by the cattle bawling in their cattle cars. On the way to the knife in St. Louis or Chicago.

Let's admit that Cheyenne is a cow plot. And Denver too for that matter. They were dropped on earth from a particular height and spread as a cow plot does in the grass. Plop plop plop. Deranged and headless, oil poured on still water; the skirt of the city with the motels, car lots, hamburger driveins, gas stations with hundred-foot-high signs visible from the freeways, and thousands of indefinable small businesses in one-story brick or cement-block buildings. In the latter dark purposes are carried out. Real estate and unreal estate. Toilet fixtures. The House of a Thousand Lamps. Brad's Steak 'n' Egg Stop. But we know all about this and there's no way to start over again.

About five A.M. I walked out to a Route 90 interchange after having a good breakfast at the Switchman's Cafe with the stools lined with railroad men in blue-and-white-striped bib overalls and engineer caps on. Pancakes with a slice of ham on top and three eggs on the slice of ham. Insulin shock and drowsiness barely after whippoorwill's rest. I stood for only a few moments with my thumb out before an

Oldsmobile, late model, fishtailed crazily to a stop. I trotted about a hundred yards and got in the open door without looking. There were three young men, two in the front and one in back, the air heavy with liquor fumes and the radio blaring Patsy Cline's "The Last Word in Lonesome Is Me." As the car shimmied and approached a hundred miles an hour it became obvious that no one had been to bed. The driver had his Stetson pulled down to the ridge of his sunglasses, driving full blast into the morning sun which was a round red ball at the end of the road. Johnny Cash sang "I Walk the Line." Nobody had spoken to me yet.

— You going to Cheyenne? I asked, voice slightly wavering.

— Yup, said the driver.

The cowboy next to me awoke with some drool coming out of the corner of his mouth which he wiped off with his shirt-sleeve. Some puke on his car window. He began singing or droning, "The last time I seen her and I ain't seen her since, she was jackin' off a nigger through a barbed-wire fence, singa kiyiyippee," etc. Over and over until the driver turned and said shut up and he went back to sleep. His boots were blue and heavily tooled with an American eagle near the top. A month's wages for boots.

We reached Cheyenne in less than an hour and I jumped out at the first stoplight and saluted with my bedroll. Jesus I might have been killed. Like the droll Yankees they watch movies of themselves and take it from there. After I saw *The Wild One* with Lee Marvin and Marlon Brando I rode a bike inadvertently through a cornfield. Enough for me. Stop this goddamn thing Oh please. I stuck with

my James Dean red jacket and perpetual sneer, a '49 Ford
with straight pipes and Hollywood mufflers that would do
seventy-five in second.

I walked up the creek until it began to narrow passing a small
beaver pond with its lodge of sticks jutting above the water
line. Active, many small trees were cut and their branches
stripped. Symmetrical cuts as if someone had wielded a
miniature but very sharp ax. On the way back from the
nest I would stalk the pond in hopes of sighting the beaver
at work. I had seen them swimming before but had only
watched them cut trees from a distance through binoculars. Alarming how fast they fell a tree. At my great-uncle
Nelse's we had once eaten fried beaver tail, a great delicacy
he claimed but Nelse was a functioning hermit and would
eat nearly anything. Drink anything too. Some loathsome
homemade raspberry wine. Maybe runs in the family. Flavor
of a popular mouthwash.
        I crossed the creek on some rocks, slipping and get-
ting one boot wet, and sought higher ground in order to
approach the nest from deep in the woods. I looked up—if
the osprey were soaring I could be spotted from a distance
of miles. Read somewhere that if our eyes were as large as a
hawk's proportionately they would be big as bowling balls.
And have three smooth holes in them. I suffered now from
a pussy trance. They come without warning in everyone's
technicolor memory—in the woods, the taiga, the Arctic, to
fighter pilots and perhaps senators and presidents. Homosexuals no doubt are struck by cock trances. No relief in

trees. A high school girl pumping at a movie, a drive-in movie with two six-packs of beer bought with false ID. Had expected the real thing but she had her period. A friend's class ring on her finger with tape wrapped around it and painted with nail polish so it would fit. That tape rubs me the wrong way darling. A change of hands and very awkward. She sips from a can and watches the movie. Hand knowingly speeds up to groans. Oh argh. Messy isn't it. She used my handkerchief without taking her eyes off the screen. A rerun later but no "head" as it was once called. I see this repeated over a nation with all those girls in pale blue summer dresses. Not any more perhaps. They all fuck like minks with the pill: revolving sexually. And are criticized as if fucking cheapens fucking. Wait until you can enjoy it in your own home with your own car in your own driveway on Elm or Maple or Oak Street.

I was forgetting to stalk in my reverie and reverence for glorious girl bum pie. Should sit and wait and listen now, not a quarter mile from the nest. Most of my sightings of animals have been accidental and caused by exhaustion — I sit down and doze or daydream until I catch my breath and often after an hour a deer or several of them appear. I saw a fox once this way playing with a mouse he had caught, tossing it into the air then pouncing on it again. And a bobcat approach a stream during a lunch break while trout fishing. Four sandwiches and as many swigs of brandy on a cool day only to awake and see this large cat gently licking water a hundred yards downstream. I lit a cigarette and looked at my hands closely. They were blackened by pine gum and the dirt it accumulates and smelled of gin, the only form of alcohol I despised. Caused by drinking a fifth and washing my hands with pine-scented soap the next day, vomiting rather forcefully against my image in the mirror. If I order a vodka gimlet or a vodka martini and am brought gin instead I suffer temporary nausea. Very temporary though. Please return and make as directed quickly quickly.

If the osprey is there I'll salute God and report it to the authorities. Few of the eggs survive; DDT has somehow affected the reproductive cycle and the eggshells are too thin to withstand the weight of the parent. Might have looked into the fact before marketing. Maybe human children with thin skulls in the future shattered by an errant marshmallow or Ping-Pong ball. Preferably stockholders' children but not possible. I put the cigarette carefully out in the damp humus beneath the leaves. A blue jay was shrieking above me but then I noticed it was a Canadian jay. They serve as an air raid siren in the woods. A few red squirrels scampered around having decided I was harmless. I never felt more harmless in my life. Not consciously killing myself with booze anyway. Wish I had some hash to make the stalk timeless. Or a moderate two peyote buttons to remember the veins in the osprey's eye or make it a pterodactyl. Even a little grass would help—I could float over the noisy twigs and leaves and brush and my stalk would be noiseless and perfect in my imagination anyway. But fuck drugs and alcohol. This brain expands by itself and sees enough ghosts. For years now I've found the earth haunted. Azoological beasts rage in untraceable configurations. They are called governments. Wounds made that never heal on every acre and covered with the scar tissue of our living presence.

The argument at bedrock: I don't want to live on earth but I want to live.

By mid-morning I was already juiced and had walked all around Cheyenne and turned my thumb down on the whole mess. In one bar I had seen the three cowboys I rode into town with but they were glassy-eyed and didn't recognize me. The singer was still singing his delightful little song. At the Silver Boot I struck up a long conversation with a florid rancher from Greeley, Colorado, and we drove over to the rodeo grounds together. He was totally unreconstructed, hating the government, religion, war, his wife and even his cattle. He liked horses though and talked interminably about his quarterhorse mare Sunstroke. I asked him why he had called her Sunstroke and he said, "That's a story in itself." Mysterious. We became unglued at the grounds by mutual boredom. I walked around to the chutes area and watched the unloading of stock. They had a semi-truck backed up to a paddock and were unloading some Brahma bulls, certainly unregenerate-looking creatures with a great hump behind the shoulders. Would ride one for a cool million in advance. Foaming in anger and red-eyed. In another enclosure an enormous top-heavy cowboy in a ragged denim shirt was sorting out broncs with a whip. They were running around kicking with their ears flattened while he looked them over. His right whip arm flexed nervously and looked capable of strangling a lion or gorilla. Wranglers rarely do calisthenics but somehow develop muscular arms and shoulders. Hard work, pure and simple. When you drive through Montana,

Wyoming or Colorado and see those immense stacks of hay
bales, dear traveler, pause a moment and understand that the
hay did not stack itself. Many of the broncs had large open
sores on their flanks where the spurs had struck too many
times; each sore the size of a hand, a raw fumarole, covered
with flies. Keeps them on their toes as it were. I've always
preferred the small local rodeo where the stock tends to be
fresher. I left the grounds and walked out to the highway. I
wanted to reach Salt Lake City by the next morning.

No osprey there. But the nest looked fresh, rather used recently. I thought I could see feathers and part of a fish tail
over the edge through my circle of leaves some fifty yards
back in the woods. A fish hawk. Once I saw one hover over
a pond, tuck its wings and hurtle down in free drop and the
last moment braking with its wings, talons extended. Hitting
the water with a blast and a foot long pike for its efforts.
    My position in a half stoop was uncomfortable. I
uprooted a large bunch of ferns and crept closer and covered
myself with them. Please no snakes. A mosquito entered my
ear and I mashed it with a forefinger. The wax in there is to
keep bugs out I understand. I would give the bird an hour
or so to appear then I would go back to the creek entrance
and try to catch a trout or two. I've always liked hawks,
even the ordinary redtail though my favorite bird is the loon.
It is the loon's voice I like—the long, coiling circular wail.
Somewhere between laughter and madness. There were so
many evenings on the lake when I was young that I heard
them and at dawn when I might rise to go fishing I would

often see them though they kept their distance. We had a small cabin my father and uncles built, with no electricity or running water and a deep well that took no less than a hundred strokes of the pump to bring up the water. Ghastly work. Took turns with my brother and it often brought fights, rolling and slugging in the dirt. We spent much of our time killing. Frogs and snakes and turtles. We weren't ever allowed BB guns so all the killing had to be done by hand. We cleared the shore of water snakes by grabbing them and whipping them against a tree or snapping them like a whip which would break their necks. We ate the frog legs in prodigious quantities, joined by my little sister who at the age of six was the acknowledged champion frog killer with a day's record in the hundreds. She would spend hours cleaning them and skinning the legs, then my mother would fry the legs and she with her friends would eat the whole lot. I had a difficult time thinking about her; she was killed at nineteen along with my father in a car accident. Both death certificates read "macerated brain" as the cause of death. They were on their way north to go deer hunting though they tended to hunt in a desultory way with more interest in the walking than the kill. Rare for a father and daughter to hunt together. By mistake in the lawyer's office I saw the state police photos of the accident, the car tipped over with its engine driven into the trunk by impact. Impossible to tell who had been driving. In one photo I caught sight of her, in a split-second glimpse — I saw her forehead upside down with a single thin trickle of blood on it, an irregular black line. A man had hit them head-on going ninety or they had hit the other car. With everyone dead the facts were difficult to establish. My initial enraged reaction was to travel north and shoot him whether he was dead or not. When the state police returned my father's wallet and, oddly, his broken false teeth I took the teeth out in back and threw them in the swamp we had planted years before with multi-flower rose for game cover. For a year afterwards I slept with my hands tightly clenched to my chest so that in the morning my arms and shoulders would be sore from the exertion.

I was still watching the nest but my eyes were sightless, thinking of my sister. I hoped she had made love to someone before she was killed. I've always felt that the draft should begin with fifty-year-old men and descend in age. Give young men a chance to live a little, taste things, before they get their asses shot off in Asia. Also draft at least 25 per cent of Congress. Let them draw straws for front line duty. I suspect then that the vote for entering a war would be a trifle more cautious. Any fifty-year-old that can play eighteen holes of golf can certainly use his weak forefinger to pull a trigger and his chubby legs to hike through swamps. Have to write some crank letters about this. Nobody's exempt. Even the president of the chamber of commerce in every little town. Considerably less American then, I bet. If they want to wave flags so badly let them wave it where it counts, in the enemy's face. Lots of whooping and whining: But I'm a stockbroker or a chemist or a dentist with my hands fresh from a mouth. Precisely. Give the young a chance to eat and fuck and drink and love and travel and have children. If they're not effective, we'll send more of these pot bellies. Of course I speak from a tender 4-F vantage point, having had my eye

nearly gored out by a broken beaker in back of a hospital
when I was five. A little girl did the job. Since then my left
eye has looked outward and upward in a googly trance of
its own. Nearly sightless it moves to the strongest light
and only sees the full moon clearly. I've often told girls
when they asked about it that it was put out in a fight with
broken bottles in East St. Louis. Then I am properly moth-
ered. Tits perk and droop and perk to caresses and sad,
lonesome tales. Eastern college girls especially like the part
Indian bit. My dark complexion and vaguely Laplander or
laplaper features have always made this possible. I vary
with tribes from Cheyenne to Cherokee to Apache. Makes
it harder to hitchhike though. Dirty minorities. I've been
asked the question a thousand times: Are you part Indian
or Mexican? Yes and no and none of the above. Was happy
in England to remind a burly cricket player while we drank
that my forefathers the Vikings had a splendid time scaring
the shit out of midget limeys. He somehow took offense.
But I reminded him that Britannia had conquered mighty
India with her starving, pathetic, pacifist millions and that
was no mean feat. Righto. And look who gave the world
kidney pudding. And fish and chips in old newspapers.
And cricket! I had won his heart. There's always some
smartass Englishman coming over here and telling us we're
mean and vulgar. I agree. But they showed their hand way
back during the Irish potato famine as instinctual Nazis.

Two hours at the interchange without a ride. All the cars
going the wrong way, toward the rodeo. I walked across

the road and into a Shell station where I bought a Coke
and asked for a map. The man charged me a dime for the
map. Little did he know that a few years later I would run
up $283 on a Shell credit card and totally outwit their col-
lectors until my mother paid them off stupidly when the
representative appeared at the door early one morning with
a phony legal document. Ho hum. I've always wanted one
of those really zippy big-time all-inclusive credit cards but
have been turned down over and over. A pickup truck driven
by an old man stopped.

—How far you going? he asked.

—California.

—That's a long ways. He actually said "a fer piece" but
no literate person would believe anyone still talks this way.
Truly literate people hang around their own kind and talk
in jingoes and arcane shorthand. Raising a single eyebrow
may involve many subtleties. That's why I always preferred
to smoke grass by myself—I simply can't bear the cultish
mummery, giggling, meaningful glances, the "oh wows" and
transference of energies by mutters. We're way up here and
ain't we neat. Not especially.

The old man pushed the pickup to eighty. Wyoming is
full of berserk drivers. Read of one who drove into a herd
of antelope crossing the road and killed sixteen. The meat
is usually too smashed up to eat. The radio was giving the
livestock report: Choice at $32 per hundredweight, com-
mercial and cutters at $24. The rancher's stockmarket. Hay
going at $22 per ton.

—How far you going? I asked.

—Creston which is thirty miles past Rawlins.

Probably a tiny town. No traffic but cars going by with blurring speed. Got there two hours later deep into the afternoon with hardly a word exchanged. He told me he was partly deaf from the First World War. I delivered some books to a VA hospital once and got a quick tour. Wreckage. Former soldiers in there for ten, twenty, thirty years, maybe only incurable fright. A friend of mine lasted only a moment in the Korean War—at the first bullet fired in his direction he said he dove under a truck and started screaming and pissing and shitting from fright. Got a medical discharge finally after they were sure he wasn't faking. A second lieutenant tried to persuade him to come out from under the truck hours later after the skirmish was over. He said he was still blubbering for his mom and dad and the good old U. S. A. He told the shrink that he was afraid of the dark, dogs, snakes, electric appliances and women, the last the only lie in the bunch. The shrink asked him then if he masturbated to which he replied, "Frequently and inconclusively." Then he told the psychiatrist that from youth he had dreamed only of marrying a pro football player and the psychiatrist said he was a bullshitting coward but he got the medical discharge anyway and with body intact. Now he is an insurance adjuster and talks about his invented war experiences. He averts his eyes when we meet by accident on our hometown streets, though he goes through the insurance man courtesy of saying, "Wanna have a cuppa of java?" No, please.

I went into a diner in Creston and had a hot pork sandwich with plenty of beef gravy. A plaque above the cash register said, "In case of atomic attack, pay bill and run like hell."

Ho ho ho. I played "Theme from Picnic" and mused about the tragic life of a wanderer. When I saw the movie I got a crush on Susan Strasberg. Maybe in some town I'll look like William Holden and a beautiful girl will take me down by the riverside and offer her own peculiar kind of vittles.

I was only back out on the freeway for a few moments when some college students with New York plates picked me up. The two of them sat in the front seat chattering about school. They were driving straight through to Salt Lake City to visit a friend, then on to California.

—Are you a cowboy? the driver asked.

—Yup, I said pulling my hat down and falling asleep.

The hawk was sitting on the nest. I cursed myself for not seeing him land. He looked around with a short jerky motion of his neck and then seemed to doze as I had done, missing his arrival. There's more than a small portion of shabbiness to my love of nature; on most pack trips I've been on I've loaded in cumbersome fifths of bourbon, so heavy but necessary. Always have to ration it so I don't get greedy and have to leave the woods early. You shouldn't ever drink while you're hunting but I often do secretively from a small flat aluminum flask. I sat in a duck blind with a friend on a very cold day and we finished a bottle and awoke in the dark. Much trouble stumbling through the woods to find the car and so cold we trembled running into invisible trees. Stopped at a tavern for a pick-me-up and discussed the non-hunt. Had ducks come in during our partly comatose sleep? Might be. We played pool for many hours and shook hands and made promises that we wouldn't drink the next time we hunted duck. Could hurt ourselves, you know. A sixteen gauge with Magnum number fours will cut a man in half at close range. What if in unsettled sleep a safety had been clicked, a trigger pulled by mistake. Blam. Or blam blam blam if it's a semi-automatic. Hunter slain in accident.

I watched the bird for a half hour and then he must have sensed my movement. He flapped upward, a five-foot wing-spread beating the air, and covering my presence in higher and wider circles. Nearly as big as an eagle which often steals from the osprey, the more effective hunter. A golden eagle from close range is awesome. In Texas there is a special club of rancher pilots who shoot thousands of golden eagles in flight from airplanes. Must protect the sheep. They have noticed strangely enough that fewer of the eagles appear during their migratory period. Be glad to be a Robin Hood for eagles and shoot their filthy Cessnas out of the sky.

Salt Lake City at dawn while lovers snuffle in pillows and wait for the alarm. The Mermaids conquered this valley thousands of moons ago, prospered by the ardent ficky-fickery of many wives, and the hard work of tilling the Indian's untilled soil. And then a great *crise*, as the French call it, arose a valley-wide horror, scarcely global, over a cloud of locusts darkening the sun. They prayed to the Angel Moroni (catch the name) and sho'nuf the seagulls buzzed in in formation, a million gobbling-bird Messerschmitts. The valley was saved and the Mermaids swore off coffee,

tea, cigarettes and alcohol. Slight misrepresentation here
but I cherish the essence of history, the main arteries rather
than the niggling individual cells. The truth is, as we know
now, that each bird ate exactly one hundred grasshoppers
and then flew away. Many prayers were offered the next
day over morning coffee which was expensive anyway, the
freight costs alone from St. Louis running about three dollars
a pound. The Mermaids gave up their expensive vices and
stimulants in thanks for the seagulls' arrival. The sacrifice
seems inappropriate in that seagulls don't drink or smoke.
Then a great tuberknuckle was built in the middle of town,
and it was decided that no one could enter this building
except the chosen. You can go into an adjacent building
and see a museum full of pioneer artifacts or hear the choir
sing "Battle Hymn" but don't try to get into the temple.
It is guarded by a giant race of seagulls trained like hunting falcons—the "white" equivalent of those ageless ravens
that guard the Tower of London. Some gossip about how
Negroes can't attain priesthood because they're children of
Ham, and not ham hocks and butter beans. The Old Testament Ham which the chosen people wouldn't eat, though
some of them secretly liked it and ate it in the night. They
were discovered and rather than giving up their favorite
recipes they traveled out of Judea, south into Africa where
years of equatorial sun darkened their skins. And that is why
they can't be priests now. Oddly enough the Mermaids are
great ham eaters now but the times change. It is difficult to
speak against these wholesome folk—I've known some of
them as friends and watched their pained wincing when I
drank coffee with cream or sugar or black. If anyone though

named Smith or Jones or Brown digs up some more stone
tablets we should put our foot down before the whole thing
gets out of control. Sanka is a moot point.

I had a quick cup of coffee then asked the waitress how
I could catch 40-80 out of town for the long desolate haul
across Nevada to Reno. She said that though she had lived
here all her life she never had gotten the roads straightened
out in her mind. She knew the road to Provo and the road
to Heber but that was the wrong direction. Her brain was
full of seagull droppings and grasshopper butter, probably
why she was a counter girl in a diner.

— Nice town you got here, I said.

— We think so, she replied covering her teeth with her
lips when she smiled. Vaguely greenish they were. Lack of
calcium?

I walked around until I found a jolly policeman and
asked him for directions. He looked at me as though my
bedroll might be concealing tommy guns and poison adders,
but he pointed the way with a courtesy uncommon in eastern
cities. Wholesome folks hereabouts I thought again — no
buggery, incest, dope, pornography, all the kitchens spic and
span and the girls fresh and capable of making their own
gravy. It took me at least two hours to get to an interchange
but the walk past dewy emerald-green lawns and cozy bungalows had been pleasant with the exception of a brush with
an early-rising cur. I palmed my five-inch switchblade and
walked backwards for a block while the dog snarled and
barked. Weird-looking hound and terrier cross. If he jumped
I would be forced to give him a single lightning slash across
his furry throat. Actually he would have had my arm before

I could open the knife. Quick rascals. And I couldn't walk
with the knife open and outstretched or every mom on the
street, awake and making breakfast, would have called the
police and my bonehandled Neapolitan switchblade is held
suspect by the law.

I stopped at a truckers' cafe near the highway, had coffee and looked imploringly at the truckers. I knew though
that they couldn't give me a ride for "insurance" reasons, a
NO RIDERS decal on every windshield. I sat down next
to a middle-aged beatnik type who glanced at me briefly
through his wrap-around shades.

— How about a ride?

— Got any gas money?

— Sure.

Finally highballing it across Nevada in a decrepit
Dodge with an unemployed musician. Didn't feel comfortable until we got past the Great Salt Lake and through Wen-
dover and into Nevada which runs Texas a close second as
the most hostile place in the nation. By the time we reached
Elko and stopped for something to eat we had talked about
jazz for four hours and were absolutely stoned on what
he called Yucatan Gold. In another twenty-four hours we
would cross the Bay Bridge into San Francisco, assuming
the car held up in the hundred-degree Nevada heat.

When I left my blind of ferns I estimated it to be about
mid-afternoon, the sun warm and hazy and a slight breeze
controlling the mosquitoes. The lake was rippling now and
the water pushed by the wind cast small waves on the far

shore. I felt exhilarated for no particular reason—for all it
mattered on earth the forest I was standing in could have
been a far province of China four thousand years ago. Not
even a jet contrail to befoul the sky, the birds in their afternoon silence and a single turkey buzzard so high that it
was scarcely visible. Maybe I'll talk in Chinese to myself
and see if the FBI has infiltrated the swamps. I thought of
continuing on around the lake to look at new territory but
dropped the idea in favor of fishing at the creek mouth or
in the beaver pond. I wanted enough fish to glut myself for
dinner, then sleep would come easily without fantasies of
whiskey.

The water near the creek mouth turned out to be fairly
rough, lacking the pellucid clarity of the morning. Writers
for "outdoor" magazines are always referring to "gin clear"
water. Switch that to vodka clear for my own taste. But
then the great majority of these writers are lame brains with
no real knowledge of the prey they speak of except how to
catch or kill it. I moved on up to the beaver pond slowly,
cautiously avoiding noise. I heard the warning "flap" before
the pond was visible. Dad beaver on the lookout and now
they're down in their lodge wondering who's interfered with
their privacy. Sounds like slapping the water with the side of
an oar. Row quietly, my father said, or you'll scare the bass.
The heat lightning scared me and I forgot. His favorite curse
came, used only in male company, "Jesus-fucking-Christ-
on-a-flatcar." I've used it to blank stares. I began swearing
at five and applications of soap and disapprobation never
discouraged me. A girl said, My dad never uses that word.
I'm not your dad or I wouldn't be humping here in a Buick

Dynaflow. Or she said in the Russian Tea Room, Sex can
be so boring. In an old-age home or with colon carcinoma.
I dug around a stump looking for a worm or grub or centi-
pede. I don't like to handle centipedes or hellgrammites but
they make good bait if your hook is small enough. Deceit
to eat. I'll trick the fish and eat its body. Sit in the swamp
until a partridge trotted out then shoot off its head, spear
the bird with a green willow stick after plucking it, then
the roasting. We always ended up eating them half raw out
of impatience. Tearing at the blackened skin in the way we
imagined savages once did where we sat. An odd sensation
when you find an arrowhead in a plowed field or in a gulley or ravine where the ground has been eroded. If you're
young you consider all of the woods a "hunting ground" and
the evidence of the arrowhead and the presence of earlier
hunters stuns you. There's almost a curse now to have read
in prepuberty Seton, Curwood, Jack London, all of Zane
Grey, Kenneth Roberts, Walter Edmonds. And I'm not even
a conservationist. My father gave his life over to the land and
got little joy for his efforts. My pitifully radical sensibilities
run to dynamite or plastic explosives. But I've no urge to
hurt people, the idea repels me. And there's more implicit
drama here than I deserve: I mean if I could blow up Dow
or Wyandotte Chemical I might if no one were to be hurt
or go jobless. Beneath the Christmas tree there are no pres-
ents, some creep has blown up Daddy's factory and there's
no money. A dinner of food surplus lard and navy beans.
Complexions turn sallow. Or on the way to the factories I'd
stop at a tavern and have a few doubles and listen to Buck
Owens sing, "It's crying time again, you're going to leave

me," lump in the throat music for me; still can't listen to
Stravinsky's *Petrouchka,* my sister's favorite record. Before
I first left for New York City we would burn a red candle
and listen to the record together. And read Walt Whitman
and Hart Crane. I was eighteen and she was thirteen. But
if you've read all those Zane Grey novels and others I've
mentioned at a vulnerable age you simply can't get along in
the present. Where's the far field? Neither can you march
even as a radical to protect your ancient turf or bring peace
to earth. I've never felt solidarity except while making love,
or with a tree or animal or while utterly alone on a river or
in a swamp or in the woods. I don't propose this as a virtue
but as a matter of rude fact. A liberal magazine once used the
word "spiv" to describe this state of being. I thought I liked
Kropotkin for a while. My ancestors, inasmuch as they were
literate, were Populists. There's no romance in being alone.

San Francisco. Now here is my golden city I hope. Look at
the people bustle at noon on Geary Street. They're wearing
wool like the guidebook instructs and very elegant. Probably
not my part of town. The musician told me when he dropped
me off that he had a "gig" promised at the Blackhawk and
to drop by. Not likely on my funds. One necktie strangled
into a rope in the bedroll which I stuffed into a locker at the
bus station. If you lose the key you're out seventeen dollars'
worth of gear. Pretty girls everywhere and I'm going to get
me one I hope. Up Polk, over Sacramento, up Grant with its
yellow threat to Green near the beach. Crossing Columbus,
nearly hit by cab. Knocking on the door where a former

friend should be and where I can lay my head. Man with girlish hair answers with suspicion. Seems my friend went to Vancouver a month ago. What will I do now? Nothing but buy a paper and look for a room.

I walked until I wanted to throw away my boots. I could feel blisters leaking into my socks. These boots are made for riding horses and nothing else. I finally found a room two or three blocks from the Opera House under a highway over-pass on Gough Street. It was cheap even considering the cars and trucks roaring overhead. I retrieved my bedroll, paid two weeks in advance, which left me seven dollars to live on forever. I drank with long gulps from a bottle of sauterne, my sleeping pill, and got into bed. When I awoke about midnight my billfold was gone from the dresser and the door was slightly ajar. How dumb. Probably someone with a small celluloid ruler slipped the lock. Sixty-six cents in change and no papers to say who I am.

I caught a mess of brook trout from the beaver pond and regretted not having my fly rod. Where are the parents of these little fish? I packed them in grass and ferns in my pouch and started the hike back to the camp. If I were a crow I could get there in a minute or two.

Something had been pawing around the tent but all was intact, the small cache of food hanging beyond any animal's reach or intelligence. A monkey would have figured out the rope. Be nice to import some Japanese snow monkeys and let them run amok up here. I stuck my head in the creek and drank, then washed myself. I fried all of the fish long enough

to brown them and ate them with salt and honey and bread.
I checked the rifle, wiping the moisture from the barrel with
my bandana, and working the action quickly to watch the
shells pop out. Eat lead death Commie, I said, aiming at my
smoldering fire. Let's control guns and stop shooting heroes.
Let only police and soldiers have guns, then they can shoot
who they want at will. Cavalry shooting with Springfields
at Indians armed with hatchets, bows and arrows. Shot a
Sharps buffalo gun once. Adequate for rhino with a shell as
heavy as a doorknob. I'm not going to shoot any presidents
or leaders may I keep my guns. Outlaw all pistols though.
Creep machines. Everyone in Detroit carries one now after
the riots. May they shoot off their toes. They aren't any
good anyway unless you have had considerable practice.
It's been ten years since I shot at a mammal. I thought of
bow hunting but even that seemed unfair. An expert archer
can kill anything, even an elephant—a liver shot with a
weighted arrow. So many deer in an unnatural balance with
all predators dead so that they have to be hunted. When you
hang up a deer and strip its hide it looks a bit too human
for my taste; in the hanging position the front feet appear
to be atrophied human arms with the skin peeled back,
striated with muscle, tendons, ligaments and a little yellow
fat. The heart is large and warm. When you reach up into
the cavity you've slit in the belly and cut the esophagus you
rip downwards and all the guts come tumbling out. Then
you carefully cut around the anus avoiding the bladder and
colon and then you have a, deer ready for butchering. The
guts always vanish by the next day, a nice meal for a fox or
two. The liver is especially tasty if the deer is young but my

favorite meal is when you strip the loins and broil them. I've eaten fried heart but its resemblance to my own took some of the pleasure from the meal. I imagine that there would be more vegetarians if everyone slaughtered their own meat. The English and French eat horse meat but when you talk to them it is subtly self-explanatory. A friend of mine in Montana lost a horse he had hobbled near a stream bank; the horse tripped in the night, stumbling down the bank and breaking its neck against the rocks in the stream. It was a beautiful horse and my friend was sad for weeks. When he came back the day after the horse was killed it was gone. A grizzly had dragged the horse a quarter of a mile or so up the creek through the brush and had eaten everything but the rumen. A feat of strength and appetite. Paw marks of two cubs too but a second-year cub weighs several hundred pounds. This may sound pointlessly sentimental but I would rather shoot a human than a grizzly or a wolf. Of course I would never shoot any of the three unless attacked and wolves never attack humans despite the falsities spread about them. Grizzlies have been known to attack humans and of course humans attack humans with considerable regularity. I don't mean during wars but in the daily life of the street. The executive bares his teeth and bites down on his partner's neck. The secretary says, Mr. Bob you've got blood on your Countess Mara tie. Fist fights. Holdups. Gang fights. Birmingham. Detroit. Chicago. Bar fights. Crestfallen wife slaps husband. Husband punches wife in snotlocker. The habit of child beating widespread.

❊   ❊   ❊

I sat there on the bed feeling very stupid, distraught, near panic: I wanted to be home in Michigan, upstairs in my own bed with my olive-colored World War Two wool blanket pulled up under my chin. But my father had said something pointed though humorous when I left: "You can stay until the piss-ants carry you out through the keyhole." Country humor, local color. This city is probably full of thieves. Cut-purses they called them long ago, lucky I wasn't stabbed in the eye like Marlowe while I slept innocently. Hope he uses the seven dollars on wine then falls neatly under a cable car, his body sliced in three sections. An old woman in my home town had committed suicide by placing her neck over the railroad track, the head dribbling like a basketball down the tracks until it rested at a crossing a hundred yards from her body. A much discussed incident. The coroner discovered that her suicide note was written entirely in consonants and wondered if a code might be involved but decided she was merely insane. Earlier that morning when I first saw the Golden Gate Bridge I thought of all those pitiful creatures who had flung themselves over the rail. From that height water is as hard as cement and if you jump too close to a piling, it is cement. Broke, thinking of suicide and far from home, finishing my sauterne. The trouble is it would hurt. During a football practice I had gotten a compound fracture across the bridge of my nose — bones sticking through and the blood a geyser. Wore an odd T-shaped cast the rest of the season. Have to meet this whole problem head-on.

I left the rooming house and walked over toward Market Street where I intended to blow my monstrous sixty-six cents on pancakes, the cheapest way to fill an empty

stomach. Starch. Manioc and pan bread, pinto beans, potatoes, pasta to swell the tummy for next to nothing. I want
a whole smoked ham like Grandpa hung in his cellar to
season. Slabs of bacon there too, potatoes and cabbages in
the cooler, deeper, root cellar. Chop off the chicken's head
and watch it trot uncackling in a parabola like a boom-
erang back to my feet and eat it fried a few hours later.
Passing the Opera House and the square with beautiful
flowers. I'll never be driven up in a limousine with Wanda
the debutante to hear Lambasta's intricate *Lo Pigro*. Apply
for a job. I'd yodel for free sir if you throw in the meals. At
the cafeteria I ordered my pancakes, salivating as I watched
them on the dirty griddle. Then a triple dose of syrup for
energy, and a cup of thin coffee stoked with chicory. Must
use the grounds over and over. Some Chicanos in the corner
laughing. Pickers no doubt up for the evening. I finished
my sickening meal and approached them. They fell silent
as I asked where to get work. They stared at me until I was
on the verge of walking away, then one of them smiled and
told me that labor trucks left daily from Hosmer Street
across from the church at four A.M. A farm labor office
was there, compliments of the State of California. I walked
over and cased the location three hours early, then walked
down Market to kill time.

   I've always liked the mad-dog atmosphere of cities after
midnight: Times Square, Rush Street, Pershing Square, now
Market Street. The maimed that come out only when the
sun goes down. Cruisers cruise. Prostitutes look for marks —
I'm only glanced at, it's obvious that I'm a poor prospect.
Movie lets out and the good citizens rush to their cars to

split the neighborhood. Don't blame them. If you take me home I'll mow your lawn. A faggot twitters hello cowpoke at me and I wish I had left this fucking stupid hat in my room but I might need it tomorrow. I want to marry adventure and this isn't it. I should be up in the Sierras standing on a mountain-top so that I can kiss dawn full on her lips. Fresh air and no blind accordionists playing "Dance, Ballerina, Dance." Should tell him that's Vaughn Monroe's trademark as far as I'm concerned.

Back at the labor office and still an hour early. A few people begin to arrive. Winos mostly. And then some black men and women with lunches packed. What will I eat—my fingers? The jobber's truck arrives, a canvas-covered flatrack. Then a rickety bus pulls up. There are at least fifty of us now murmuring in the half-light. The Catholic church across the street is pink stucco and the first pale light strikes the belfry where dozens of pigeons are cooing and chucking. The jobber is a mountainous black who tells me to get into the truck after making sure I'm not drunk. Three winos have been rejected and stand at a distance cursing. It is dark in the truck and I can only see the tips of lit cigarettes. The truck starts and we pull away. I watch the street recede and wonder where I'm going, what I'll be picking in what field. I ask the man next to me on the bench where we're headed and he says in a ghetto gibberish I can scarcely understand that you never know but you're always back in Frisco by dark.

I got up in the middle of the night and started a fire after hearing what I thought were footsteps in the brush. A dream

I suppose. The fire burned quickly and with a roar, big
chunks and strips of dry pine ripped easily off a stump. The
tree cut how long ago? My mind was sinking into a small
black ball. With no prospects how will I ever travel first class
anywhere? I want to go to San Francisco again someday
and stay at the Palace or Fairmont or Mark Hopkins or
the St. Francis. Fuck steerage and the contempt of everyone. Held for vagrancy in Fraser, Colorado, once because
I lacked two dollars of the needed amount to make one an
ordinary citizen. And in a small town outside of Topeka
questioned by a bored deputy in an old car with "Deputy
Sheriff" hand painted on the door. He only wanted to talk.
And the usual homosexual ride that begins with "Do you
have a girl friend?" Yes of course and a ponderous cock and
you can't have a single solitary bite. They're uniformly nice
about the whole thing. Pun intended. One in Waltham with
a St. Christopher statue on the dashboard. Should have a
tiny blindfold so he doesn't have to watch blowjobs. Saints
deserve some consideration. And an actual pass made by
a war-torn veteran who had to speak through a battery-
operated amplifier held against his throat. Sounded like a
faulty growling tape recorder — the obscene question drawn
out, a forty-five rpm played at thirty-three. Would have been
more interesting if the machine accelerated the voice into
insane chipmunk talk. My brain shrank perceptibly again. I
felt a whirling sort of nausea, facing the fire in the darkness
and wondering if I were meant to be one of those fragile
individuals who shrink into dustballs from generalized pain
and are swept into asylums. No Heathcliff with ten hounds
and vast moor. Where is a "she" to retrieve me, draw me

out of the riddle that only leads to another. I have lost my faith I thought in "figuring things out," the various tongues in my skull that spoke daily of alternatives, counterploys, divisions, instructions, directions. All the interior sensuosities of language and style. And I live the life of an animal and transmute my infancies, plural because I always repeat never conquer, a circle rather than a coil or spiral. I've talked myself into the woods up here and will there be a common language when I return? Or is there a need for one or was there ever such a language in any world at any time? I think so. Before the gibbet or guillotine the cheers take the same arc of sound and come from a single huge throat. No king to require a spokesman. Off in the dark there is a wolf who speaks his limited instincts to another. I imagine he knows that there are few of his own kind left. On Isle Royale they control their population without help. I'll talk to Villon or Marlowe tonight when the fire goes out. I've only floated.

My next few days revolved around trips to Stockton, Modesto, San Jose and their limitless hot string-bean fields. I picked very slowly, fatigued by the heat and scratching all the itches caused by the bean dust and pesticides. When I filled a basket full of thirty pounds of beans I would get either sixty cents cash on the line or have a ticket punched. The grower's man preferred the tickets to keep pickers around. The first day I brought four dollars and twenty cents back to Frisco with me. After that day and its initial boredom and exhaustion I averaged about seven dollars a day. Many of the Chicanos made fifteen dollars a day but they had the truly

questionable benefit of years of experience. I was bullied by
the jobber a great deal but only grinned like an idiot. Later
when I became straw boss on a farm in Michigan I acted
the same way, walking around swearing at the dawdlers.
Picking apples is the only civilized form of such work—it
is fall, the weather is cool and no stoop labor is involved.
Cucumbers are lowest on the rung of preference.

On the fourth day I didn't take the truck back but
instead walked the half dozen or so miles into San Jose. I
stopped at a store on the outskirts of town and bought three
grapefruit which I ate on the way. There was a continuous
rustling in the ditch which would stop when I stopped. I
spotted the small lizards that were making the noise and
threw a few stones. No one would pick me up and a car
full of teenagers having fun threw a firecracker, narrowly
missing my head. I looked at the car closely thinking that
I might meet them in San Jose and get the chance to kick
the shit out of somebody. The grapefruit were delicious,
the juices soaking my shirt front, my best white shirt which
had hung on a fencepost all day while I picked barebacked.
There was to be a dance that night and I wanted to look
good. I felt flush with a twenty-dollar bill in my right sock
and a few bucks in my pocket. A diesel truck passed me so
closely that I teetered in the wind. Pigfucker might have
aimed. I felt a great empathy then with all the cocoa-colored
people in America. Work hard and try to play hard. Scorned
if you don't save the meager wages and live like they do in
Middletown, U. S. A. I thought of one of my uncles who
lived back in the woods preferring the company of his red-
bone and bluetick hounds to people. His lovely wife, my

aunt, died of cancer and his oldest son fatally injured in a car wreck. No marks on his body, the neck broken neatly and invisibly. At the funeral I looked at him closely and decided he wasn't dead. When his mother died, though, there was no mistaking it—she had dropped from a hundred thirty to seventy pounds, dying at home on the couch while her children played pinochle next to her. They were able to kiss her goodbye.

I got a very cheap hotel room after being turned down at two places for unknown reasons. I took a bath and looked at myself in the mirror. Color of coffee and the grapefruit stains dry. I walked over to a park and sat on a bench beneath a palm tree with a copy of *Life*. A family I picked with waved to me and I felt good about it. I know somebody out here in the golden West. The magazine made me feel that I was missing opportunities—a special on this year's crop of starlets, one of them beautiful indeed. She has since dropped out of sight. Where do all the starlets go that drop out of sight? To Vegas and Manhattan where they command fees of five hundred dollars a night for perverse gymnastics involving electrical apparatus and hundreds of yards of mauve velvet. When I'm chairman of some kind of board I'll meet a has-been starlet, twenty-seven years old, and propose something truly infamous, an act so imaginative that her eyes will pop out like Satchmo's. Have to involve pushing a dead cow off a skyscraper roof. A gray-haired gentleman with jism splotches all over his cotton trousers sat down beside me. Go away or I'll call the vice squad, I said. Wonder how much movies have directed my affections, heartsick with love for screen stars; chronologically, Ingrid Bergman, Deborah Kerr (in

Quo Vadis when she is almost gored by the bull), Ava Gardner, Lee Remick, Carol Lynley, and years later, Lauren Hutton who is a model and comparative unknown. If they only knew how pleasant my company would be. Uta Hagen, Shelley Winters and Jeanne Moreau scare me. Catherine Deneuve is too aggressively depraved in that Buñuel movie.

The next day I got up about noon with an incredible hangover. The dance had been a relative flop; the girl I had spotted in the field and so carefully nurtured with polite talk had a boy friend. The Mexican music was too melancholy and I spent most of my time and money in a bar next door to the dance hall. I drank tequila and played country music on the jukebox and talked mostly to a drunk Filipino picker who claimed the Chicanos were against him. Then I ate a huge combination plate at a Mexican restaurant and had difficulty finding the hotel. When I flipped on the light switch exactly ten thousand cockroaches dove for cover. Lucky I'm not shy of bugs, even spiders. Before I fell asleep I heard the ticking sound they made when they dropped off the ceiling onto the bed. I yelled "shoo" but it didn't disturb them. I took a bus back to the city, deftly seating myself next to a pretty girl who refused to speak to me. Yes my little one I am a psychotic and rapist and thimble freak. Back in my Gough Street room I watched the taxis and trucks pass and the lordly messengers on their high monkey-bar motorcycles. My bedroll was intact in the closet and I was a week ahead on the rent with seven dollars again to blow on the delights of the city. Early next morning I bought a city map and started walking.

❖   ❖   ❖

There is a constant urge to re-order memory—all events
falling between joy and absolute disgust are discarded. Some
even favor leaving out disgust. I think often though of rather
ordinary kindnesses, a waitress letting me sleep on a table
in the back room of a restaurant outside of Heber, Utah.
Or sitting with a rancher's children in the back of a pickup
on hay bales and the way he passed back a bottle, driving
full tilt through the Uinta and Wasatch mountains. Or an
old high school friend sending me fifty dollars because if
"you go into art you can have a bad time of it." The friend
had recently seen a film biography of Vincent van Gogh. Or
a woman I met near Sather Gate at Berkeley when I was
roaming around and fearfully trying to use the university
library. No one asked questions though. She was an assistant
librarian and spent hours digging up material on Provencal
poets for me. I wasn't interested but it seemed like a good
idea. During a noon hour I talked to her walking around
through a garden near the library and offered to take her
to dinner. We sat on the grass and she finally said no, that
I probably couldn't afford to take anyone to dinner. I said
I was saving money by living in an abandoned apartment
house off Green Street with eight or nine other bums, mostly
young and rootless tea heads. She was a trifle homely but
very pleasant. After work we went to her apartment and I
took an hour-long shower and put on her husband's pajamas, while she washed my clothes. They were separated and
getting a divorce. She was about thirty-five and a little bit
plump for my taste but strangely the best lover I've ever had.
Very straightforward with none of the oblique difficulties
of young girls. When I left after a week I felt no particular

loss because I had never really been attracted to her—very adult with a nice kiss of farewell and the bus back across the bay, at least seven pounds heavier from decent food and soapy smelling from daily showers. Sated.

Odd about older women, I mean between thirty-five and fifty or sixty. It's nice to be appreciated and not practice hours of beggary to get near the snuffbox. There's no condescension here at all, only an observation arrived at at age twenty-one. None of those long agonizing sessions of petting and waddling home with the ache of the malady known as lover's nuts. Swollen with no release. Probably less of this nowadays with the mink culture going full tilt. I remembered standing in a bookstore and reading the entirety of *Lolita* in two hours, then walking out onto the street with glazed eyes, a full-fledged ravenous nympholeptic. The power of literature. Or what did Earwicker say in *Finnegan*—"I learned all the rules of the gamest of games from my old Norse Ada." We all know firm young tanned or pink unblemished bodies are sweet, peach melba or crepes suzette. But they involve a Don Juanish career that wastes a lot of time and there's something suspicious about always wanting to poke the unpoken. Bob said I was first I was first I was first as if a country or a vaccine had been discovered. An archeologic instinct I suppose. An urge to squeeze rather than plunge in; and how can you be less than adequate if you're among the first to tup the heifer. I remembered the year before coming up from Barstow by bus after midnight through the invisible greenery of the San Joaquin Valley, sitting next to a girl fresh out of Vegas and a semi-pro with white satin dress and glass high heels. Long brown legs. I don't know why I do this, she said after an hour's prattle and we began necking. I burned my fingers holding a marvelous french kiss all the way through a cigarette. Couldn't drop it on her dress. Difficult to operate on a bus seat, finally impossible for more than her deft palm. Disgruntled senior citizens surrounding us in the dark. Three of my fingers were wet, salving the burn—a revolutionary medicine, healed by dawn.

I got back to the Hanging Gardens and found that my bedroll had been stolen. Went down to Broadway and Columbus with a friend from Albuquerque and we panhandled enough money for some food, a matchbox, and a gallon of wine. A week before we had stolen a gallon of wine from a grocer but that involved a ten-block full-blast run through Chinatown and my friend lost one of his sandals. We stashed the food except for a package of sweet rolls, the grass and wine and climbed up to Coit Tower for a little picnic in the shrubbery. We got awesomely high and drunk at the same time watching a huge Matson Line ship back out of the dock far below. Someday this will all be yourn May Lou. All of it. Two police coming toward us in the shrubbery and Walter swallowed the last roach. What are you guys doing? Looking at the beauty of the city, officer. It sure is a lovely view up here. Best to be coquettish with the police—it often flusters them. They might be former marines but they remember the playfulness in the tents back in their Boy Scout days. Walter handles them beautifully—they move on in search of actual criminals which we are when Walter offers to recite a poem he has spontaneously written called "The Men in Blue." They tell us to get out of here or we might get mugged. Golly it's dangerous in this city, I said.

We walked down the hill and over to the Co-existence Bagel Shop where an English reporter bought us beer and macaroni salad for the real lowdown on the recently vaunted San Francisco Renaissance. Walter claimed that the true Renaissance was in Kansas City and that he should catch the next plane before it disappeared. I had another quick order of the macaroni salad before the patron disappeared. A man sitting at the next table in a business suit hid behind a newspaper. We told the reporter that he was a federal narcotics agent and that as an Englishman he could be deported for carrying a full kilo in his briefcase. We left and stood around on the corner in front of the shop for hours talking to unnamed acquaintances. The most interesting of them was Billy the Pimp who often bought us meals for companionship. He had a common-law wife who worked the conventions for fifty-dollar tricks. A few times he gave me a twenty with a reminder that some hard work was behind the money. Billy also had two college girls "turned out" in secret whorehouses in Chinatown where he said they would be held for at least two years. By then he could depend on them since he was the only white man they ever saw. He claimed he usually grossed five hundred a day which I believed, in that his heroin bit cost him at least a hundred and he was always beautifully dressed. I had dinner with him and his wife one evening and we talked most of the night popping bennies. Billy maintained that as long as his wife balled for money it was OK but that if she ever went to bed with anyone for free it would be adultery and need punishing. The whole idea boggled my Protestant mind. Truly depraved people and I'm sitting in the room talking to them. She laughed and told stories about the "Johns," how most of the paunchy conventioneers never even got hard-ons but wanted their friends to think they were cocksmen. Easy work, she said, and they always begged her not to tell on them. Who would she tell? she wondered aloud. I left when I got angry about the college girls who were trapped. Billy said they got used to it and looked forward to his weekly visits but if they somehow got away he would "cut" them—this meant a slash with a knife or razor along the nose and through the upper and lower lip. Difficult for a doctor to mend neatly and Billy said this was the usual treatment for extremely recalcitrant whores. I was repelled I think more than I had ever been before. Poor girls with a line of Chinese. Snow pea breath. I avoided Billy after that evening.

We leaned against a car and talked about the St. Anthony's Mission where a free lunch was served at noon every day. Some of the bums brought jars to take home the food their rotting stomachs couldn't receive. I had eaten there several times with Walter and other malcontents from North Beach and enjoyed talking to the monks. You got a vitamin pill with the meal and often a dish of ice cream. But the life of the streets had begun to pall after a few months. At a party in Fillmore that had lasted three days I had witnessed an unsavory gang bang. The girl was too young and completely out of her head though very lovely. Bongo drums and gin and the whole bag. I looked into the bedroom where her blond hair was spread out damply on a pillow and her eyes squeezed shut in apparent pain. There were five or six still to be served. I left at about three A.M. in order to catch the labor bus and earn some honest money to rent a room of my own again, Maybe go back to Berkeley and try to

start up with the librarian. Or earn a small stake and hitch
back to Michigan.

I worked four loathsome days with a group of Okies
who lacked the Chicanos' grace and good humor. They were
living in Oakland and hadn't lived in California long enough
to collect welfare. I remembered going through Atlanta in
a bus late at night and seeing them with their pale faces
and long sideburns and thin lips. The oldest Americans.
Standing in front of a honky-tonk smoking, the musicians in
string ties taking their break. But I like the music and if you
could fold over the country horizontally in the middle you
would find that northern rural people mirror their southern
counterparts. Poor. Often vicious to outsiders. Contempt for
the law. The mainstay for some is alcohol, for the others,
that "old time" fundamentalist religion. I liked a few of them
though, a vague sort of recognition when we talked about
hunting and fishing at noon. They were quick to admit they
hated Oakland but there was no work back home. So they
came west. That Big Eight-Wheeler Running Down the
Tracks. As the Joads had come thirty years before and had
adapted to chrome and neon instead of gutted cotton land.
Ignorance only gradually accrues, builds up—as sediment
collects at a river's mouth. The poor are instinctively suspicious but then so are the rich, and the middle-class more
suspicious than either.

That night around my fire I heard howling far to the west
of me, perhaps several miles away. Sure as God a wolf. All
my side trips had been east to the lake or southwest to the

car. Tomorrow I would go up to the higher ground to the
north and west of my campside. They figure Indians took
copper out of this area four or five thousand years ago,
before Jesus rode the donkey into Jerusalem for his last
session of confrontation politics. Any radicalism in my head
was got initially from the Bible. Coming to maturity in the
full syrup of the Eisenhower lassitude fed the fire. A moonless hiatus when energies built in people to whom life was
merely a succession of injustices. A false period of light and
comparative quietude with the powers in the nation playing
golf and collecting billions, Congress collectively picking
its nose, oinking out grotesqueries and sloth. The nation
continued shitting in its own sandbox and only recently has
noticed it. And this long after obvious greed had been purged
and was merely called business. The business of business is
business. Sowing wind. Hard to understand how a nation
conceived in rapine and expanded in slaughter could last
anyway. But there's no sense of Old Testament doom — the
doom is contemporary and earned daily. Pull off the face
and you see the skull is Naugahyde. Cheyenne autumn. And
the holds of ships with millions of slaves mentally rotting
toward servitude. With a base this questionable, how can
one conceive of a nation at peace? I saw a picture in the
paper a week ago of the President and the Vice President
at sport. They looked like barbers on a Sunday outing, tits
sagging a bit in their golf shirts. And a supercharged cart
behind them to carry the eminences from hole to hole. The
world with wall to wall war, the ocean lidded with oil and
most whales dead. Her prophets whine and play patty-cake
patty-cake. M. L. King dead after seeing God's face, his

eyes seeing the glory. The dead-end apocalypticism of the young fed by hard rock and amphetamines. And though I'm barely over thirty I come from the nineteenth century and a somnolent world with a top on it. I feel destined not to do anything about anything. Perhaps resuscitate a few animal skins stolen from coat racks and parlor floors. Pile them in a giant mound by the thousands until I sense that there are enough for a proper funeral. Douse with kerosene. Light it with a burning arrow of course and sit with my dogs and watch the conflagration and if I have had enough to drink I'll take off my clothes and dance around this monstrous fire, singing and howling with my dogs until the animals either come back to life or I watch their souls and ghosts float upwards in the plumes of smoke. I'll roll in the ashes and it will begin raining and never stop.

I looked at my tattered map and plotted the next day's trip, how far and in what general directions I would walk and where I might find water or catch a few fish. Someday I intended to walk the circumference of Lake Superior. Maybe walk straight north to the pole, or walk into a cave and refuse to come out until the back wall of the cave reflected a livable earth, or the brilliant orange anti-shadow of the earth exploding.

I threw another log on my diminishing fire and went down to the creek to prepare for bed. First a long drink and a wash with the small sliver of soap I had left. I was giggling about my romanticism and wondering if my brain would ever be able to expand beyond all those oblique forms of mental narcissism I practiced daily. And did I feel deeply anything other than an urge to survive. Yes. Add eating, drinking and fucking, and a peopleless forest. With a weekly visit of a beautiful maiden who would float down the creek to me in gossamer on a raft made of rushes and bound together with human hair. She would look suspiciously like my mental image of Ophelia and we would make love until, naturally, we would bleed through the eyes and pores. Various animals would sit in a circle and watch—raccoons, opossums, coyotes, fox, deer, wolves, and many varieties of snakes and insects. When we finished making love we would bathe in the creek in the dawn light and she would lie back down on her raft and float downstream out of my field of vision. Then I would fill a huge golden bowl with milk from which all the above creatures would drink in harmony. If an inept viper or mouse fell in, a fox would gently lift it out. Then I would sleep for three days and three nights and roll the stone back up the hill until she arrived again.

In a week of stupefying labor I managed to save forty dollars. I hitched into Frisco to collect my belongings and to spend two days saying goodbye to inanimate presences. I spent a day in Golden Gate thinking this was the end of it all. I could hear the Pacific out there while gliding through all the crazy unfamiliar flora and fauna. A dozen or so motorcyclists passed me on a bordering street with "SKULLS" on the back of their jackets. Sleeveless leather jackets and hairbands with hair flowing out behind, a bush-league Gestapo. I re-entered the tropics following some faint music, arriving at a sunlit bandshell where there was a Strauss concert in progress. I waltzed a little and an old couple sitting on a bench grinned and waved at me. I signaled to the old lady and she got up and we made a few gliding slow trips around the bench while her husband clapped. I actually hated waltz music but it seemed appropriate today. Farther on I sat down on the grass and turned to look up a pretty girl's legs. White ninety-nine-cent lollipop panties. Oh darling if only. Thighs ever so slightly parted and eyes closed in rapt attention to the music. Should crawl over there barking and mount. I went into the DeYoung Museum and looked at the Medici statue. Power, that's what I wanted. With power I would fly home rather than hitchhike. Slight chance though that during the Renaissance I wouldn't have been a prince but would have been up on the Baltic in a smoky log hut. At the end of the park I looked out at the Pacific and greeted her with a sigh. Across there in the Orient the Orientals are being Oriental. Huge breakers swept in. Two girls were racing down the beach far below. The whole continent is at my back I thought and I turned and left.

Out on Green Street I couldn't find anybody in the floating world to say goodbye to. The Hanging Gardens were empty—probably someone got busted and they all left. I walked down Grant to Geary then over again through the garden giving the Opera House a wanton high sign. Fuck opera. Who needs it? *La Bohème* indeed. With a garnish of resolute turkey cream pie. I bought an old metal air force suitcase thinking it would help get me rides in preference to a smelly bedroll.

I caught a ride on 80 to Sacramento with a businessman who thought I was in the air force and perhaps on leave. I said no and he accused me of false advertising. He was in the service during World War Two, he said, and always liked to give our boys a break by picking them up when he saw them hitchhiking. I told him my father had died on the Bataan death march which changed his attitude. He patted my arm and said that Burma took a heavy toll. I had become OK with a gratuitous lie. The Nips sure were a tough bunch of yellow bastards. He went on and on while I dozed. By Sacramento I felt sick with what I suspected was mild food poisoning. It was late evening and I snuck across the State Capitol lawn and vomited in the bushes repeatedly. I finally curled up on the grass and slept fitfully wondering if a policeman would disturb my rest.

I emerged from the bushes early and thought how appropriate a place to get sick I had found — I was amused even though I had mild stomach cramps. All state houses should be turned into vomitoriums and then they could start over in a place that didn't overwhelm them. Say in a big field all votes would be taken while the lawmakers were crawling naked on their hands and knees yelling yes or no. A new perspective. Proper humility in their concerns for millions of helpless citizens. If you've ever taken a trip to Washington you perhaps may gather this meaning — how can anything less than pompous or idle or torpid result from that giant cluster of marble and monuments. The buildings create a self-importance that is destructive. I propose that the whole compound be leveled except the Lincoln Monument and the mall and pond in front of it. And that some adept sculptor do a prone M. L. King to lay across Lincoln's lap in the manner of *La Pietà*. Only with a big hole in the head. We are mortal O lord. Trigger fingers itch and squeeze, itch and squeeze.

In the first light I had three cups of tea at an all-night cafe and read the Sunday paper without remembering anything but a bikini clad model in the travel section who said in an artful blib, "COME TO BERMUDA." Be glad to. O island in the sun chigadigdigdo. I caught a ride across the Sierras from a Frisco cab driver with two days off and headed to Reno to beat Harold's Club with a new system. Upon my promise not to tell anyone he explained the questionable mathematics of blackjack and gobbled up a hundred miles of fine scenery. He pointed out the gorge where the Donner party had come to their end eating each other. Literally. Have a piece of Mama's liver, Brad. John Muir walked around here peacefully years ago but now people trample each other and scramble for campsites. In Rocky Mountain National Park I was way up in the "high lonesome" sleeping near a glacier when I heard the strains of "You Are My Sunshine." Nice family packing in a battery-operated record player. From Scarsdale no less. I was sixteen at the time and feisty beyond belief and told them that I was going to kick their little machine to pieces if they didn't turn it off. On the way out of the woods I was stopped at a ranger station and asked to fill out a long questionnaire on the general quality of the services and pleasures in the park. This request got a shrieking "fuck you" and the other campers that had gathered and the ranger gave me that look of "Well here's a mad dog let's hope he goes away." The hotel where I worked had recently fired then rehired me over my abortive attempt to unionize the dining room labor. We all worked a triple split shift and the manager of the hotel offered me three hundred dollars to call the thing off. The option was a quick and forceful trip to Denver with a local deputy. I called off the walkout but didn't accept the money which was a fortune to me at the time. I felt laved in honor and pride. They're not buying off Reuther Junior goddamnit. I hoped Steffens and Herbert Croly were watching me from Labor Heaven. Of course I was a chickenshit and should have taken the ride to Denver with the cop. But he might have hurt my body. I got back at the management by organizing pilferage, pulling the plug on the ice machine, and serving raw eggs on my room service trips. I was ashamed during a room service breakfast trip to betray a homely old lady who had treated me well in the past. I served her two absolutely raw eggs then raced back to the kitchen to the phone in order to receive her complaint. Seems her husband who I had heard showering didn't like his eggs raw. Would you please bring two more. Yes of course in a concealed voice then to the refrigerator for two hard-boiled eggs and sending them up with another waiter. Desperation would set in but then a fifteen-hour day wasn't my idea of acceptable working conditions. My most courageous action was the dropping of a full tray of silverware during a muted lovely dinner hour with the sun glinting off Longs Peak. Horrid noise with diners' necks jerking around. Might cause whiplash. I picked up the silverware slowly while the maitre d'hotel and the headwaiter stood nearby cursing.

In the tent cross-legged looking at the maps in the dark by a gradually dimming flashlight. I plotted a ten-mile circle which would start out toward the west, then north and back

east and south back to the tent. It wouldn't be a bad walk
assuming I began at dawn and assuming again that I didn't
get lost. I turned off my flashlight and lay back on my sleeping bag. I seemed to be losing weight but it might just be
liquid from not drinking. I felt my chest and stomach and
their layer of fat which had gathered slowly over the years.
From the vantage point of 1970 it appeared that all my
movements since 1958 had been lateral rather than forward.
I had printed three extremely slender books of poems which
took up approximately an inch of shelf space. A succession
of not very interesting nervous breakdowns. The reading
of perhaps a few thousand books and the absorption of no
wisdom at all from them. I no longer carried books around
as a walking blood bank, a purgative for sorrow. Swallow
when needed. Take when lost and Bo-Peep will find you as
she finds all lost sheep. I heard of a man who traced man-
dalas by riding the New York City subway. I had become
covert about the past to the extent that my interest in it
slackened. And the future was even more oblique. Not that
I was unhappy or particularly upset about its prospects. I
had once planned to walk the periphery of the United States
but then I had also planned a trip on the Trans-Siberian
Express, the Orient Express, and a tracing of Rimbaud's
path into Africa. But these intentions had become all gaggle
and gilt from planning. I was twelve years old again sharp-
ening broadhead arrows in my bedroom while someone said
downstairs that Ike's going to get us out of Korea. Where
and why was Korea or Panmunjon? Across the flat blue
ocean on a map, across the Marianas Trench. Stop in Hawaii
where there were bared belly buttons. I knew I was dying

daily day per day. At an acceleration rate of twenty-four-hour units. A trip to Jerusalem to see where Jesus walked. It occurred to me that I was still an orthodox Christer and believed in the Second Coming. Lion of Judah. I still read the last book of the Bible with fright, the Book of Revelation. I had lost my urge to chat with Gandhi or Ramakrishna. Only Shakespeare or Apollinaire would do and the exchange of information would be nominal and diffident. They would be curious about color TV and freeze-dried foods as great artists always seemed to devour particulars. If I found wolf tracks tomorrow or even spotted a wolf or found the impossible den that would scarcely change the fact that my first love had betrayed me. My real griefs were over the dead and the prospects of a disastrous future; my affection for the presentness of the woods was easily accounted for. Trees offer no problems and even if all wilderness is despoiled I'll settle for a hundred acres and hide within it and defend it with howls perfected by operatic training. I'll hand-roll Bugler tobacco and become a hermit. They'll parachute starlets into my outpost to be reseeded—the poor girls will wander about aimlessly for a few hours wondering what the hell it's all about and I'll follow them like a male Rima the birdman sizing up the cut of their haunches. Sex enters. To mate not once but a thousand times. And one turns out to be quite enough if you give yourself over to her and if you can give yourself over to anything. The urge seems so atavistic and never leaves for more than a day at a time except during illness and then the lovely worm stirs again with no sense of aim. I sat up trying to catch a new sound, almost a bark but guttural. Probably a bear raiding a honey tree at night

and getting stung around the nose and mouth. I cut a honey
tree down during winter when the bees were sluggish and
almost dormant, dropping out of the hole to the ground
where they froze instantly in the near zero cold. I chopped
with an ax until I reached the cache of honey which was
after all their food. I took off a glove and scooped up a handful. Not very good, almost rank with a buckwheat flavor.
Put sticky hand back in glove and walked away on my snow-
shoes. You spot honey trees in the summer and come back
when it's cool enough not to get stung. Rabelais said a cunt
was a honeypot, but no bees of course. The first time you
enter and the breathless hammering of your heart in your
chest. Dwell on the sexual as it is not yet totally atrophied
by our progress. We would be looked upon strangely by
those in the past who might be busy building a civilization.
How to make bricks with no straw they said in Egypt to the
Pharaoh before the long walk out and north. I ran my hand
along the barrel of the rifle and thought of its pitiless machinery. Leakey crept up on a deer and stabbed it with a
knife chipped from stone to show it was possible. The final
sport will be throwing stones at stars, super refined with an
earth population of fifty billion and the falling stones bringing an anonymous and non-selective death. I turned over
in sleeplessness, reached out for an imaginary bottle. Jesus
wants me for a sunbeam. Even earth is a she. Millions kissed
her daily before it occurred to Raskolnikov as an act of
penance. Real grass still grows. That girl you knew in 1956
lasted a year with heroin until she was found in the East
River her head nearly severed from the body. Not dooms.
Hapless accident walked into if you turn tricks for any habit

as my brain shrank with a succession of jobs in pastel offices here and there in cities. If the wanderings were traced on a map I would hope the connecting numbers would spell something but I'm sure they don't. Mouse or ground squirrel outside the tent. God I told you I didn't want a full moon tonight or I wanted it covered. The woman I read about in the Brooks Range, now littered with oil and barrels and derricks, had her howling answered by wolves. Silver light through tent front. I got up into a crouch and loaded the rifle, then crawled out of the tent. No clouds or slightest breeze. Wolfbane blooming in the Carpathians. I sighted on the moon with the rifle uncocked then racked a shell into the chamber, aiming at a gray mottled area on the moon's surface. If I squeezed now I would see blue flame and hear the noise until morning. I gently released the hammer and added a log to the fire, chilled now with only my shorts on. I tested the rifle's length for suicide turning the end of the barrel against my forehead where its cool tip further chilled me. Thinking of how Hemingway in unthinkable pain, mental and physical, picked the shotgun from the cabinet that morning. I smiled to myself. How far again I was from taking my life with the woods covered with the skin of moonlight. The log began to take, a flame shooting up from one side of the bed of hot coals. I squatted close to the fire and then stood and took off my shorts and squatted again as near to the flame as I could bear. I looked down in a vague wonderment — walking around putting that thing in girls. How pleasant. I thought of howling against the improbable chance of getting an answer but then I knew if I howled I would frighten myself. I remembered wrestling with a friend after football practice and a quarrel and getting a chokehold on him, holding it until his face changed color. I was afraid, losing my anger instantly. When we got up he looked at me strangely and we scarcely ever spoke again. Something moved in the brush and trees near the creek and I wished that I had brought along my predator call which is a small wooden whistle-type object that when blown into properly makes the sound of a dying rabbit. A horrid strangling sound, closest to high-pitched child-weeping. A porcupine when mortally wounded makes a similar sound when he falls from the tree. They are vastly overpopulated because their predator, the marten, has been trapped to extinction for its beautiful fur. Hard to get close to one—I've pulled quills from a dog's mouth a number of times. You trim the ends to let air into the hollow quill then twist and jerk. Out comes the barbed quill and a gout of blood, very painful to the dog but they seem to know the process is necessary. I want to draw false conclusions about everything and obvious scientific facts will not change my weak mind and its continuous droning monologue against itself. I left the circle of light the fire cast and walked slowly toward the creek to find the source of the noise. Nothing there—probably moved on when I arose. If I were to live here long enough many of the animals would adjust to my harmless presence. Many frogs along the creek and the raccoons eat them. And are always cleansing themselves as a falcon does to avoid fleas. I went back to the tent and got into my sleeping bag which was cheap and serviceable but useless when the weather turned cooler. Sleeping in a down mummy bag in the Absarokas thinking that a grizzly might tear off my face

as one did to those two girls at Glacier. Sleeping on picnic
tables in Hastings, Nebraska, and near Brainerd, Minnesota.
Better sleeping with that girl who wouldn't sleep when I
awoke in the morning and I was a house guest and she was
nimbly curious. Only fourteen and I didn't enter but may
as well have, when she brought orange juice and coffee. Me
with the sheet bound around my feet when she entered the
room and the pillow over my eyes, daughter of an acquaintance when I read poems in Wisconsin to a collection of
general dimwits, speed and acid freaks and dazed graduate
students. She's looking at my lighthouse giggling. How old
are you. Fooling around necking. She held it too hard. What
if your parents. I never tell them anything they're creeps.
Dress so short and when I push it up I bury my face then
pull off panties. She's laughing because it tickles. Of course
it does and she has too many teeth and I can't hold anything.
I'll suffocate here now that she is silent and wriggles like all
her older sisters on earth and then when I finish she is on
her hands and knees still squirming. After I wash myself
and come back into the room she is on her back, dress still
up, looking at the pictures in my billfold, panties around an
ankle smiling at me — "That was fun I love to pet." Maybe
I wasn't first I didn't ask. We used to say seventeen will get
you twenty and meant statutory rape is frowned upon but
how can you tell nowadays anyway? Put it there for a moment
rubbing it back and forth madly with her legs up as we kiss
open mouth and nearly enter the nether place to conclude.
Frightened but she wasn't at all, only saying your coffee is
cold now I'll get you some more. I love you of course I
thought and will return when you're less old enough to be

my daughter or were half my age. More fleece. Will you be
spoiled and I have spoiled you. John Calvin is back there
in my brain and sweating in guilt a dozen times since. I carry
a small school photo of her with her small empire curls before
her ears and light brown hair. Smooth, brown, strong, she
played tennis all the time but her buttocks so white. Should
confess to her parents and whisk her to Virginia where that
age isn't rare and fuck until my brain is sated and built of
honeysuckle flowers which was her scent. First color of
dawn now and I can't bother with sleep if I'm going to make
my circle.

Reno, Fallon, Austin, Ely. God I took the wrong way with
nearly a week to reach Salt Lake City again. I see why they
test atomic bombs in this state — if they didn't I would, only
in more central locations. Reno a remuda of divorcees. I arrived at noon with three dollars and by one o'clock I had only
fifty cents what with the nickel misery of slot machines and
an aluminum roast beef sandwich sprayed with tabasco to
make it a tabasco aluminum roast beef sandwich. And iced
tea in a small foggy plastic glass with a trace of lipstick on it.
Whose lips and I wonder who is kissing her now and where
precisely. Out on the hot asphalt street a policeman parked
at the curb looks at me from an air-conditioned squad car. I
mill about close to a tourist family staring in shop windows at
cowboy hats and beaded moccasins and turquoise amulets.
Through the door of a club I watch a woman working two
slot machines at once with a big pile of silver dollars. Probably from Dayton, Ohio, come here for a divorce because

marriage hasn't in fifteen marfak years fulfilled her life or
widened her horizons. Turning around I see that the squad
car is now on the other side of the street and I'm sure now
that I'm being watched. His small face and big sunglasses
remind me of an enlarged photo of the head of a fly. A fuzz
buzz. On the corner in vacant lot there is a mobile glass
cage. I walk up to it and smell the cotton candy, caramel
corn and hot dogs. I ask a girl in a white uniform for a glass
of water and she says, Coke rootbeer orange Pepsi RC Dr
Pepper Seven-Up lime cherry cream soda.

    —I'll just take a glass of water.

    —No water, she says looking a half foot above my head.

    —Coke with no ice.

    I drink it in three gulps and hand her the cup. She
points wordlessly to a garbage pail on my left.

    —Water, I ask.

    She fills the cup with ice water.

    —We can't make a dollar on water.

    —Thanks.

    I begin to walk away when I hear a "hey you." The cop
of course. I sit in his chilled car while he pokes around in
my billfold. I explain the theft in San Francisco thus little
identification. The radio rasps. Nice cool place to sit. He
calls in my name and then we wait for fifteen minutes or so
until I am cleared from nameless deeds.

    —I'm going to give you a ride.

    —That's nice of you.

    —Don't get smart.

    When we drive away I nod at the pop-stand girl and
she waves, smiling.

—Where we going? I ask.

He doesn't answer. He drives with his left hand and keeps his right on his holster. A quick-draw champ no doubt. Matt Dillon and Robert Mitchum in a hundred-thirty-pound sack of kidney beans. If one were interested in martyrdom it would be nice to quietly draw a Beretta out of your pocket and fan him six times in the bread basket where the badge wouldn't deflect the lead. But then he is probably a Methodist and church usher and an Eagle, Moose and Lion with a wife and little eaglets at home who love his steely bravado. At the edge of town he tells me to get out and start walking because hitchhiking is against the law. I stand there while he turns the car around in a swirl of gravel and dust and peels a few yards of rubber on the way back into town. Oh for a bazooka. Or to pull the pin of a grenade as I got out of the car and just as he shifted into second to see and hear the car shatter in an orange explosion. I started walking and with only forty cents after my Coke, at least a hundred degrees of heat and my mouth already dry as the pavement. About two thousand miles from home.

So dumb of me to take 50 on the split instead of 40-95 up through Winnemucca and Elko, the main route. A ride into Fallon for buying some teenagers beer and I wasn't twenty-one myself but evidently looked it. Two cases and a buck for the effort. I walked around Fallon then out the other side standing a few brief minutes until I got a lift to the entrance of a secret air base where two guards stood in the heat with white helmets glinting. I walked down the road a few hundred yards farther and began to wait. The desert around me seemed so immense, hostile, nature at total war with herself and the road such a thin strip of civility through so many measureless miles of sand and umber rock. I've been told there's life out there and the desert owns all these mysteries but they aren't my own and I must have green. I stood there twelve hours with only three or four cars passing, until my bottom lip cracked and I became dizzy from the lack of food and water and though evening had come the air had not cooled. Breathing in a furnace. Holes out there that go down to the center of the earth. I crossed the road and began to walk back toward Fallon and I could not quite feel my teeth or tongue or my hands swinging at my sides. After a few miles I heard a car coming but doubted my senses — earlier in the day the few cars seemed to ride on a cushion of air, a wave of heat. But they stopped. A man and his wife and when I got in they looked at me and she said, Jesus Christ. He gave me a lukewarm can of beer which I drank in a few swallows and then another. No more you need water, his wife said, look at your face. I looked in the rearview mirror and my lips were black and had cracked in three places and the whites of my eyes were shot with blood. Toasted. They let me out and I went into a cafe that was half casino. I drank water until I was swollen after ordering a cup of coffee. The place was nearly empty and a man came over to me while the waitress changed the grounds in the coffee maker. He asked if I had gotten stuck out there and I said yes. Then he said the northern route is best and I answered that I had by now figured that out. I asked him about the telegraph office and when it opened and then went over and made a collect call to Michigan to an old friend. Couldn't call my dad as he usually had less money than I did. I told him I was stuck in Fallon, Nevada, and then to juice it up a bit I told him the police at gun point said I had to be out of here close after dawn and that I only had thirty cents. He giggled and asked if there were any whorehouses in the town and I said yes but not for a man with two bits. He said he would wire two hundred dollars right away and I said make it a hundred fifty. I went back to the counter and had some more water and started talking to the waitress and the owner. She put a hamburger before me and I said I had no money. He waved his arm and said he had heard my call and the bus didn't leave until ten next morning and I could pay him back after I cashed my wire. Three Paiutes entered and bought some wine to go. They were nearly in rags but one had an unblocked Stetson. When the owner got back from selling them the wine he told me a story of how he got out of the army after World War Two and was hitchhiking back home when outside of Topeka he lipped off at two cops and they beat him until he had to have his jaws wired back together in a VA hospital. All this after he had taken part in the Normandy invasion and swept across France and was one of the first to enter Paris. He said he always did want to get back to Paris because he drank himself silly and fucked the thankful French girls until he lost ten pounds. Then he said he always planned to take his antelope rifle, a .270 Weatherby back to Topeka and get both cops in the cross hairs of his four-power Bushnell scope. They would be head shots. But he never got around to it. I left the casino after he told me I could sleep in the park and if the police came to tell them "Bob" had sent me over. Some fine people left, a bond of voyagers no matter how far in the past it was.

Funny how many people with tattoos and muscles give you rides. Not afraid of anything. I remembered how with a few friends we had terrified some college students at a bar. It was summer and I was chewing tobacco to try to kick cigarettes and the students were slumming and rather deftly beat us at the pool table. My friend stooped behind the most arrogant one and I pushed him over and spit tobacco in his face then my friend planted a boot in his ribs. We were ashamed after they fled. Bad losers and we were part-time students too only hated it. When we had a few more drinks my friend said he wouldn't have put the boot to him but was trying to kick off his fraternity pin.

I watched the locals leave the second movie — one girl in particular with long blond hair and incredibly tight Levi's. Take me home. The marquee lights went off and a pickup roared down the main street narrowly missing some movie-goers. I walked a few blocks over to the park. Nice with a cool breeze and clumps of cottonwood trees. I hear crickets and cars accelerating from town which is an orange haze. It is moonless. There is a street lamp at the entrance of the park and beer cans all over the ground. I lie back on the picnic table but then am startled from the beginning of sleep by some roaming dogs. Out with the knife. The largest of them, part collie and part shepherd I think, approaches the table snarling. I say, Come boy, in a soft voice and he starts wiggling and wagging his tail. Now four of them are around the table all jumping to be petted. Then a car swerves into the park and the dogs run off. Country music again from the radio and two couples drinking and I'm in their headlights now. A man calls out,

Hey kid, what you doing? Sleeping. They laugh and tell
me to get out because they're going to have a little party.
I get up and walk out of the park as far from their car as
possible. No trouble please — so tired that if someone hit
me I would put the knife in to the handle. I walk a dozen or
so blocks until I reach a school and walk across the green
lawn to the bushes that surround it. I crawl into the shrubbery and make myself comfortable watching the same four
dogs trot down the middle of the street. My friends. School
daze. The girl in those Levi's now or beneath lilacs in a
greener country. Take bus the hell out of here and sleep all
the way to diesel roar on the back wide seat. Think I can
smell chalk dust and cleaning fluid from the building. All
schools smell the same, don't they? Hope that there're no
rattlesnakes in town like the one I saw crushed on the road
covered with flies. Fat with large head. I cut off the stinking rattles and put them in my pocket. Rotten cucumber
smell. Won't rattle them now or its brothers and sisters
might hear and come in from the desert for a visit. Strange
to wake up with a blanket of rattlesnakes. Or a large ball
of hibernating rattlesnakes for a pillow as they get in a
ball to hibernate in prairie dog holes. Scare people in town
when I carried them in for breakfast. Little sleep for four
days and my adrenaline glands as large as a baby's head.
Girl with Levi's will find me but we'll discover the trousers
won't come off and I'll have her between the breasts like
the Berkeley librarian in the morning and I could watch
each involuntary mindless thrust. I want some fried eggs
or a steak. I turned over and faced the street and slept with
my blind eye open to the lamp on the corner.

❀   ❀   ❀

I ate a tin of Argentine beef and kicked some dirt over the coals of the fire. Smokey the Bear is always watching. Canteen full and only a package of raisins and peanuts in my pouch with the fish line. I made another inept attempt at a compass reading—perhaps I would miss the juncture of my circle and be lost all night seven hundred feet from my tent. I was lost at twelve in an impenetrable swamp, my clothes covered with ooze, and then I heard a car on a log road only a few invisible feet away. And how could I be truly lost when there was only a tent to find and it was summer and there was food in the woods and I could make a lean-to out of cedar or birch poles. Being lost somehow presupposes a distant location that you are trying to find, a warm center where a door will open, a screen door at that with a piece of cotton on it to keep off the flies, and into a yellow kitchen where a woman is cooking at the stove. When she turns around you'll be able to tell if it's your mother, wife or mistress. Or some dark lady you haven't met yet who will lead you to another, more evil life. When I set out toward the hills barely visible in the west I had the feeling that I wouldn't make it back to the tent that evening. I was momentarily angry at the wolves—I knew they were out there and they were aware of my presence but had learned through generations not to reveal themselves to anyone who walks upright. I felt peaceful again when I thought of the Arctic wolf that had weighed a hundred ninety pounds, exactly my own weight. How pleasant to have him as a companion walking with you, his back higher than your waist and his head and teeth rubbing and caressing your shoulder. They can be vaguely domesticated but only on their own terms and should be left where they belong. Of course they only knew it weighed that much after they shot it. Heat rising to the head now, a thin red line of anger encircling my vision of the woods ahead of me. I could do less with my life than go to Alaska and shoot down the airplanes from which they shoot the wolves. I think here I have found a worthy cause, a holy war I can adapt myself to—I suppose it would be less significant than taking part in the other horrors but it's something I might do well.

Chapter 4

New York City

Midnight now. Only for you Lucia I'll take my wounds from the light. Here in the rain and half asleep. Then from the hill in the first milky light I could see the cars leaving. All the sailors were gone and only one toll booth on each side of the turnpike was open. There was a fine needle mist in the air—it had rained sporadically through the night with some thunder and lightning in the distance dimming the flames of the steel mills, dimming the headlights of the trucks, the arc lights above the booths, brightening the grass and the leaves of the elm under which I lay curled and wet. Late the night before there had been too many hitchhikers, mostly sailors, so I had walked two miles back along an access highway toward Pittsburgh and bought a hamburger and a pint of whiskey. Then back to the hill where I lay in the first drops of rain hoping the May night would stay warm, drinking the whiskey in sips and thinking that for a dollar extra I could

have bought a brand that wouldn't burn and stop at the back
of my throat before it went down. In the future all amber
liquids would be silken and come in crystal decanters and
be poured for me by Annabel Lee. When the whiskey was
gone I slept then awoke thinking the sailors might be gone
but there were still five of them so I went to sleep again to
the sounds of crickets, arc lights hissing in the rain, a single
whippoorwill somewhere back in the hills behind me, and
the huge diesel trucks switching gears a dozen times to reach
their running speed.

She had asked me to come in a letter with a single paragraph on stationery that was off-pink and smelled of nastur-
tiums or skunk cabbage. I suppose violets were intended. I
thought about her for several days then hurled my school
books off a bridge — I was studying art history and working
part time as a carpenter. I had chosen art history because
it involved sitting in a large darkened room and looking at
slides of paintings and buildings I someday wanted to see.
I had saved a thousand dollars two years before to go to
France but blew it all on an involved eye operation. Took
three years to save the money and the kindly surgeon got it
all in three hours for an incredibly unsuccessful hatchet job.
Nice that he should get three hundred and thirty-three dollars an hour for knowing all about eyeballs. He considered
me pointlessly hostile — no promises had been made. I left
on a Friday after I picked up my check which was small
because we had been rained out for several days. I tried to
borrow enough to take the bus or train but my few friends
were broke and the bank asked me what I had to offer as
security. On foolish evenings I had planned bank robberies

with a friend and I thought when I walked out of that particular bank after being refused I would come back one day
and hold it up. Remember me? You wouldn't give me a loan.
Blam blam blam blam capitalist pigfucker. Maybe I would
simply fire into the floor near his feet. I didn't want to hurt
anyone. But so far the trip had been pleasant and the rides
easy. I liked the verdant Ohio countryside, the hay dryers
giving off their smell of rotting alfalfa. A green, hot smell.
Even Pittsburgh looked kindly for a change, a stiff breeze
blowing the filth elsewhere. But now hung-up because people always pick up soldiers and sailors first. America first
or IMPEACH EARL WARREN, as the signs say outside
of Kalamazoo—"Kalamazoo" is Indian for "sneeze" and
"stink pot."

At last the fighting boys were out of the way and I
walked down the hill and vaulted the Cyclone fence, something I can't do any more along with hopscotching parking
meters or chinning myself a hundred times with one arm.
My how bodies calcify then rot. Within a few moments I was
picked up by a chemical engineer who was very methodic in
his questioning. Where was my suitcase? Stolen. Satisfied.
What did I do? I worked for a demolition company tearing down old buildings. Hard work? Yes a twelve-pound
sledge tends to get heavy. Good pay? Yes four dollars an
hour. Then he says the unions are going too far too far too
far. How much do you make? None of your business. Oh.
Where were all the unions going? I wondered. Then he said
if there was a radio in the car we could listen to music or a
ball game but it was a company car. I said you should unionize and demand radios. Wise guy, he said. Then he began

his life story as if it were obligatory—his rise through the
management ranks of a Cincinnati soap factory and about
his three children and how property and income taxes were
a real pinch. Also a convention he had been to in San Francisco that was a real ball and I mean a real ball with beautiful
high-priced prostitutes. You rich guys have all the luck, I
said, getting to travel and putting ass on the tab. Golly. But
we work hard and have to let off steam and by gosh when
it comes down to brass tacks soap means a lot. Very handy
to wash with I thought to myself. He sighed and asked if I
had many girl friends. I said only one and we were saving
ourselves for marriage. I didn't want to get into an aimless
sex conversation. I began to doze, the chill going out of my
wet clothes which were drying in the sun coming through
the windshield. I thought of her in odd ways—she was bird-
like thus became a bird, her head jerking and darting as
she spoke. Her panties looked heavy with feathers beneath
them and her breast was large and single, soft with down.
Then soapy said the weather has been rainy in Cincy and
sports in general and then we had a long argument on farm
parity. I thought of her again and who I would see first and
whether I would ask Barbara if the child was mine or skip
seeing her altogether. There's a mindless promiscuity girls
from Mississippi or Louisiana develop when they get to New
York. Need for warmth I suppose after a secure home and
good schools and money and all they have left in the city is
money and their instinctive charm and aimlessness. He lets
me off in Harrisburg even though I know he's going farther.
All the jackoff business types and I wish I were that sure
of myself. Wanting to know if I took "dope." Of course of

course and lots of it. Well, he says, I'm a chemist and it's a scourge. Nice word scourge, I said, but I thought you made soap not dope. I'm management, he says, and work downtown, the factory is on the outskirts. I only waited in Harrisburg a half hour before I caught a ride from a young man with a package of Luckies rolled up in the sleeve of his T-shirt and an eagle tattooed on his forearm. He had the radio turned on too loud for much talk except when the hourly news came on and then he would talk. He was fresh out of the navy and said all the women in Norfolk, Virginia, were clapped up but if you went to Richmond on a weekend pass you could score with a nice country girl. I had never been to Richmond but as we talked I began to believe that I had been there and agreed with everything he said and added my own obscene embellishments. Later that evening when we had reached Staten Island I hoped that someday I might go to Richmond and meet fresh country girls who weren't like the clapped-up fat-ankled hogs in Norfolk.

At Staten Island I caught a cross-island bus and walked to the ferry from town after having a few drinks. The bartender asked if I had been to Florida what with my nice tan and I said no I had been working outdoors where the sun tends to be most of the time. He sagely agreed. I waited about an hour for the ferry in the cavernous terminal, keeping an eye on one group of Negroes who were terribly drunk but laughing, and two pasty-faced sullen young men who glared at everyone with little eyes set in pizza faces. When we boarded I immediately went up the stairs and out to the rail where I watched the dimly lit island recede, and then to the prow where I watched Manhattan slowly draw closer.

Such black, black water beneath us. I've little confidence in the ability of any boat to float. How old is this ship sir that I've been on dozens of times with this and that girl? The first time with a girl I was living with and telling her I had seen a real author that day during noon hour: Aldous Huxley standing tall and gaunt and foggy-eyed on the corner of Fifty-seventh and Fifth, with a young girl holding his hand. She was very pretty, the young girl, and I followed them down Fifth until they turned down Fifty-third and went into the Museum of Modern Art to which I didn't have the price of admission. I wanted to overhear their conversation — to see if he said witty things as he did in *Crome Yellow* and *Point Counter Point* and all the other books where the young men of my age had souls that were "tenuous membranes." I had fashioned myself on one of those young men during my last year of high school adding a large dose of Stephen Dedalus for a *bouquet garni*. I only saved myself from being a snot and prig by moving on to an absolute absorption with Whitman, Faulkner, Dostoevsky, Rimbaud, and then Henry Miller who was like a continuous transfusion, food to avoid melancholy. If you're eighteen or nineteen you read for strength more than for pleasure. On a string stretched across my little room I had taped two portraits, one of Rimbaud and the other a yellowish line drawing of Dostoevsky with his high globed forehead containing it seemed all the evils and joys man had ever known, a simultaneous jubilance and doom. But then the primacy was always owned by life herself and if you're a busboy or you're hoeing or bucking hay bales the presentness of the labor overwhelms the loftiness of your reading. To an outsider from the midlands who

WOLF   157

is broke the first hot pastrami sandwich at a delicatessen is
an unbelievable wonder. Why don't they make this sort of
food back home? Or the lions in front of the library seemed
so magnificent and the idea that I was allowed to wander
around the library at will where I saw a manuscript in the
handwriting of Keats. Truly a golden city I thought. And
the splendor of my first marijuana in a dark corner of the
Five Spot where Pepper Adams was playing with Alvin
Jones taking thirty-minute drum solos growling and sweating all the way through his blue suit until it turned black. At
eighteen I was ill prepared to absorb anything and walked
around in a dreamlike stupefaction with the city.

    And now two years later on the ferry drawing closer
to the Battery the city looked flat and painted, a decal on
the horizon, suppurating in filth and cold evil. No promise
or future in her. I would get in and out with dispatch after
two short visits. Or I would be happy to see her leveled
by a giant tidal wave caused by a comet plunging into the
Atlantic a few miles off shore, the harbor clogged with dead
squid. The water beneath me was dank and smelly—the
engines roared in reverse as the ferry nosed into the berth.
I'll catch a train to midtown and walk around until dawn.
Oddly I've never felt threatened in New York City. Perhaps
my innocence while walking around Harlem and Spanish
Harlem and the Lower East Side, and of course shabby,
anonymous clothing makes you appear a poor mark. Even
sitting on a park bench in what I later found out was Needle
Park. Talking easily with the whores and junkies, curious
to see how they live and think. A friend told me that I was
never approached because my googly eye made me look

hostile and criminal in itself. How many times have I asked
strangers questions to startle them and to watch them look
over their right shoulders to see if I'm talking to someone
else. Anyway I felt safe. And never hesitated to go where I
wanted. In the three times I've lived in the city I've only been
involved in two incidents that could be thought of as violent.
On the way to a party in Far Rockaway some young hoods
were tearing up subway seats with their knives and then
after we were well into Brooklyn they pried a door open and
brought in some snow from the platform. There were five of
us, three girls from Barnard and a friend of mine, a sandal
maker from the Village. His girl told one of the creeps not
to throw any snow at her which he immediately did just as
we reached another stop. We chased them out of the car and
down the platform where my friend upended one of them by
the hair and I chased the other off the end of the platform
where I yelled, I hope you hit the third rail, cocksucker. But
he ran across the tracks and climbed a fence. When I got
back up the platform the conductor was holding the train
and the other creep was sitting on the cement blubbering.
My friend stood there waiting for me with a handful of hair
he had jerked out when he had stopped the chase. He said
he slapped him a few times but that was all. When we got
back with the girls, mine told me that I should never do that
or I might get stabbed. But then I had seen within a few
months the most insane brutality on subways without a conductor or any subway employee ever interfering. The other
incident was unpleasant inasmuch as it was my own fault. I
was sitting with some people at a bar that was popular with
painters. I went to the toilet and a well-dressed man standing

next to the urinal said, You queers really like this bar don't
you. I hit him full blast in the ear while he was combing his
hair then a few more times about the head and shoulders
and kneed him in the solar plexus on the way down. I then
stomped on his glasses which had fallen to the floor. He sat
there looking stupidly at me holding his hands out and said
again I was a queer so I stuck his head in the toilet bowl
which had something in it and walked out and back to my
table. But then he emerged and talked to the bartender who
came over and said that I shouldn't have beaten up a regu-
lar customer. Then one of the painters said that it was the
guy's "bit" to get beat up in toilets. I felt very embarrassed
but then they went back to talking about de Kooning and
let the subject drop. I've always hated any sort of violence
to the extent that I feel vaguely jittery and nauseated when
watching a fist fight.

After a few hours of walking in a generally westerly direction I realized how hot it was going to become. The Huron
Mountains are on approximately the same latitude as the
city of Quebec but when the wind off Lake Superior ceases
the summer weather can become dense and unbearable. The
year before camped on the pine barrens of the Yellow Dog
plains I had spent much of my time lolling in the cool river.
The heat was so intense and the forest so baked and dry
that a single match would have created a firestorm, an animal
Dresden with the fire moving at two hundred miles per hour
in great orange leaps, the same speed incidentally as an ava-
lanche moves. Some false conclusions should be drawn from

this. Never forget that ontogeny recapitulates phylogeny. And vice versa. Gourd in her great widowdom creates worlds daily with mathematical verisimilitude. A plowed furrow resembles an open vagina and so on. A rifle is a false prick and a prick is a false rifle, useless if the Nips invade California. I was told only last week that we live in apocalyptical times. Perhaps the "last days." Yes of course, I'm making a caul, a necklace with a pendant built out of a chocolate-covered horse turd to ward off evil. The problem is suffocation by chintz not apocalypse — too many rats in the grain bin and many are becoming enfevered and will die from stress, death of the mind first, the body goes more slowly. I climbed a hill with effort, up through a windfall of poplar and aspen, until I reached the summit and sat down on a moss-covered rock. Nothing but green, encircled by forest and no sign of man visible though they were out there somewhere cutting pulp for the paper mills. Or cutting cedar logs to build cabins for auto workers in Detroit a comfortable six hundred miles south of me. When I caught my wind I headed north down the hill toward a small lake I spotted perhaps three miles distant. Take a dip there and turn east. I noticed that I had forgotten to smoke for several hours and looked down at the cordovan tobacco stains on my fingers and the way my shrinking lungs had to suck in air to feed my heart oxygen. A short fit then as I stomped on a half pack of cigarettes and ground them into the dry leaves. Ugly package. I knelt and scooped a small hole with my fingers and buried it knowing that I would regret the action by the time I reached the lake. I began to feel a total enervation again and thrashed through the woods as fast as I could walk. The anger fed by the thought of a girl trying to guess my birth sign. Fuck horoscopes. But I remembered dreaming of running through a swamp as a centaur, then plunging into a river to wash the mud from my flanks. Also taking the bow from my shoulder and unsheathing an arrow which I shot at a tree for no particular reason. But it's the daily gab and trash of the astrology thing. The alchemists had sense enough to conceal themselves just as the true satanists remain anonymous and work their wonders privately. I said I was a spy thus revealing that I wasn't despite my Luger and Burberry trenchcoat. The black arts including astrology require an apprenticeship and great study from their novitiates. Then you discover that there are no secrets or true mysteries but a Secret, no holy books but the unwritten one hidden from us at earth's center. The dark side of the moon is merely dark and cold and Jupiter and Saturn only distant flecks of brain hurled out before time was. I lost control of my feet and slid down a ferny bank and into the trunk of a tamarack knocking myself windless. I lay there wheezing and soaked with sweat, the local mosquitoes and flies finding me effortlessly. Are you a Pisces? she asks. No, I say, slapping her face with a schmaltz herring swung deftly by the tail. Can I eat your Libra pussy, RSVP? Backscuttle your Scorpio bum? Drive Mr. Powerful down your silly Taurus throat? I rolled over reaching automatically for the cigarettes that wouldn't be there. Maybe I could climb back up the hill and find their little grave. Salvage even one. That will teach me. I could see the sunlight barely reaching through the ferns and the straight, slight stalks. Mary Jane and Sniffles the mouse go down the hole in the

stump. Miniaturization by magic sand. No one ever sticks
his hand in the dark hole of a stump. A witless naturalist
maybe who deserves a bite on the fingers. I thought of the
mountain lion bounty hunter I met near Duchesne, Utah.
Long greasy hair down over his shoulders and a stained
buckskin shirt. While we drove along in his ancient Plymouth he complained that none of the Mormon women would
fuck him because they stick to their own kind. When the
mountain lion business got slow he would catch two or three
burlap bags full of rattlesnakes and sell them to a college in
Provo for medical research. Five bucks apiece. We failed to
make one mountain grade but a county road truck came
along and pushed us over. He said that he usually lived with
his brother who was a rancher near Roosevelt but he preferred sleeping outdoors. He could ride seventy-five miles
north into Wyoming without seeing a soul. Or south farther
than that along the Green River and Tavaputs Plateau. He
gave me the address of a girl in Vernal who might just pos-
sibly be "nice" to me. But my next ride had been a Catholic
priest who let me sit in the car in Vernal while he ate. Trusts
me in the car with the keys in his pocket but won't buy me
lunch. His voice was highly nasal and he preached to me
until it sounded like a duck's voice, either Donald's or
Daisy's. But then we became friendly after he bought me
dinner and I told him about all the lies Baptists used to
spread about Catholics — the tunnel between the nunnery
and the monastery with the tunnel floor littered with the
bones of babies. He took this very seriously and said we
must pray for them. Lying in the ferns I was happy that
there were no poisonous snakes this far north. Otherwise

I wouldn't be able to wallow around in the leaves with safety or impunity. I finally got up when my sweat had begun to dry and I had eaten some raisins with a slug of warm water. Oh God I'd give a healthy tooth for a cigarette. My hair flopped irritatingly across my eyes and I stopped and took out my knife and cut the front shock off, then made a sweatband out of my red handkerchief. Natty Bumppo wants tobacco. And a porterhouse and a bottle of Chateau Margaux and a horse to ride back to camp where he would pack, back to the car where the horse would be abandoned and the car driven straight through to New York City to the Algonquin or the Plaza where he would send an underling over to Bonwit's Bill Blass shop with his measurements and get out-fitted for outrageous high-class low-down gluttony and fuckery. Tiresome. I mean fine places and coming down to the Edwardian Room for breakfast, forgetting your tie and having the waiter whip one on you before you could fart or whistle. The rich never forget their ties and my dad tied mine for me until I was nineteen because I simply couldn't get the hang of it. I was walking into a lower, swampier area and knew the lake couldn't be far away now. I skirted the swale for a few hundred yards then plunged in, in despair of finding an open path to the water. I reached a knoll and shimmied up a birch tree from which I spotted the water not far ahead. The birch was too thick to swing from—it's a dangerous sport in that if the tree is a bit too thick your downward swing stops too far in the air and there is no retreat. You have to drop. Be smart to break a leg here and crawl for a week to reach the car. My boyhood hero Jim Bridger would never be caught in such an act but neither would he have entered the Plaza without

a tie except perhaps to set a fire or hit somebody. Still some
of his kind left. A friend had seen a halfbreed near Timmins,
Ontario, portage two miles with four hundred pounds of
moose meat on his back. I reached the lake and spotted a
sand bar to my left down the shore where I could sit and
take off my clothes for a swim.

I went into a bar near the Battery and had my pastrami
sandwich and five double bourbons. Health creeping back in
the blood stream after last night's chill and discomfort. There
were only a few nondescript old men in the place mumbling
to themselves—New York has the highest concentration
of mumblers per square acre in the world. A Bulova after
working for the city until sixty-five and then the mumbling
begins. Shirts spittle-flecked from it. The bartender was
intently watching the Jack Paar show where a celebrity was
lashing out at the phoniness of Hollywood. Yum what wit. I
want to go out there someday and take a room and wander
around and challenge Esther Williams to a swimming race,
three miles into the Pacific with the fate of the world as a
prize. A thousand movies have poisoned the mind. James
Dean, O James Dean, where are you now? Six feet under
Indiana's lid. I'm not like Robert Mitchum in *Thunder Road*.
We didn't get a TV until I was on the verge of leaving home
at eighteen. Still don't like it because the screen is so small
and the people might be that size if you went into the studio.
I asked for a glass of water and popped three bennies. Here
we go folks. Out onto the street and toward the subway and
the hum beginning.

I got off the train at Sheridan Square and walked
down Grove to look at the building I had lived in the year

before. Tears of stupidity formed. As they do during the
national anthem at a football game. I looked at the Bar-
rymore house and then turned around and went back to
the Square where I had coffee at Rikers. A queen next to
me with false eyelashes asked for the sugar. Flutter flutter. I felt warmly toward him—why should we care who
they fuck and why. All the legislatures with their Robert's
Rules of Love. I have it on good authority that there are
proportionately more transvestites and flaming rim queens
in Congress than in Laredo, Texas; Springfield, Mass.; or
Malibu Beach. A *sub rosa* report filed under "China" at the
National Institute of Arts and Letters, the collective wisdom of which organization could varnish a Ming vase with
bubbles. Of course singly the members are alpha types but
at election time the daisy chain sets in and whirl herself
nose picks the unworthy first. Finished my coffee. Three
bennies were two too many. If I walk at the speed of light
it's my business. I was aiming generally at Sullivan Street
where she lived in the squalor she loved and deserved. If
she wasn't there I would lick my name on the door and she
would never know unless she got there before the saliva
dried. Down West Fourth with all that apparel to determine
the real you. Opera buffs eating manicotti, breaking into
song spontaneously with their mouths full of marinara sauce.
Music comes from blood-soaked holes. If I were drafted I'd
carry catsup and play dead until they let me go. A girl at the
mailbox on Sixth Avenue, led there by her elegant Afghan
hound. So beautiful with long legs and high butt and hips.
Please be mine and would someone introduce us right now.
She walks away with her globes rubbing each other where

my nose or hose could be. Wish I could ditch the chemistry
and come back to earth. I want to go back home and pound
nails into two-by-fours and carry my empty lunch bucket to
the car and have Mama say how did it go today. Bad very
badly. I hit my thumb twice and very hard. Tore off three
fingernails the first day on an irrigation job. A scream across
the dry field which the water sprinkled and dispersed in my
blood. Finally across Washington Square and to her street.
People playing chess in the dark and a dozen studs along
the meat rack. To be yodeled for a fee. I bought a sack of
pistachios and sat on a bench to collect what was left of my
thoughts. When I'm rich I'll hire a Pulitzer winner to do
nothing but shuck my pistachios. The rest of the time must
be spent in the henhouse clucking. He will not be allowed
to touch the eggs.

Up the stairs. Zero hour and not a sensible word form-
ing in my throat. Perhaps a Zen "I'm here because I'm here
because I'm here." And then the master will run out of a
broom closet and cudgel me to the floor with what is the
sound of one flap clapping. Knock. This place smells of the
usual cabbage soup. Knock. And fish and Roman Cleanser.
A fat girl with puffy eyes opens the door.

— You woke me up.

— Swell. Is Laurie here?

— Who are you?

— Swanson.

— She gets off at three-thirty.

She begins to close the door.

— Wait a minute.

I push past her through a narrow hall and into the arty living room. There is a sofa along the far wall and I sit down then lay back.

The fat girl shrugs her shoulders under her robe and walks into another room. I try to close my eyes but they are gritty. There are books and records and magazines strewn over the floor and theater programs pasted on the wall. And a Moses Soyer painting of a girl whose thighs are askew where they enter her red dress. Larry Rivers print. An imitation Chaim Gross piece on a corner table. Laurie is a counter girl at a big East Side delicatessen catering to the rich Temple Emanu-El crowd. I met her the first time I came east when I intended to go to Washington and had a letter recommending my character from a prominent businessman to a Congressman. But I got sidetracked in Philadelphia and pawned my high school graduation Wittnauer watch and came to New York City. The room grows dimmer, my nerves die a little, my body softening into the couch. Fatty puts a record on in the next room — low and sweet and Latin and I see Mexicans and am back in San Jose covered with palm fronds. Standing then in the hot asphalt parking lot of the bus station. Palm trees with naked trunks like elephant hide and pineapples. Eating tripe stew, *menudo*, I love to eat *menudo* with the kernels of hominy and red peppers.

Laurie wakens me. I know I've slept only a short time but my neck aches from the cramped couch. She is a trifle thinner and her freckles don't seem to show as much. She smells of tongue and pastrami.

—What are you doing here?

She speaks softly, her voice always sounded like a child's, a baby-oil voice.

—I was resting. I take her arm and move over so she can sit on the couch next to me.

—Did you get married? she asks.

—I just hitched in. Took me four days.

—Let me change my clothes. She walks over to a rickety wardrobe and takes out jeans and a sweater. I feel sleep coming on again but then her white uniform drops to the floor.

She stoops and picks it up. Oh my God.

—Why don't you come here a minute?

She turns and smiles and walks over to me in her panties and bra. How lovely her belly. She stretches out along my side and we kiss and don't stop kissing while I undo my belt and push down my trousers and her panties and take off her bra and rip my shirt off, my hands against her breasts. Then she sits up and grinds it in and smiles at me again and then leans down and we kiss until we are finished. I am overwhelmed with love for her. I've never felt distant after making love to her because I loved her. We talked pointlessly about what had gone wrong before. Me. I hated New York City and I slapped her one day. And I met her parents who hated me and wouldn't speak—I wasn't Jewish. I kissed her neck and she slid down my belly and aroused me a second time with her mouth. I kicked off my boots and trousers and entered a second time rocking slowly with her heels in my back and kissing again. Then I slept.

❊   ❊   ❊

I sat on the sand bar and smoked an imaginary cigarette.
It must be seventy-seven degrees and I stood and shed my
clothes and did a little circular toe dance on the sand. Dum
dum dum dum I'm a thirty-two-year-old Indian and nature
herself sees my berserk bare ass and doesn't care. Enough
of a breeze to keep the bugs away. I walked out into the cold
water with an involuntary shudder. Like peeing outdoors
on a cold day. A Cheyenne Indian at that because they had
the finest country to live in, Montana for a few thousand
years before it was Montana. I let go with a long Cheyenne
shriek and dove into the water swimming under it with eyes
open to the blurred bottom. I popped up and looked back
to shore, not bad. When we were twelve we swam around
our lake twice without parental knowledge or consent and
it took nine hours. He said to her, "Do the backstroke."
Bad thing though to put the firecracker in the frog's mouth.
Where did the frog go? Everywhere and in pieces.

I swam idly out into the middle of the lake and looked
down at the black invisible bottom and wished there were
a sea creature to struggle with. When I swam back to shore
I got a cramp in my left calf and let the leg trail slackly. Lay
back on the sand with my head on my clothes and massaged
the muscle until the cramp disappeared. Peter will get sun-
burned a bit. I raised myself by skull and heels. Where's
my squaw now that I may diddle her? Pocahontas and her
splendid cartwheels. It's a matter of contention now who
got fucked over the most, the blacks brought here as slaves
or the Indians who were totally dispossessed. Sand Creek.
Harper's Ferry. Like asking who in a war was murdered
the "deadest." Tell those who pass by I lie here, my skull's

mouth open in perpetual curse. All coming true and without romance. Why can't they learn to be nice boys and girls? Blankets purposely infected with smallpox, rapine, marches, slaughter, greed, and a hundred million pelts shipped back east. Those Paiutes let me off then turned left onto a gravel road which went thirty miles into the desert where they lived in metal government surplus Quonset huts. Had a tendency to stay hot in summer and cold in winter. We passed a bottle, laughing at a song on the radio sung by a champagne lady. Car filthy and heated smell of exhaust fumes and raven black hair. I wrote my first name on my stomach with a handful of sand. A low-flying plane will read it and be alarmed. The dark orphaned prince is on the loose again. Lock up the women and children. Form a posse. Like Cleaver he is to be considered armed and extremely dangerous. I rolled over in the sand then rolled like a log into the water and drank some. Delicious. A spring-fed lake. Wish my dad were here, bringing fly rods to see if there were trout. He would emerge from the woods in the hunting clothes he left in on that November morning. And my sister farther back in the woods could pick flowers and then some mushrooms to eat with the trout. Seven years ago. I wouldn't tell anyone they were still alive. Or that they could walk on the water and over the tops of trees in long floating strides. Or Dolly Parton, my favorite since Patsy Cline died with Cowboy Copas in the plane crash, sings, Daddy come and get me, it's not my mind that's broken it's my heart. The point is that she's love crazed and is in an asylum. Meaulnes never found the girl again and when Heathcliff dug up Cathy it was cold necromancy. Still chills me to think of it or when the mastiff bit her lovely leg. I paddled over to a patch of reeds and looked at their stalks and roots under the water.

When I wake up this time I'm trembling. Poisons in the body. Laurie comes into the room and hands me a cup of coffee. Then she walks over to a desk and intently rolls a joint tapping some crumbled hash in it, wasteful way to use hash but nice. She lights the joint and hands it to me.

—It's all yours. I had some while you were asleep.

I drew heavily and choked holding the sweet smoke as long as possible, exhaled and then drew again. Finally down to the nubbin and I chewed the bitter resinous roach. Now I am way up in the air but nicely this time. I get up and go into the toilet and wash my distant face and hands which don't belong to me and look at my red eyes in the mirror. And my chest—my tits could be mistaken for baboon eyes I think and my belly button goes through to the other side. When I come back the fat girl is talking to a young man with a stringy yellow beard which should be torn off immediately. Creep clergy out of Chaucer. They look at me, I'm naked, and disappear. I glance down at my worn-out cock and it appears to have been recently tied on. Laurie begins talking of the past year and I don't hear much of what she says. I drink coffee from the stained plastic cup and watch it run down the pipe into my stomach where it makes a small black lake.

—What have you been doing?

—What?

—What have you been doing?

—Nothing. The usual.

—Oh.

Then she began talking of an affair with a painter and that it took a few weeks to get used to the way someone else made love. And a man tried to attack her in the subway but when his pants dropped she pushed him over. Almost a nervous breakdown and now she carries a long hatpin to discourage such people. And remember how we used to carry the mattress up to the roof on Grove and roll a bomber and ball to the street sounds and soot settling on us if we stayed too long. I remember how the roof was coarse to my bare feet. I could feel it now like walking up a warm plank in bare feet or scratching a blackboard with my fingernails. She was sitting next to me now crying and sniffling and talking in a choked voice about how I should stay this time and it would be much better than before.

—You got anything to eat? I asked.

She was startled by the obtusity of my question and shook her head. I said I would go out and get some Chinese food and I dressed quickly putting on my boots without socks. Buttons gone on my shirt, three left.

—You'll be back?

—Of course, don't be stupid.

She followed me to the door and kissed me. I walked out without looking back and by the time I hit the street I knew I wouldn't return. I wandered around looking for an uptown train. On a corner three junior delinquents lean against a mailbox and nudge each other as I approach. My body seems to tighten though I'm still floating from the hash and I put my right hand in my pocket and cradle the knife. When I pass one of them spits and narrowly misses my boots. I walk on waiting for any footsteps. Be strange to catch three of them with one wide swipe. But then I might get it too and I could almost feel the stitch of pain in my side that a knife or zip gun would make.

Now up in the East Seventies where everything is sweet and safe. The first door was open but the second was locked. I look at the names. Number 24. I press the button. A walled city.

—Yes? from the speaker.

—It's me.

The door buzzes and clicks. The lobby is marbled and smells of precisely nothing. Two tricycles in a corner for fun. I press another button and hear the self-service elevator sliding down toward me and cables rattling. Near dawn now and not very many birds singing. Up in the pastel cage with a mirror in the corner to see if a rapist is crouched drooling. Go away bad man. Your dingle dangle is not wanted. Elevator stops. She's standing by her apartment door smoking a cigarette. Well. We embrace but my eyes are open and I watch her outstretched hand keeping the cigarette away from us. Then we break away and go into the apartment. She looks at me closely.

—You're stoned and you smell.

—Nice place you got here. Raise in the allowance?

—Yes but they don't want me back if I bring the baby.

—I want to see it.

I follow her through the bedroom into a smaller adjoining bedroom thinking the apartment must cost at least three hundred a month or perhaps more. My dad's house payments were only sixty-six dollars. There is a crib in the corner and other baby accouterments and that strange generalized sweet smell that a baby creates in what surrounds "it." I hear breathing but I don't really see the child. Vague outline of a little head.

—Is it mine?

She lights another cigarette and we move quietly back into the living room. Her robe is a beautiful yellow pattern and the carpet is thick and very soft and I feel weightless. We sit down and look at each other.

—I guess I don't know. My parents think it is.

—How many possibilities are there?

—None of your business.

Her face becomes flushed and she looks at the ceiling. The room is at a dead stop.

—Can I have a drink?

She pours me some bourbon with an inch of water on top and no ice like I used to drink it. She begins talking about her problems getting help to clean and stay with the child and cook dinner. There's an extra bedroom but nobody will "live in." I feel very concerned and attentive and drink the bourbon in a few swallows. More chemicals and my body is shredding itself in fatigue for beef jerky. She's still looking at the ceiling and now talking about how much she loves the baby and about her parents' last visit and how she might move to San Francisco and find some sort of career. The robe is parted to her knee and despite the action with Laurie I'm beginning to warm up. I walk over to her and lean down and kiss her throat. Salt and perfume.

—You should sleep.

She stands up and leads me into the spare bedroom. I take off my clothes and she tells me to take a shower or I might permanently harm the room. In the shower I nearly fall asleep in the rain of steaming water. Back in the room she watches as I dry myself and get into bed where I fall instantly asleep.

When I got out of the water I could see by the shadows the sun cast that I was well behind my schedule, the intended circle only half completed. If I began jogging now I would be lucky to reach my camp before dark. Then I ate the rest of my raisins and thought how totally unimportant the problem was; true wilderness might destroy me within a month if I committed such fuckups. The only points in my favor were nonchalance and reasonably good health but I had none of the constant wariness owned by all good woodsmen. A case here where God doesn't love fools and drunks. Or care if they make feed and fertilizer for the beasts. At the far end of the lake I saw a flash of a black animal. Harmless black bear that didn't catch my scent until he reached the lake's edge. I simply didn't have the functional intelligence of the explorer, the voyager and had only met a few people who were unilaterally stable in the wilderness. You have to know a great deal about food and shelter and the stalking of game and many of the aspects of this knowledge come only through astute, almost instinctive openness to your surroundings. In Montana I nearly walked off a cliff dreaming of the peculiar flat shape of a whore's ass. Too much muscle like a ballerina. Next time I go back I'll pick a different one and then before my feet a thousand-foot gorge of nothing. What roots do I eat? What does my body live on after I use

up the twenty pounds of fat around my belly? Spare tire as
they say. I imagined myself crawling around in hunger and
in a snarling rage attacking a sick old opossum and losing the
fight. Paws and face badly bitten by it. I cast out my sinker
and line hoping that my swimming hadn't driven all of the
fish to the other end of the lake. Then I went back into the
swamp and began to gather as much firewood as possible
for what I knew would be a long uncomfortable night.

Barbara woke me up with tomato juice and coffee and
two aspirin which she felt with accuracy that I might need.
Late afternoon and a rusty spike driven into each temple.

—Bring me a drink.

—No. Eat something first.

—No. The water.

She brought me a glass of ice water and sat down on
the edge of the bed. I put my pillow over my face and started
moaning. I needed chemicals.

—Shut up. The maid's still here.

An old Negro woman poked her head in the door and
said the baby was asleep and that she was leaving. Barbara
left and I turned over and listened to my brain cry and rub
and creak. My stomach was bilious and I could still taste
a mixture of hash and bourbon in my throat. I got up and
brushed my teeth and noticed that my skin had a yellowish cast. Back in bed I wanted the bed to be my own and
I peeked out beneath the pillow to make sure again where
I was. O God I'll never put anything in my mouth again
except food and water. In painful dark. Squeeze the eyes
and see stars and red dots and little filaments free-float in
vitreous humor. Blind eye sees more interesting things when

closed tight or can turn around and paint on the back of the skull. I heard the door open again and lifted the pillow. She handed me an eggnog.

—I'll buy you a plane ticket.

—Oh fuck off.

—I don't want you to stay here. I can't stand it.

—I'm not. Cramp your gentlemen to have me sneaking around.

—Shut up.

—You already said that today.

She looked like she was going to cry so I turned over and asked her to rub my back. She went into the bathroom and got some lotion and began a long slow massage of my lower back and shoulders. We used to massage each other and pretend we had no sexual intentions until a moment would arrive and we could no longer bear to wait.

—You can sit on my head if you want.

—No.

—Why?

—I don't know. I don't feel like it.

—Please.

—Why should I?

—Because you like to be licked.

—You have a filthy mouth.

—Then blow me.

—Can't you be nice?

—It would be nice of you to blow me. My head hurts.

She got up from the edge of the bed and went to the windows and drew the shades. I could hear the rush hour, the cross-town traffic. Home for dinner in scab city after a day of

boredom and paper burns. Bob lick these envelopes and fill
the water cooler with ink. Yes sir. She knelt beside the bed
and drew back the sheet. My toes are going to curl and do
at the first wet heat and nudge of tongue and teeth. Farther
please and I like the warm noise. A finger where it ought to
be and thumb twitching. Please get up on the bed and I'll do
you. Muffled no. Say Patrice Lumumba or Robert Ruark like
the old joke. Wordless. I watch then as best I can in the dim
light but can't hold it long. Vision makes me explode. She goes
into the bathroom and I hear water running, my hangover
considerably diminished, and the pillow back over my face
in perfect, soft darkness. Barbara comes back into the room,
turns on the light and smiles. I feel the ache I often felt the
year before. She's lovely, winsome, demure, and her brain
is a shabby, torpid mess; enough money goes to her analyst
per week to support someone handsomely. And her diffidence about who she gave her body to not so much that it
hurt her but that it abraded my vaguely Calvinist center. She
said she would stop if we married but that many of them were
merely old friends from Atlanta. And she couldn't deny them
because they were so sweet and had been her friends so long.
She came to the bed and asked me what I wanted for dinner.
I couldn't think about food or going home or anything else. I
took her wrist and drew her down toward me; she resisted.
    —No.
    —Why?
    I forced her onto the bed. I thought that I only wanted
to see her body one last time but I knew it was a lie—I
wanted revenge for being cuckolded, for the sheer exhaust-
ing hours of jealousy.

—Will you take them off?

She stood and quickly took off her skirt and sweater then walked toward the lamp in her undergarments. The panties were a pale blue.

—No. Don't turn it off.

She stopped with her hands on her hips and then turned and walked back to the bed with her head down. I knew she was beginning to cry. I got up and took off her bra very deliberately and then kneeled and pulled down her panties. She was standing very stiffly and wouldn't move her feet so I tore the panties in half while I was kneeling there. I kissed her with my hands on her hips—her sex tasted deliciously of the violet bath salts she always used. Then I kissed and licked her in every position I could think of for I don't know how long. She finally relaxed but said nothing. She acted like the ballerina I had seen in the movie of *Tales of Hoffmann.* I put her on her hands and knees and kissed then entered her with force watching myself, her smooth buttocks and my hands against their whiteness, and her lovely back. I withdrew and slowly entered her anally which I knew she despised. She was crying and I began to lose heart. I sat back on my heels and she collapsed onto her side. We looked at each other for several moments and then she held out her arms to me.

I lay there listening to her in the bathroom again and I felt so generally melancholy that I couldn't swallow. She passed through the room in her yellow robe without looking at me. I got up and dressed and lit a cigarette and looked out the blinds at the street below. A French restaurant across the street and people getting dropped at the curb; a nasty place

where I would be seated in a toilet stall and the food heaved
over the top. We ate there with her parents and they were
gentle and kind to me without condescension. Surprised me
as her father was a broker in Atlanta and apparently didn't
have to work. But they probably knew that she had been
sleeping with blacks and I appeared as a perhaps obvious
improvement. They seemed sad but then she was their only
child and I supposed at the time that no matter how much
money and power you have your children will bring you
to grief over and over. My own parents were poor and I
managed nicely to make them unhappy. Her father asked
me what I was going to do with my life. Or do without it, I
thought at the time, because we were on our fourth bottle
of wine and had guzzled several martinis before dinner in
the first nervousness of meeting. I announced that I planned
a career in the United Nations. It simply came out of my
mouth and the three of them looked at me strangely. Her
father said that the UN would provide an interesting if not
very profitable career while I ate a chocolate mousse with
a fork which I bit uncontrollably with each mouthful. I
wanted to tell them that their daughter had bought me the
sport coat I was wearing that morning at Tripler's. I stood
outside the store and waited for her. And I didn't have the
guts to tell them I intended to write an epic parable on the
decline of the West not to speak of the North and South, in
fact the whole fucking world. Her mother was unspeakably
elegant and showed no sign of the amount she had to drink.
We parted affably outside after Barbara arranged to shop
with her mother the next day and off they went to the Pierre
while we went back to the apartment and dog-fucked in

front of the hall mirror. The United Nations indeed and she asked me to give a sample speech. I pretended I was a giant and my cock was a microphone and I gave a speech about what the world needed was desegregated toilets. Never mind food. That would come naturally afterwards.

I went into the kitchen where we ate some scrambled eggs and bacon. We talked idly for a while then I went into the living room and picked up my jacket. At the door we kissed and she asked me to accept sixty dollars to fly home instead of hitchhike. I looked down at the three twenties and kissed her again with the choking sensation returning. I wanted to tell her that I still loved her but it was assumed and pointless. She walked me to the elevator and my last look was her yellow robe between the doors as they slid toward each other.

Enough wood gathered to keep a fire going all night and I wished that I had brought a sweatshirt along. I tore off dead twigs and branches from a pine tree for kindling. I had at least two more hours of daylight but I wanted to be completely ready. The moon was already over the tops of the trees at the far end of the lake and I could see through her as if she were a disc of tracing paper. My trotline moved and I grabbed for it but there was no pull at the end so I drew in the line and rebaited. Something out there hopefully not a minnow. I watched the line carefully — the prospect of sitting up all night on a totally empty stomach appalled me. Heard that lily pad roots were good food but the evening was cooling and I didn't want to go back in the water. I

would spend the night watching the moon bury herself in
the water and wish I were elsewhere, even on the moon in a
space vehicle while she buried herself in the lake. Drowned
on the waterless moon. I started the kindling and slowly
added sticks and rotten but dry stump slabs until the fire
roared and then I pushed on a huge piece of driftwood
which I knew would burn all night. I began to think of
venison chops and then a saddle of venison I had eaten at
Lüchow's. Nearly destroyed the meal with their swarm of
minstrels. I had hoped the huge Christmas tree would fall
over on them. The line moved again but this time the hook
caught and I had a small brook trout. It would take ten of
them to make a decent meal but I took a green stick and
shoved its pointed end through the trout lengthwise and
began roasting it. Very clumsy and if I had taken some foil I
would eat finely steamed rather than scorched fish. And if I
had salt with me I would have eaten the fish raw; I had done
so a number of times with a little vinegar and salt after the
experience of eating in a Japanese restaurant. The herring
we always ate on Saturdays and Sundays were raw in their
soup of brine. My father ate sandwiches made of the roe
with raw onion, and my grandfather would often eat fried
salt herring for breakfast. Strange how he lived to eighty-
eight eating so much fried pork and side pork too, which is
unsmoked bacon. And his cheek always filled with tobacco
and steady quantities of cheap whiskey neat. A neighbor
went blind over a bad batch of the homemade but then
he already had a metal plate in his head from World War
Two. Not much mourned—we suspected him of poisoning
dogs and exposing himself to school children and screwing

his Guernsey calves. I never had an urge for animals but I've read that it's not unusual. Urp. A nice sow. Pigs are so frantic and the boar shudders convulsively, kicking his pink legs when he's all done. A chunk of smoked ham would be nice now, chewing on it without cooking and snarling into the dark beyond the fire. Mine mine mine. My pigmeat. I've always liked pigs and wish the radicals would call cops sheep or zebra or robin redbreast. The first robin means a snowstorm within twenty-four hours. I eat my tiny fish even though it is only partially cooked. Take a caravan out for salt for Christ's sake. I move further back from the fire and lie down on the bed of ferns I'd gathered to protect myself from ground moisture. I want my sleeping bag and my rifle because I'm afraid of the dark and the moon is still almost full. Or maybe the *Vogue* model will walk out of the swamp and coolly ask where the hell she is. She'll think I'm a dark, incredibly romantic savage and we'll play wood nymph. A short doze then awake to some noise back in the brush, my knife open and outstretched before I'm fully conscious. No noise. I need a bodyguard. My body is sore and covered with bug bites and I need lotion and cigarettes and a night light. I stood up and stretched and checked my line again. The moon had moved fifteen feet and was under water again. This time I had a larger trout and cooked and devoured it with great haste. A plate of pasta with a garlic sauce and grated aged romano please. Not cool fish flesh tasting of smoke. I stirred my big driftwood log and propped it with another log to give it more air. I did a little dance around the fire and howled as loudly as I could. I howled and howled until I felt sure that all beasts in my area were adequately

warned. Couldn't do this in New York City or the zebras
would say we better haul this fucking howler up to Bellevue.
Visited Cindy Blank (must protect her identity) after she
had overdosed on downers. Seems she didn't want to live
any longer which I understood. She was brilliant but very
homely and kept trying to change her life style in order to
get a permanent lover. I told her that when she got out I
would make love to her for seven days and seven nights but
I could only muster a single trip. I'm very selective and must
have a Beatrice or a Juilet. Throw in an Anouk Aimee. I
curled up again on my ferns in love with the warmth of fire.

I had a small room on Valentine Avenue in the Bronx for a
few weeks — I was eighteen and had moved to New York
City to live forever away from the vulgarities of the Midwest. It took only a few days for me to realize that the
Bronx wasn't exactly the center of cosmopolitan activity. I
only stuck out those few weeks because I lived three blocks
from Edgar Allan Poe's cottage where he had lived with his
thirteen-year-old bride. Besides I didn't have any money to
move and I was waiting for a delayed pay check for some
construction work in Michigan. And so I waited and it was
July and miserably hot and I took the D train to Manhattan several times but no one would hire me because I didn't
know how to do anything. The room was about seven by
ten with a single chair, a dresser and an uncomfortable bed.
The window looked out into an alley and another row of
tenements precisely like my own. My food allotment was
only a dollar a day and after I bought a quart of Rheingold

which I would drink quickly for a buzz I had only enough money for a sandwich. I lost weight at an alarming speed even though I spent most of my days lying in bed and sweating or walking over to the Botanical Gardens. Sex and power fantasies—King of the State, then the country, then the world. Or to be simply a financier like the one I had seen in a limousine on Wall Street talking on a phone in the back seat, giving no doubt global instructions before he returned to his penthouse to fuck a beautiful girl many years his junior. Sold my high school graduation suit for five dollars and pawned my watch in Philadelphia. I once had an honest-to-God pen pal in Davenport, Tasmania; we exchanged small photos and she was fairly pretty. I wanted her to be with me on Valentine Avenue but we had been out of touch for several years and Tasmania is further away than Mongolia where old men hunt wolves using golden eagles as falcons. I spent a lot of time with the lights out trying to get a peek at a naked woman across the alley but everyone's shades were drawn and most of the women I had seen on the streets I didn't want to see naked. I created varied lives for myself to take place in Argentina or Florence or, and this was the best one, Thessalonica, though I knew nothing of the place but was attracted by the name. I would have tended goats or sheep or juniper trees or spent ten hours a day casting out nets and drawing them in laden with the fruits of the sea. Fish are unmistakable and if you fish all day your continuous sanity is assured. Or even in northern Michigan for which I felt the acute pain of homesickness: I would have dogs and cats and horses and children in a big dilapidated farmhouse. I would have a yard covered with tangled laurel and lilacs and quince and flowering almond but behind the house the ground would be scratched bare by the chickens. I would like a barn with a fat rich manure pile and cows and near the manure pile the grass would be a richer and darker green. Some of the boards on the barn would be rotten and the red paint would be faded flaking off in small red bits at touch. There would be a small orchard which I would prune each February and I would prune my grapes back late in the fall, each brown corded vine being limited to seven shoots for maximum health. In the orchard there would be goldenrod and Queen Anne's lace and brake which smells like thyme. Next to the granary there would be a small pigpen because I like to watch pigs eat, the way their powerful jaws strip the kernels from a hardened ear of corn and chew the corn with crunching smacking noises: they root in the mud and when their snouts get covered with mud they blow out their noses to loosen the mud clogged there. My wife would be a buxom hundred and sixty-six pounds and laugh all the time. I would be lazy and giggle much of the day and night and only cut enough hay for the horses, plant a few acres of oats and few acres of corn for the hogs, plant a small garden which my wife would tend — sweet corn, string beans, peas, tomatoes, radishes, potatoes, cucumbers, leaf lettuce, cabbage and some turnips. I would spend most of my time walking around smelling the lilacs and watching the swallows swoop, drift and float and flutter around in the barn, ride my horse around the edge of a lake always in about a foot of water so the horse could bury his feet in the cool mud. I would watch the nests of birds and when I walked through the woods among the ferns and wet matted leaves the scream of a blue jay would follow me and I would wade knee deep in cedar swamps and watch the water snakes glide and wiggle over the green skin of algae. There would be a single cow for milk and each fall a hog would be slaughtered and most of it hickory-smoked by a neighbor. And fifty gallons of apple wine: to the juice in a wooden charcoal-lined barrel add twenty-five pounds of sugar and five pounds of raisins. Wait three months and drink in large quantities. Very nice but such dreams are long ago. Speaks of softness, is dulcet and umbrous and I'm suffocating in geometry. Soft ripe grapes, sweet scent of rotting pine on the bottom of the wood pile, soft yellow belly of the garter snake, the flank of a horse sweating and corseted with muscle, the green moss wavering in the current of a creek and the sound of ten million bees in the lilacs and in the field of flowering buckwheat across the fence. Though I know this life I always leave it and where do I live when I leave home over and over on small and brutally stupid voyages.

I spoke to the landlord daily and he reminded me that I had "kitchen privileges" but I had nothing to cook, didn't know how to cook and had no utensils to cook with. He was Italian but most of the tenants were Jews. He warned me of the Irish girl next door who though only fifteen had showed him her breasts when he painted the apartment. He giggled and told me to tell no one. With whom would I share this secret? I told him that I had got a note from one of the occupants saying that I had used his frying pan and if I did so again I would be sorry. I collected a handful of dead roaches and went into the kitchen and sprinkled them in his frying pan. The common toilet is always unoccupied and I suspected that most of the tenants, at least the ones I saw, were too old to use it. I felt that they had ceased to function as complicated biological organisms and that they were aged dolls. If they tripped and fell on the sidewalk they would break revealing either cotton stuffing or a rubberish-smelling dust. I was enfeebled too. At absolute zero where the body is likely to crystallize and shatter. Flakes of bowels and iced splinters of throat. I thought I could descend no further and had the constant image in mind that I was pelagic and would one day soon rise up through the water from the depths at tremendous speed disemboweling whales or sharks or any other creature that blocked my inevitable ascent.

During my third week my luck changed a trifle. A woman down the hall asked me to take care of her child for several evenings and to take her over to the park in the morning so that the woman could sleep. She was blond and frowsy and chain-smoked. She called me "kid" which vaguely offended me but the baby-sitting money allowed me to eat better and wander around Manhattan during the summer afternoons. The child was a little girl of three named Sharon and was easy to care for. It took me several days to realize that her mother was turning tricks rather than acting as a hostess in a restaurant. One night she returned late and very drunk and offered to lay me for ten bucks. I tried to explain that I didn't have ten dollars to spend but she kept on saying blearily, "What are you, queer?" until I walked down the hall to my room. I lay in bed depressed at being called a queer but wishing I had the money to go back down and bang her. I had seen her nearly nude several

times when I would pick up Sharon in the morning to take
her to the park. She would unlock the door and flop back
into bed while I gave the child some cereal and dressed
her. By the time we would leave the apartment, perhaps
within fifteen minutes, Carla would be snoring. One especially hot morning I studied her pink dimpled ass from a
range of three feet while Sharon ate breakfast. Too many
puckers on it. How many men have plumbed there for how
much money. I carried Sharon piggy-back to the gardens
pondering the dimples and patch I had seen. We found a
deserted well-shaded place which was easy on weekdays,
almost like not being in New York. It was beginning to get
hot and I was already hotter than a two-peckered goat as
my dad used to say from seeing Carla's ass. I dozed on the
blanket while Sharon picked dandelions; she picked them
until the blanket was covered and her hands were yellow
from yellow stains. Rub them under your nose and see if you
eat butter. Down the hill on a sidewalk a girl was pulling
a small boy in a red wagon. She turned onto the grass and
started to pull up the hill but she had sneakers on and her
feet kept slipping on the grass. Sharon was near them so I
walked down to get her out of the way. When I reached them
I saw that the girl was pretty and that she wouldn't make it
up the hill without dropping from exhaustion so I grabbed
the handle and pulled the wagon, nearly running, up to the
shade tree where our blanket lay covered with dandelions.
She kept saying no, no, no as I ran and I turned around to
bawl the kid out when I saw that his legs were withered and
short, protruding weakly from his hips. He smiled at me and
shrugged. I was embarrassed and turned to her to apologize

but she smiled too so we sat and talked and shared a Coke
I had brought along. Sharon began filling the wagon with
the dandelions from the blanket and the little boy said thank
you with each new handful.

Cold fog. Awake and damp and cold. The fire was nearly out,
faintly smoldering and hissing, the log devoured. I heard a
loon, the cry muffled by the fog from the far end of the lake.
I was curled and shivering but accepted the loon as a good
omen for the day. I got up and then noticed three deer at
the lake's edge not a hundred yards away. We stared at each
other for a moment and then they disappeared soundlessly
into the brush. I threw some kindling and sticks onto what
was left of the fire and then hopped around to get warm. Get
your knees higher, said the coach. When my blood warmed
up I checked my line. Nothing. No breakfast for the poor
wayfaring stranger. Shit. The Indian needs food for his hike
back to the tent at least ten miles to the southeast. I felt giddy
from hunger, a slight headache just above the eyes. Oh for
a cigarette. When I got back to camp I intended to smoke
ten in a row until I fell into a terminal fit of coughing and
nicotine poisoning. Trade many dollars and shoes and shirt
for tobacco. I took off my shirt and waved it over the fire
to dry and stood close enough to nearly scorch my pants.
Then I scooped sand over the fire to make sure it was out
and set off for my long, hungry walk back to the tent. First
a hot pan of refried beans into which I would dump a tin
of beef and chop some onion over the whole mess and pig
it down in minutes. I reached the edge of the swamp where

I had entered the day before and took a compass reading. I trotted the first mile with my pantlegs wet and flapping from the dew and my lungs heaving for air. I had stupidly forgotten to fill my canteen before leaving the lake and was already thirsty from exertion. Short prayer for a creek and a permanently healed brain.

Luck changed—the check came and also an odd-looking package from a friend in New Orleans. I opened it to find only a pack of Cajun cigarettes but then upon opening them I found that I was the proud owner of twenty round, fully packed fat joints. I sat in my room and smoked one lazily and looked at the check which was for nearly a hundred dollars. Moving money. I went downtown immediately with a tremendously aerated brain—my first D train while absolutely stoned. Naturally took a lot longer. I found the room on Grove Street with no difficulty, first looking at a larger room on Macdougal which was too expensive but strangely the place I would end up with Barbara six months later. I paid for the room for a month in advance before I could blow the money, then went back up to Valentine Avenue to get my belongings. Rush hour and packed in like an anchovy tight against a skinny man face to face who peered fixedly over my shoulder. Jesus how terrible to ride this thing every day and I don't understand anyone who would put up with such punishment. I stopped at a place on the Grand Concourse and ate an enormous meal, my first in weeks—some kind of strange Jewish flank steak and some barley soaked with beef juices and garlic and strawberries with sour cream.

These bastards knew how to cook — back in Michigan you
have a choice of cheeseburgers or chicken fried in rancid
batter. When I got back to the room I packed hurriedly
stuffing everything in my large cardboard box and binding it
with clothesline. I felt terribly sad for a moment — my father
standing with me on the platform of the Greyhound bus
station and my kissing him on the forehead to say goodbye.
When I finished packing I treated myself to another joint
which I smoked all the way down to a very small roach,
popping it in my mouth with a glass of water. No matter the
wild hum, whiskey's still my medicine. Can't help it. A little
rest and dreams of my new room and Europe. I lay back on
the bed and desperately wanted back the grand I blew on
the operation. Take a boat. Too stoned now to do anything
but lie back in this rank heat. Cross the big water for the
first time for anyone in my family since Grandpa came over
from Goteborg in 1892. When they reached the basement
of the ghost ship they passed through the galley where tall
thin Negroes in red stovepipe hats were boiling tripe for fifth
class passengers. Much of the tripe seemed to be slipping off
the formica counters onto the bloody and onionskin-strewn
cement floor. The bottom of a ship shouldn't be cement?
The steward paused long enough to strike the handsomest
cook lightly across the neck with a handful of chits. They
gazed at each other soulfully and the cook said, "De often
dat gar bis bis," in a heavy Cruzán accent, his face shiny with
tripe steam. What did he say? I wondered. But the steward
was far ahead with his flashlight beam in the dark corridor.
Led into the dark room then the steward said, "Everything
A-OK?" Found a cot and listened to the choke and bark

of the engines above me, the steady hummer-booger-rak hummer-booger-rak-rak of the pistons in the night, or day, who knew? Then morning, a dim light from the hall under the door. Water rushing past the closed porthole. Below waterline. The cabin was four by six and the light switch was on the floor under the cot. Another cot next to mine with a crone either asleep or dead beneath a sheet printed gaily with blue flowers. I arose from the cot and opened the porthole hoping to see at least a fish but the water rushed by too quickly. I pressed my fingers against the cold moist side of the ship and it crinkled like an oilcan.

I got up and looked out my window for the last time. Must be about midnight. I left a note with my forwarding address on the bed for the landlord and my room key. I carried my box down the hallway and knocked on Carla's door. She answered quickly and I could see the "gentleman" on the bed behind her. I said goodbye but she was merely pissed off at losing a baby sitter. I walked over to the Concourse and caught the downtown train making sure my new room key was safely in my pocket.

I reached the tent by late afternoon, my clothes soaked through to the skin — it had been raining lightly but steadily since mid-morning. My feet were a mess. The wet boots had ground and rubbed large blisters in each heel. I stopped and put on some filthy but dry clothes and ate the refried beans cold out of the can. No dry kindling in the tent. I'm going to get out of this fucking place. I smoked three cigarettes in a row and felt a little better though I was dizzy from hunger

waiting for the bean energy to occur. Rain pattering on
the leaves and tent roof. I opened a can of tinned beef and
finished the whole thing in moments with salt spread on it
like a white crust. On the way down to the creek for water
I crossed some deer tracks—they had snooped around in
my absence. Probably a doe. A buck sends the doe along
or across a clearing first as a decoy to make sure the path is
safe. Sensible. I wanted though to be a lion in the hot Kenyan
sun napping while my assorted mates brought me a juicy
gazelle; my only function would be to roar warnings to any
intruders and screw and eat. Maybe help out with a sturdy
Cape buffalo or charge an Abercrombie Fitch hunter from
deep cover and bat off his head with one swipe of a paw. I
had been in the store a dozen times in the past decade since
Barbara first took me there but never had the money to buy
anything but a few trout flies. Condescending employees,
some of them anyway. To one in the camping department I
had said, Look asshole I've been in the woods since I was
five and I don't need a snakebite kit in Michigan. Alarmed
him. In six days I hadn't so much as seen a wolf track, only
the perhaps imaginary shadow crossing the log road near
the source of the Huron. I should have stayed there all night
and looked at the tracks in the morning or driven the car up
the road and looked at them in the headlights but I hadn't
thought of it. They certainly had a right not to let me see
them. My scent has a bad record for potshotting anything
that moves. I checked the tracks again in Olaus Murie, the
only book I had brought along.

As it began to get dark I managed a small fire despite
the dampness. There was a slight warm breeze from the

south but not enough to drive away mosquitoes so I gathered
some ferns to smoke them away. I sat by the fire thinking
of how few women I had truly known in my life. If you
stood on the corner of Lexington and Fifty-seventh for a
day a hundred beautiful women you might wish to know
would pass. But the greatest share of them might be vapid,
torpid whiners with air-brushed brains. So why should one
know many women. A few of my friends were known as
"cocksmen" but there was a particular form of boredom
that always seemed to accompany their success. Perhaps I
was naturally monogamous but it was frightening in some
respects to be owned by a single woman. I had no taste
though for more than one over any period of time. I was
either trembling like a whippet dog over some girl or almost
completely turned off. How many endless love letters have
I written and I could list those to whom they were sent and
the list would number less than ten. When I think of the
snickering, giggling, elbowing, guffawing that goes on in
bars, barbershops, locker rooms, club-houses, dormitories,
I'm appalled that I've habitually taken part in it. Simply part
of not growing up assuming there's a point to grow towards.
Never read anything very sage on the matter. Testing one
two three. Distances. Coming together but one of you is still
on Saturn and the other on Jupiter. Bull elk bugling. We
could hear it miles away in the Tom Miner basin. Who wants
to come challenge me for my absence of harem. I should be
one of those Indians who combined magic and witchcraft
and buffoonery by doing everything backwards.

I lit the only cigar I had brought along. Addictive. Used
to smoke twenty Dutch Master panatellas a day. I explored

my muscles again—they were strangely more there than six days ago but then I must have dropped ten pounds of lard out here looking for a beast that is said to exist. Not even a scat. Melancholy. Laurie's plump butt, white teeth, precocious senility being beaten down to insanity in New York. As I had gone goony for sequences in my life and would only refer to myself in the third person and change my signature every day. Or where are the three of them now and does it matter? Think of the grove of willows by that creek and the tubular stalks of what we called snake grass. Her wet violet smell and the light from the next room passing between her thighs through which I could see the couch and a book on a pillow. I'm never cool enough but jerk around, a horse in double hobbles. That girl in high school burned me but got knocked up by a fireman and is probably happy now. Perhaps Mrs. Chief. The great gush out of the pig's throat when Walter cut it and again the wet throat of the stillborn calf in a pen in the barn, the mother bawling horribly. Twenty-five years later I can hear her bawl and I told grandfather I was sorry he lost the calf while he ate his herring the next morning and I carried the slop pail to the hogs. Nature doesn't heal, it diverts and because we are animals too all this silence is a small harmony. If I stayed I would go berserk and shrink into a wooden knot. I once thought there were only two natural courses for a man, savior or poet; now at its vulgarest level either voting or not bothering to. I don't care about anyone's problem only the occasional luminescence we offer to each other. Fifty grand worth of creature comforts. Yes of course but a poor thing to trade a life for I think. And do options exist and

if they did would I see them? When I proselytized I gave
bad advice from boredom with giving advice. Taught one
course but I can't be a walking blood bank. I let myself be
transfused by winter and seven feet of snow and crossing
comparatively trackless wastes in both winter and summer.
Barring love I'll take my life in large doses alone — rivers,
forests, fish, grouse, mountains. Dogs.

    I thought I heard something and received the accom-
panying split-second shot of adrenaline, the hand reaching
for the rifle. Nothing beyond the pale light of the fire. And
a hundred years ago or more I might have been the sort of
person who fucked it up for the Indians blazing ignorantly
the way for waves of settlers to follow. Or I always wanted
to be a cowboy but those I know only break horses, adjust
the irrigation, put up hay, drink, and hit each other. Inside a
butcher shop I see a side of prime beef on a huge maple block.
Crawl up on it and start chewing with a case of red wine
and a salt shaker and see how much I could eat. Then have a
three-dollar Havana cigar, purged of human problems; only
beef problems and those briefly solved with the taste of steer,
wine, salt and fine Havana leaf in my mouth. And the smell of
the cedar box the cigar came in. Then a lovely janitress would
come in with her broom and see me there and I'd push what
was left of the carcass off onto the floor and she would get on
and draw off all the poison left. I told a girl once that it backs
up and gives you migraine headaches so please co-operate.
Push her off onto the carcass when we finished. Not quite
a prime beef janitress. Picked cherries all day once thinking
of Laurie a thousand miles away, a hot afternoon, hands and
arms sticky with red juice, clothes wet with itching sweat. I

climbed up the water tank used to fill the sprayers and slid
into the water down to the bottom, looking up at the wide
circle of light above me and wanted to be a fish.

I met her in Bryant Park behind the library where I had
brought a sandwich during my lunch hour. First three doubles at a White Rose on Sixth then a sandwich in the park. I
was reading Henry Miller's biography on Rimbaud and she
was with a group of a half dozen young people who were
obviously what the press liked to call "beatniks." She came
up to me and said directly into my face, "I've read that book."

I was so startled I couldn't answer. She was very pretty
and you usually have to approach pretty girls, they don't
approach you.

—We're going up to the park. Want to come?

—I have to work.

I paused then and looked at her closely to see if she
was putting me on. The rest of them approached us and
started talking about Miller and Céline, then about Kerouac
whose *On the Road* had appeared that year. They seemed very
friendly and intense but unassuming.

—Wait three minutes. I'll tell my boss I'm sick.

I ran across Forty-second Street and told my boss at
Marboro's where I worked as a stock clerk that I had just
puked all over the park and was going home for the afternoon. He waved me away with a "so OK." I rejoined them
in the park and we headed up Fifth.

We were together constantly after that initial meeting.
I stopped seeing a girl from Nebraska who lived on Perry

Street and who was only using me anyway—her fiancé worked out on the tip of Long Island and every Friday afternoon we would have a drink at Penn Station and say goodbye for the weekend. And I had already met Barbara but it was only for one night and day and I had no idea she would reappear. I had moved out of my Grove Street room for the better one on Macdougal with its little black rat hole in the corner over which I put the grate from the oven.

We stuck it out through a mutual sense of melancholy, a total unhappiness with everything. She was much brighter than I was and had read more of everything. So we made endless trips to everything that was cheap especially the Metropolitan Museum of Art. She was the first Jewish girl I had ever known. She wasn't terribly interested in sex but I was insistent in my own neurotic confusion—a number of homosexuals had made passes and I had worried that there was something in my conduct that made them see the potential homosexual in me. So I was bent on proving I wasn't queer to myself by getting into every girl in the Village I could get my hands on. I was very close to proposing when Barbara entered the store on an October afternoon and coolly took over again.

I began packing at dawn. It was cold and very windy, the weather changing in the middle of the night. February and November have always been my worst months in Michigan because of the wind. It deafens and depresses me and I can usually do nothing but drink and look out the window waiting for a change. If I didn't despise the act of asking for help I long ago would have asked a psychiatrist if climatic changes affected many people. I knew that a disproportionate number of people died between three and five in the morning. Stig Dagerman whose work I was very much taken with committed suicide in the winter even though Harriet Anderson was his lover. I had absorbed too much Strindberg and there were many suicides in my family history, either by the long route of alcohol or the short one of the shotgun pressed to the head. Bang, his brains were still hearing it, synapses ringing, as they flecked the wall. Wish I could ask him what he's doing now. Absolutely nothing. Seven to one odds on nothing, over and over. Keep the bet open. I gathered everything into a pile and rolled up the sleeping bag and tent—the tent was too goddamn heavy and wet, a surplus pup tent and I wondered if any soldiers had spent their last night in it before emerging at dawn to slay either Nips or Nazis. O Tojo. What fear we once felt at his name, apocalyptic samurai. I stomped on and crushed the tin cans and then with a great deal of effort and broken fingernails dug a hole with my hatchet and hands. I hacked away at the ground as if I were trying to murder it until I had a hole deep enough to cover all the refuse with a foot of dirt. In high school if I felt bad enough I would come home and dig a garbage hole at the end of my father's garden deep enough to bury myself. Digging soothes as does crawling. Stalking a fox as a recipe—crawl a hundred yards through brake, sumac, vetch and when you stand again your brain will be at ease. Wish I could jettison the tent. The total pack weighed over sixty pounds and ditching the tent would cut the weight in half. Fucking wind rising to thirty knots from the southwest—look at those tree tips bend with gusts and the roar of it. Even with two pairs of dry socks my heels ached from the blisters.

By mid-morning I was ready, with the campside looking as if no one had been there, the effect I wanted. No scars. I think of my brain as striated with scar tissue the color of the marl you can dig up from lake bottoms. I even dusted the ground with a handful of branches.

The pack had a body-formed aluminum frame but after three miles I was in wheezing pain. I lay back on it against a birch tree and had a cigarette and then had to struggle like an overturned turtle to get up. My feet seemed wet and I was sure the blisters were raw enough to have started bleeding. I headed more directly west hoping to pick up the log road and follow it south to the car. There was a vague chance too that I might see some tracks crossing the road. God send a helicopter and I'll become a missionary to the heathen wherever you want me to go. Accept this small bribe and you won't be sorry. Silence except for wind's Wailing and I looked at the dark cumuli scudding above me. And don't let it start raining until I get to the car, that's an order gourd and salute. A sense of blasphemy from all that time spent with the Bible—at fifteen I intended to become a Baptist evangelist. I stumbled onto the log road sooner than I expected so I stopped to take a compass reading—it might be the wrong log road. But it ran north and south so I figured it had to at least lead to the right road. Within a few hundred yards I came upon an old bulldozer the pulp people used to reach new stands of timber. LeTourneau diesel. Wonder if I could start it—used to be able to hot-wire cars. I shed

my pack and got upon the seat. Rummmmm rummmm,
I yelled, tinkering with the throttle and the two steering
handles and the handle to hydraulically lift the blade. Then I
rememberd that bulldozers of that size have a small auxiliary
gas engine to get their huge diesels started. I got down and
found the small Briggs-Stratton but the gas tank was empty.
I impulsively dumped a handful of sand in it and another
handful in the diesel oil tank. Could see it thrashing to a stop
after a hundred yards with all that sand in the workings. Ho
ho. Don't cut down my trees even if they're useless poplar. I
thought of dropping a match in the oil tank then hesitated—I
didn't want to start a forest fire. I smoked another cigarette
sitting in the comfortable seat and making noises then got
down and unstrapped my tent and threw it over the seat. A
gift to the pulpers to keep their seats dry. The change in load
made me happy and I quickened my pace despite the pain
in my feet. I sang the national anthem but forgot the words
toward the end and invented my own. I sang Buck Owens'
"It's Crying Time Again" and Dolly Parton's "Blue Ridge
Mountain Boy" and finally Schiller's "Ode to Joy" from
Beethoven's Ninth, and hummed a Schutz and a Buxtehude
piece. By the time I reached the car I was just finishing "The
Old Rugged Cross" after a quick run through the Jefferson
Airplane's "White Rabbit." I was considerably more than
ten feet tall. I quickly took off my clothes and ran down the
creek bank and jumped in beneath the waterfall. The water
seemed colder than three days before. I rubbed my hands
and body with wet sand then got out and sat on the warm
car hood until the wind dried my body, raising goose pim-
ples. Where's my coryphee now that I want her wantonly

here—into the warm back seat for pushups and pushdowns
and other good time-proven variations the Creator put in
our heads to cause joy. My small share in it must be enlarged
I think, pleasure up thirty-three points on the small board.
And the use of dynamite. For charming nature back to her
own sweet self. Take that rush of water as an exhilarant. A
premier danseur of I'm not sure and perhaps never will be.
Light fuses alone with a single match. Romance. Bloodless
though as too much blood has been let. Just a few dams,
bridges, signs, machines.

When I left New York City after my first nine months I
had only two people to say goodbye to, a tribute to my own
grotesque hostility and to the skin of ice that covers nearly
everyone there. Acrid is the word. And talk because there's
no other movement to make and the subways are clogged
with geese. I watched them ice skating at Rockefeller Center
and at the mangy terrifying children's zoo in Central Park.
Tchelitchew-painting children with glass brain covers. A
city of clanking manholes. We dragged an old man into the
store who had been blasted up onto our doorway by a taxicab. The driver naturally said the "fucka" crossed against
the light and I said there was no light out there. Meanwhile
blood and vomit were pouring out of the man's mouth and
around a metal book rack. Blood out of the ears and nose
too. DOA at bookstore and a crowd looking in. I opened his
jacket and saw that his shirt was wet; he must have turned
and caught three thousand pounds in the chest. When the
police ambulance came there were no witnesses not that it

mattered. I went over to a bar near Forty-second and Eighth Avenue and put my brain to sleep.

Things were over with Barbara. She had left for East Hampton two weeks before with a junior broker type from Mississippi. She called me at the store and asked if she could come back and I said no very kindly and that I would call her if I ever returned to the city. I called Laurie three times over a period of days before she would consent to say goodbye. We had coffee at a White Tower restaurant near Hudson Street, and then went over to the White Horse where she asked for a Coke and I had a half dozen Margaritas. Then we had a very strained, expensive dinner where she was weepy and barely touched her food. I was all packed and was in the process of spending my bus money. I'll have to hitchhike home and she won't even eat the food. In fact I took a train to Philadelphia then walked all the way up Broad Street to Roosevelt Boulevard where I stood for two hours before I got a ride out to the turnpike. When we said goodbye I told her that I would come back in a few months and marry her. I liked happy endings especially when drinking.

Chapter 5

Home

Certain memories have the quality of an alabaster trance —
you float into their places in the brain where they sit, a white
temple or pavilion in a grove of trees. After I started the
car still shivering a bit from my bath I totally lost my sense
of panic and realized I had been worrying about whether
the car would start without consciously knowing it; the
threat, a fifty-mile walk, was too grand to even consider. I
began driving very slowly and came to a full stop where the
shadow had crossed the road three nights before; no tracks
but with the wind blowing this hard and then some rain — I
couldn't prove to myself that I had seen a ghost. I remembered Barbara having nightmares and deciding to sit up all
night because if she slept during the daylight she thought
the nightmares wouldn't return. And I awoke to her voice
thinking a visitor had come but when I opened my eyes it
was dawn and she was sitting in a chair before the window,

the open Venetian blinds casting stripes of pink light across
her body, one stripe across her hair, then her throat and
breasts and stomach and knees. I called her over to the bed
and she fell asleep instantly. I felt sorry then looking at her
face against the pillow for all creatures who are afraid of the
dark or the things that must be "in" the darkness. Another
such memory only involved lying on the grass at the Clois-
ters with my head on Laurie's thigh listening to a Gregorian
chant and watching a maple bud fall out of a tree above us,
falling with infinite softness toward my head and missing
it by a few feet but in a split-second pause in the music I
heard the bud land on the grass just as I had once heard a
sparrow's feet touch a limb while sitting in the woods. The
third temple involved a sort of terror I couldn't bear, the
mixture though they were years apart of two visions which
had married in my brain: the first in Nevada, washing my
face in an irrigation ditch and suddenly seeing a rattlesnake
close by and my exploding backward up the bank; the image
of this was accompanied by being lost while deer hunting
when I was fourteen. It was dark and cold and the trees
were black columns in front of me and when I fired the
agreed-upon three quick successive shots blue flame came
out of the rifle tip and blinded me while the delayed sound
deafened me. Then before the echoing stopped I heard my
father's rifle answer and I quickly turned toward the source
of the sound so I wouldn't be fooled by echoes.

Driving out of the woods I felt a new and curious calm
but doubted that it would last: I had changed my life so
often that I finally decided there'd never been anything
to change—I could make all the moves I wished to on the

surface as if I were playing Chinese checkers but these moves were suspended on a thin layer that failed to stir anything below. A sort of mordant fatalism I lived within concerning geometrical matters—jobs, alcohol, marriage and the naturally concomitant joblessness, drunkenness, infidelity. Perhaps all true children of Protestantism are victims of such self-help—the notion of the law of life involving steps, paths, guideposts, ladders. St. Paul out in the red rock wilderness trying not to think about women. Just as I thought now of whiskey. When I reached the main road I would stop at a gas station and make a reservation at a hotel in Ishpeming and when I got there I knew I would shower and go down to the bar and drink myself into the comatose state I knew I deserved. Consciousness is simply the kind of work I can't make a continuous effort at—a disease causing giddiness, brain fever, unhappiness. Maybe King David drank heavily in his canopied tent the night before battle.

There were washouts in the road where there hadn't been seven days before. I took the first few too fast and on one bottomed out on the gas tank. I got out to check damage but there wasn't any other than a raw scrape. Relief. I proceeded more slowly until I came over the crest of a hill where the road crossed over an unused beaver dam with a swamp on the left and a pond on the right. An overflow from the pond had worn a deep trench in the road and I knew I hadn't the slightest chance without an hour's work. I cursed the loggers for not grading the road I didn't want them to use. I tiptoed down the hill in my bare feet—I wanted my red heels to dry—and looked at the miniature ravine and the trickle of clear water flowing into the swamp. I heard a splash in the pond and saw the widening ripple and then farther out another occurred. Trout. And no rod. I felt pissed enough to shoot at them with the rifle. The last-minute claustrophobia that made me leave things behind in hopes of discovering something else. Fuck all gurus on earth and advice and conclusions. I put my boots on with considerable pain and began dragging any dead logs I could find down the hill, trimming the dry branches with the hatchet. I was so angry my vision seemed rimmed with red and I took off my shirt which had become soaked with exertion. I filled the hole in about an hour, gunned the car as if I were on a drag strip and crashed over the pile, nearly losing control. There was an ugly clunking sound as I drove on, either a wheel bearing or the universal joint. I had hated cars all my life; a friend and I had dismantled a '47 Plymouth years before at sixty miles an hour while drunk. We were working as carpenters at the time and we flailed away with hammers at the windows and dashboard and when we got to his place shot out the tires with a pistol.

I checked the speedometer. I figured it was about thirty more miles to the main road and mid-afternoon. I would reach Ishpeming in time to buy a clean shirt and pants. The hotel catered mostly to mining engineers or those who had business with Cleveland Cliffs. The ore had finally become low grade but someone had discovered the taconite process so the town was booming again. I once noted the resemblance between Ishpeming and Houghton and English mining towns: even the people had the same denuded, milky-eyed look of those who spend a third of their life underground. Part of the reason there are so many strikes is that miners reach a point occasionally when it's no longer possible to continue the life of a mole. Calumet-Hecla had closed a copper mine after a two-year strike. The mine filled with water and the lives of thousands became virtually dead.

I slowed down again to cross a rut and thought I saw some tracks in the reddish sand. I took the Murie book from my pack but they belonged to a coyote. I was still generally angry and it occurred to me as I finally drove out on the main road that I felt none of my usual fears. A cautionary feeling. Fuck the dark, cars, electricity, fire, police, Chicago, Agnew, universities, pain, death, Marine mentality. Even the earth as a rotting tomato, death by implosion, slow rot at the core. I turned on the radio and caught the end of a Creedence Clearwater Revival hit. Strutting music. Who can put on his grandpa's boots? Or is this again the cowboy stupidity that brought us to where we were? I stopped at a gas station and made a phone call for reservations. My first words to another human in a full week were "Fillerup check the oil."

—Why don't we get married?
    —Because you're a whore.
    —I'll stop being a whore.
    —You can't.
    —I'll get a job or money and we'll go to Mexico.
    —I don't want to go to Mexico and we don't have a car.
    I only wanted a 500-cc. Triumph. I had three dollars and they cost eight hundred. I turned in the bed and looked

into her eyes which as usual in these discussions were twin pools of hazel tears. Hazel eyes are rare.

—I don't want a job and I'll never have one.

—I don't think you love me.

—Right.

I got up and drank a cup of lukewarm coffee. Total mess everywhere—the remains of a party and stale smoke sticking to the skin. I went out into the ozone air and walked over to Fifth. Servants entering apartment houses for the day's work. I looked across the street at the Metropolitan and at the third step where I had sat so often with Laurie, and out into the park beyond. Not a square inch without a cigarette butt. We made love against Cleopatra's needle and against benches and fences and on the grass, behind rocks, against trees. Once we almost tripped over a faggot daisy chain over near Central Park West. Ho hum. I walked down to the East Side Terminal and caught a bus for La Guardia. Forty-eight hours to find that I'm in the wrong place at the wrong time for the wrong reasons again. I was stunned with boredom and slept all the way to Detroit, the most wretched of our cities. Then a flight to Lansing with some apparent legislators who looked even more bored. It was March when everyone is bored and wants to emerge from a cold muddy hole and shed a skin. My last exploratory trip. On the phone Laurie's mother wouldn't give me her address with a nasal Bronxian "Haven't you done enough harm." No, of course not. Ill return as a five-star Wac and then you'll be sorry. Mrs. Menopause. Mothers protecting twenty-year-old daughters with daily litmus tests to see what they've been up to. I got into my car and drove home,

picked up my gear in total silence and headed north. Then
turned back south when I saw how much snow there was.
I slept for three months before making another move.

Standing before a full-length mirror in the bathroom with
new chinos and a Hawaiian style short-sleeved shirt, a three-
dollar special on the shirt. In the mirror I saw the same me
with a bit more tan and windburn and perhaps ten pounds
lighter; a characterless slack jaw and the left eye bobbing
off on its own sightless adventures. Five grand minimum
for a cornea transplant. I wanted to be in San Francisco
with a necklace on, fucking a starlet with a hash pipe still
smoldering in an ashtray. Dopey dipadick. You can't take
everything at once, Brad. Settle on your poison. I got a bad
table in the corner in the dining room, reserved for criminal
types and less than stylish fishermen; in fact the same table
I had two years before. I held up a forefinger and a waitress
approached.
    — Planked whitefish and a rare T-bone.
    — Both?
    — Yes.
    — At once?
    — And a triple bourbon with water and no ice.
    — Appetizer?
    — No.
    I drank the bourbon with three long swallows. Oh what
incredible, easeful warmth. Up with whiskey. Within a few
moments I got what my druggie friends call a "rush," a slight
dizzying hollow vacuum in the brain pan. Feet numbing. I

ate the fish first and with haste in great gobbling chunks, then loitered over the T-bone. Rare enough for a change and coolish in the center, I picked up the bone and chewed on it to the disgust of Mr. and Mrs. America at the next table. Mom's birthday or an anniversary I bet. Get her away from that old hot stove for an evening and let her put on the Easter dress and hat. I stood and loosened an uncontrollable, resounding belch that echoed back at me from the far end of the dining room. Many stares and I salute with slight embarrassment. Sorry folks. Now for a walk and buy all the magazines and newspapers available in this company town and tour the bars.

Life, Time, Newsweek, Sports Illustrated, Playboy, Cavalier, Adam. I passed over *Outdoor Life, Sports Afield* and *Fortune.* Wish they had some clam magazines. I forgot what one looked like. Three bars so desolate and crumby it was hard to finish a drink and Finnish accents sing-songy, stumbling in the air. I returned to the inn and the bar on its first floor with its beautiful gleaming murals of trout fishing, and mining machinery. I was greeted with an affable "Hello sport" from the young bartender.

— Double Beam with water and no ice.

— Catching many?

— Only small ones.

We lapsed into an involved conversation about U.P. rivers and several other men entered it too. All the names, so beautiful and round to the tongue: Black, Firesteel, Salmon, Huron, Yellow Dog, Sturgeon, Baltimore, Ontonagon, Two Hearted, Escanaba, Big Cedar, Fox, Whitefish, Driggs, Manistique, Tahquamenon. I told a moderate, polite number

of lies and they returned equally specious tales of fishing.
Very friendly buying of rounds until I felt my brain was
numb enough for sleep. Into the room dumping the sack
of magazines on the bed and a single nightcap swig from a
fresh pint for the drive tomorrow. I thumbed through the
magazines from pictures to news to sports to air-brushed tits
and jokes that weren't funny. Another drink. I didn't want to
be here. Where is my musty tent—over the bulldozer seat.
And where is my mind and why won't it die now. Fantasy
of British Columbia and packing in for three months with a
.44 Colt Magnum in case of feisty grizzlies. Take the coast
boat to Bella Coola and set out to the east, guideless, with
pack rod and dried food. A hermit. Five pounds of tobacco,
Bugler, and Zig-Zag papers but no grass or whiskey. Meet
Indian girl and ficky-fick. Prick dead. Or get back with wife
and forget a decade, written off as they say, a bad time was
had by all. I want twenty years ago and milking cows in
the evening before dinner, pitch the silage in trough before
stanchions. Oats for horses with the hay. Alfalfa too thick
to walk through now. How long has it been since I've been
home where no one lives now anyway?

An average hangover breakfast with too many glasses
of ice water. I asked for ham and eggs and potatoes and a
double bloody mary.

—The bar's closed.

—May I see the manager?

—He isn't here.

—The assistant manager?

I got the desk clerk who went downstairs and made
the drink. I tipped him a buck and leaned back in my chair.

Two men at the far end of the dining room reading their separate *Wall Street Journals* and so far from New York. They glanced at me with evident distaste when I entered and I gave them a quick finger but they were back at their papers and didn't catch it.

I made the Mackinaw Bridge in record time driving at eighty in my old car and finishing the pint in the first hour. Nice buzz now. Hello woods and water and hello bridge. I crossed it with averted eyes — I'm terribly afraid of bridges especially the Verrazano Narrows and the Mackinaw. Too long. Somehow the Bay Bridge and the Golden Gate seem sturdier. Maybe I'll move to Frisco and take dope but I need seasons and the alternating rain and fog depress me. I reached Grayling by dinnertime and detoured to pass the house I was born in but was disgusted with the way the merchants had attempted to turn the town into an "alpine village" by putting false-front shingled mansard roofs on their stores. Holy shit upon birthplace but I felt nothing and continued south after buying another pint.

My father placed me on the bank near a black hole in the bend of the river and I was told not to move. It was scarcely daylight and I stayed in the same place until later afternoon when he returned with a creel full of trout. But I had a half dozen trout and a few suckers which he threw down the bank for the blackbirds to eat. We drove back to the cottage from Luther to Bristol to Tustin to Leroy to the lake and ate the fish. Two parents and five children in a small cabin shingled with asbestos. We slept for a while then near midnight got up again to start bass season which began at twelve. I rowed around the lake and he cast hundreds of times with his favorite plug which was a jointed minnow. He caught four and I caught one. We ate them for breakfast with eggs and potatoes. I slept with my brother under the bare beams of the loft and the heat traveled up to us as did mosquitoes and the smell of wood smoke. And often rain beating madly on the roof a foot above my head and when it stopped, more rain blown off the tree branches in gusts. I never thought at the time of the people I was connected with—the family below me and the brother in bed. Or the ceaseless droning gatherings involving my mother's relatives or my father's relatives or the large yearly gathering of Mennonites we were connected to through my father. Related to hundreds of people with an old photo of Lincoln and in the background an ancestor smiling through an elaborate beard. And when my father died I stopped being connected to any of them, without effort except for an occasional funeral. I couldn't bear the way his mother, my grandmother, had an enlarged photo of him on the wall with old college photos surrounding it and sprigs of dried flowers and newspaper clippings. Some shrine she looked at until she died. I think families based on kinship are disappearing—slowly to be sure but they are still disappearing.

Cadillac, after Mancelona and Kalkaska, then Leroy and Ashton where I turned left on a gravel road for a quick detour to the lake. But I stopped after a few miles. It was over ten years since I had been there and I decided against seeing it again.

Three blue herons were always in a particular giant fir across
the lake. Two readily identifiable loons, male and female, a
limited number of large snapping turtles which were nearly
familiar enough to be named. And the first few years after
the war a family of bobcats back in the woods with their own
particular music, a high snarling shriek. Perhaps it meant I
love you in bobcat language. I made a U-turn nearly getting
stuck in the ditch. The second pint was beginning to do its
splendid work. Then I became sensible again and threw it
out the window into the ditch though it was half full. It was
evening and I wanted to sleep. I parked in a farm lane and
curled up in the back seat in my sleeping bag. If I want to be
nothing it's my business. Absolutely nothing to which I may
add something later but at the moment nothing. Wish I had
some boiled pig hocks with bread and butter and hot mustard.
Tentative: maybe I've had enough to drink like the apparent
though mythic number of Chinese orgasms. My father and
I had built a dormer on the house, an extra bedroom and a
garage with a screened-in porch and patio. Took over a month,
and then I stood on the roof we had built and decided to go
to New York City. We sat in the yellow kitchen at the yellow
kitchen table.

    — Why do you want to go to New York?
    — Because I don't want to stay here.
    — You've been there once.
    — I want to try it again.
    — Where will you work?
    — I don't know. I have ninety dollars.

    Then I went upstairs and packed the carton. A few
clothes that were ill fitting. My typewriter which he had

bought for twenty dollars two years before. And five or six
books—my Scholfield Reference Bible, Rimbaud, Dostoevsky's *The Possessed, The Portable Faulkner,* Mann's *Death in
Venice* and *Ulysses.* Exactly. I got some clothesline rope in the
basement and bound up the carton. My father was sitting
at the kitchen table.

—You can have my suitcase.

—I can't get a typewriter into the suitcase. Besides
you need it.

—I wish I had some money to give you.

—I don't need any.

We sat at the table and I drank a can of beer. We talked
about the addition to the house we had built during his
vacation. Then he got up and took a bottle of whiskey out
of the broom closet and we each had a few shots. He went
into the bedroom and got two of his ties and knotted them
for me. I wedged them under the lid of my carton.

In the morning my mother and brothers and sisters
wept because I was going away, except for my older brother
who was in the navy and stationed at Guantanamo Bay, and
my father drove me down to the bus station.

—You're always welcome at home.

I awoke in the middle of the night in the back seat with
a very dry mouth and a measure of self-disgust. I started
the car and turned on the radio to find out the time. Only
eleven. The Everly Brothers sang "Love Is Strange." Yes it
is providing you can manage it. I drove back through Reed
City and had coffee at a cafe where twenty-five years before

I had eaten cereal in the dark before going trout fishing. I
was the envy of others in the first grade because I got to tag
along like a dog on fishing trips. Buckhorn Creek and only
a few small ones. Quickly past the old house and the violet
glade near the row of huge willows. Nothing is haunted
and sentiment is a lid I don't need to manage the present.
Repainted linoleum and a pantry. Small hospital behind
which in a woodlot and a pile of cinders my eye was put out
with a broken bottle. Didn't seem to hurt but when I walked
home there were screams. When I was "saved" at the Baptist church I stayed saved for two years and read the Bible
a dozen times—church twice on Sunday and Wednesday
night prayer meeting when people gave testimony to the
matchless grace of Jesus in their day-by-day lives. I spoke to
a group using Paul's Ephesians about putting on the whole
armor of God. Religion enlivens loins—when it's forbidden
even a small peek up the dress means instant hard-on. I wish
you were hot or cold in Laodicea but since you're lukewarm
I'll utterly cast you out. Torpor. Disinherited children. How
true. Milling about the country, the pilgrims of the age who
don't want to be insurance adjusters. You only say no, said
someone, and the whole bloody fucking mess passes you by.
Don't let its slipstream catch you. At the after-hours place
in Lansing the Negro said to me, Don't cross that line and
drew an invisible line with his foot. And I didn't but we got
drunk and forgot about it. Ate big buffalo which is carp.
But I'm not sure of myself like the young are. Pre-*Sputnik*.
Can't manage to stay married. There is a woman out there in
the passing dark I know but doubt it. There never was any
question of co-operating after reading Isaiah and Jeremiah

anyway. I heard there are Jesus freaks now but my mind
is set convexly against the grain so keep out of my room.
A true lapsarian with bugle breath. Horrified by Cain and
Ishmael's mother. How could Abraham be willing to kill his
son? Then I went to Colorado and lost my religion when
she pulled down her Levi's in the abandoned fire tower. At
least ten seconds of pleasure, then again and again. New
discoveries. I pulled into the parking lot of the tavern in
Paris, Michigan, a town of about two hundred. Another
thirst coming upon me.

I slowed down by the fish hatchery. Despite night I should
make them open it up at gunpoint and let me see the two
sturgeons and all the huge brown and rainbow trout they
use for breeding. Who said the predator husbands his prey?
We didn't or said so because they weren't. I quit art history
in disgust when I learned the temples hadn't been white
but were garishly painted. Diana's red spangles and blue
hounds. Years later I liked the idea. In an alley in New
York the only time I sniffed cocaine I walked through a
metal fire door into a room where in a far corner a man held
a baby and seeing me, dropped it. The baby was yellow
and I think a fake because its hollow head broke open on
the floor. When I looked back up the man was gone and
when I looked down the baby was gone. I was sure then
that I hadn't seen anything but I turned around and the
door wasn't there, then farther around and the room had
disappeared. I clenched my fist but didn't have any and
my teeth wouldn't click either. I wasn't any longer. Bad

stuff, cocaine, and what is the American urge so stupidly put over and over: "I'll try anything once." The man who lived behind us had his ears flooded with gas in 1918 and never heard again but tended the largest raspberry patch in town. Across from his house in a meadow there was oil-drilling equipment and a steam engine you could climb into and lean against the boiler holes. Shot an arrow into the air and it came down sticking into my sister's head which was to be macerated fifteen years later. At the fish hatchery my uncle had been caught trying to pull a trout with hook and line up his pantleg in broad daylight. But the fish was too large and flopped madly and wetly around his cuff as he tried to run from the conservation officer, dragging the fish by his ankle. Poaching as always. Shining deer. Running into a grocery store with an oil truck. My dad tipped over a beer truck and spent a day cleaning up the mess at the main intersection in town. And he told me he once got drunk and crawled under another beer truck in the parking lot to go to sleep. Said somebody drove the truck away and the tire tracks missed his head by not more than three inches. Says the song "Everybody wants to go to heaven but nobody wants to die." Ho. The tavern was empty except for one table of men playing euchre at the end of the bar. I had a double and bought some cigarettes, recognizing the bartender from years before. Might be a third cousin. We talked for a while and then played three games of pool and he won two. The house "stick" knowing even the slightest imperfections of the table, which cushions were dead, and where a ball would roll falsely because the table wasn't flawlessly level. I left at closing time with

no sense of being juiced. I couldn't seem to get the whiskey
past my Adam's apple so I drank several ginger ales.

Two years after I had seen Barbara for the last time I had
a note forwarded with a "Just to let you know I'm married now and we have a son." Husband named Paul and
the same apartment. Then I heard through a friend that
Laurie was married. And my Worcester girl was married.
And my wretched high school cheerleader sweetheart with
her candy heart and sissbooombahs. Hands above the waist
mister. There is something peculiar in the institution that
makes talking about its problems bathetic. All the average griefs of the mating process. Smoke gets in your eyes.
And the whole "our song" bit as if that were the end of the
organic process. Cottage with myrtled lawn and cones of
mauve wisteria. I've been an attendant in several divorces
and it always resembles the kennel master or the veterinarian
examining the puke or shit to see what's making the dogs
sick. A thirty-three-foot tapeworm with sapphire eyes of
course. All those people colliding and sticking for wordless
reasons. The GNP people. I am one and over and above
the average simplicities of love monogamy usually involves
retreat and cowardice. Necessary. To be sure. Sirens and
lotuses strewn. A mechanistic coil which has taken place,
we're told, in only the last one-thousandth of human life of
earth. Must carbon-date marriage, rain, homesickness, the
hearth. Better to run around the tent three times and start
over in the dark with no street lights, factories or bungalows.
A Spanish cavalier. Strange how you can't say anything to

most people without their assuming you mean it didactically as law. Thus I express a seven-word sentence about the Bill of Rights and a man turns from a bar stool and says, "You Abbie Hoffman commies ought to go to Russia." I offered obscenely to kick in his fat face. I'm talking about my own particular, harmless sort of freedom. I don't want anyone to adopt my mannerisms, or opinions. If I had those instincts I'd run for office. My interests are anachronistic — fishing, forests, alcohol, food, art, in that order. Kropotkin is fine but Nechayev is too programmatic. I don't think I'm meant to be part of anything or to raise my hand and ask a question.

I backtracked as far as the road that led past the house. No one had lived there since 1938 but it was still standing with a yard full of weeds, and glass from the broken windows, fallen eaves-troughs among the burdocks. A neighbor farmed the land desultorily but let most of it return to fern, sumac, canary grass. I turned off the car lights and sat in the total darkness listening to the engine ticking as it cooled and the crickets through the window. Something dank and sweet in the air, cattails and wild clover from the marsh across the road. And someone had taken in hay. My dad had been born in the house. I wanted the impact of this to sink in but nothing happened; further back in time his great-grandfather had homesteaded here after the Civil War but this meant nothing — I didn't remember the man's name. I didn't know my mothers ancestors either; if I ever went to Urnshaldsvik in the north of Sweden on the coast I might find out. But it isn't the sort of journey I'm liable to take. A towhead comes over to escape the draft thirty years after another walked north exhausted from war. They settle finally thirty or so miles from one another, not knowing one another, and years later I am begot by their accidental conjunction. A lumberjack's son marries a farmer's daughter after meeting her at a dance in a roadhouse along the Muskegon River. Still nothing stirs; it would if I had a journal of their individual voyages, a topographical map of the clipper's route or a photo of a man walking. Where did he stop in Kentucky and Ohio each day? What did he eat and drink and what were his thoughts; and with the other, were there storms in the North Atlantic and what was the character of his fear? A grandfather and great-great-grandfather. Nothing could be expected, nothing in particular had been accomplished. A heritage of sloth and witlessness and poverty. Seemed splendid. A new freedom as when the father dies there is no one left to judge even though he didn't judge before death. An implicit "Do as you will." Generosity and arrogance and strength. In that farmer's house the mongoloid child sat with its forehead against the coolness of the pot-bellied stove. We pumped some cold water and they talked while we sat at a table covered with an oilcloth. A sticky fly strip hanging from a string, coated with trapped houseflies. The child crawled over and leaned its Oriental head against his father's knee and kept on staring at me. The house smelled like cow shit and milk and kerosene, a cream separator in the kitchen. I turned the one at my grandfather's then carried the pails of skimmed milk out to the calves and pigs.

Barely a quarter of a moon. I think of those years 1957 through 1960 as unbearably convulsive but then the years after that seem strangely blank and a few of them have no isolatable events. When books were physical events and capable of overwhelming you for weeks; they entered your breath and you adopted their conversational patterns and thoughts as your own. Tintype Myshkin. The laughter, actually extended hysterical laughter, when the funeral director said that all "cosmetic" efforts had failed and both caskets would have to be closed. Why not? A carcass is a carcass, asshole. A wish now to be in Antwerp in 1643. As our preacher said that Golgotha was in reality Jerusalem's garbage dump and I never went to a garbage dump again without thinking of that sermon, however obtuse and antique it became in my memory. Miscarriages, greenish lamb bones, entrails of goats and perhaps lepers wandering about with their bells tinkling, and the small hill or knoll with the crosses. Who could truly envision the crosses and this was the base of history since then. Someone said the science of what happened only once. You came over in the hold of the ship only once and you died in the hold of the ship only once. A sailor was drunk and gave you salt water by mistake. The squaw slit her baby's throat and then her own to avoid the indignity of capture. Twice in dreams the dead had become birds, one a mourning dove and the other a crow though both with human faces and flew away when I tried to talk to them.

I started the car and turned on the radio again. Three. It would begin to get light in another half hour; I turned on the lights briefly to see the house. The front door was open and I could walk through that black hole if I had any guts but the floors may not be solid and I would fall through to the basement and its dirt floor might give way to yet another,

deeper basement . . . A kerosene lamp at the table with the
wick burning brightly. I was fifteen and they took all my
money playing poker and tripoli. My father and two of his
brothers. A quarrel about who got "into" a girl first twenty
years before. Cheap A & P beer and a fifth of rye. They were
experienced and got my money after I drank too much of
the beer and then a single shot of rye sent me puking out
into the snow which they thought was very funny. I went
up to the loft and in the morning tried to avoid going hunting by saying I was sick. More laughter: Get up it's only a
hangover. God it is cold. And when we left I was the only
one without a deer. I missed three running shots.

    Whippoorwill now. Always thought them eerie. Only
snow haunts—if I were here in winter when it was below
zero and the snow was a bluish white drifting across the yard
into the open door and broken windows. Old newspapers
in one of the upstairs bedrooms will reveal that nothing has
changed except the entire world and at the speed of light.
I was at the other place the day after the barn blew down
and my grandfather was already salvaging lumber to build a
garage. He was straddling the ridge beam and we all asked
him to please get off the roof because he was eighty-five and
senile. He wouldn't come down so we went into the house
and had a nervous lunch while he tore off roof boards from
his precarious height. An aunt reported the progress of her
father from the window with her mouth full of food. He built
a garage against the back of the house, out of plumb and tilted
crazily and leaky. Then he drove into it too fast one day and
wedged the car hopelessly against the side. He died two years
later after walking home twelve miles in the middle of the

night in his hospital nightdress. Buried him in a small country cemetery next to his daughter Charlotte who died from the flu during World War One. Many graves added now. I thought stupidly that when everyone I know is dead there will be no more cause for grief. Up the road in the schoolhouse there were Communist Party meetings during the Depression.

A little light in the east now and I got out of the car and stretched, wishing I hadn't thrown away my bottle. Like burying the cigarettes that morning. Willing to shed this old skin and add a new one within hours. Exhausted from volatility. I want something more final but doubt I'll get it barring dying. I walked from the cottage to a farm to pick up a sack of groceries the farmer's wife bought for us in Ashton and on the way back I took a shortcut through the woods. It was very hot so when I reached a favorite clearing I picked a milkweed pod and sat down and broke it open; glaucous milk and sticky with light fluffy down on the inside and a nest of dark brown seeds. Then the breeze changed and there was a stench in the air and I walked over to the far edge of the clearing toward a mound of fur: a deer with eyes gone and insects in the sockets and grizzled muzzle from age, a cavity torn open in the stomach probably by a fox and in the cavity an incredibly thick pile of white maggots working at the meat. I remembered that in the grocery sack there was a can of lighter fluid for my father. I knelt and ripped and dug the dry grass away and took out the can of fluid from between the hamburger and milk and squirted its contents all over the maggots and the flies who bred them and then touched a match to the whole mess and backed away. A horrible stink from the burning which didn't last long. I walked back over to the carcass and already live maggots were working up through the scorched surface of the dead ones. When I got back I told my mother that the woman must have forgotten the lighter fluid. Odd to remember something for the first time—no particular hate for the maggots but a curiosity about burning them.

I lit a cigarette and had a fit of coughing which left my throat raw and dry. There was more light in the air now, smeared and pearlish. A cat crossed the road behind me. Ground mist was floating across the road and around my waist from the marsh, past the car and through the weeds around the house, one slender flume entering the door. I lit another cigarette and wondered why I was standing before an empty house at dawn as if I expected my father to appear at the door in his cavalry breeches from college inviting me in for coffee. He wouldn't recognize me as his son because of course he wasn't married yet and I'd already be ten years older than he. His own father would be up getting ready for the rural mail route he got after the timber gave out. He would tell my dad to take off those goddamn silly breeches and to cultivate the corn on the front forty. I would follow my father to the barn where he would spend a half hour harnessing the horses. Then while we were talking he would lean against the fencepost and tell me he would be glad to get back to college because farm work was boring. I agreed—it was hard and the pay was low. Then he would hitch up the cultivator and walk off with the horses and I would say pleasant talking to you and walk back out to my car.

Someone drove past on the road and beeped at me. I waved. Another early riser. I got back into the car and drove off back toward Reed City.

In the spring of 1960 I went back to New York City for want of any place else to go — I had gone generally berserk in three consecutive Februaries and had grown to expect it. I had found two girls to love back home and when I thought of them they seemed to resist each other's presence on earth with perfect balance. And the duplicity had settled in a sweet contradictory syrup in my brain so I chose the alternative of leaving them both. I walked from Penn Station down to East Eleventh Street and stayed overnight with an old friend, a brilliant homosexual who taught design at Cooper Union. We had had many quarrels and discussions about his sexual tastes — he was terribly handsome and I thought if I were that handsome I would have only the finest of women. Even on a purely physical level men offered one less possibility, a missing orifice. But he claimed he had known he was homosexual at thirteen and began having "affairs" at that tender age when most young men were still jacking off over Miss April.

When I arrived he and two friends, a lover and a young French girl who was living with them, were getting ready to go out for dinner. They dragged a mattress out of the closet and made up a bed for me on the kitchen floor and left me alone with no invitation to join them. Probably going to a freak orgy. I snooped around with a tumbler of vermouth in hand. Nothing but vermouth and gin in the cupboard.

While looking through some books I found a manila envelope of photos, Polaroid photos of naked men. There must have been a hundred of them and the background in the pictures was easily recognizable as the apartment I was standing in. I immediately envied this rapacious sexuality. A uniform set of silly grins, some with organs erect, others at limp rest. My goodness. If I started at that moment and devoted all my time to it, years would be needed for that many conquests. I drank the whole bottle of vermouth and went into the bathroom and looked in the mirror. I'm not handsome—maybe a few grand worth of plastic surgery. Tsk. Then I went back to the photos and mused about all the extant cock myths. None of them were particularly large when erect. I looked out the window feeling moderately juiced and high average. Using it not owning it, that's important. For years now all over the world people are doing it to each other, gland in gland. In caves and in mountain top chalets in Switzerland; fifteen minutes before death by stroke old Mr. Piggy Businessman is banging away and squealing. Give my love to a perfect rose.

I overcame my aversion to gin by mixing it with some bitters and fruit punch. When I finished the half bottle of gin I washed up and prepared for my humble bed on the kitchen floor. Another peek at the photos and I lapsed into uncontrolled giggling. There must be more to do on earth than wag our humble tools at other girls and boys. I thought of all the times when deep in romance I had gazed at a girl with heat, all asmarm with lust and bleary-brained. Goodrich rubber love. Launch with an ooga ooga and perhaps the mind on a movie star. Was it good indeed? Cornstarch with water for your thoughts.

I heard them enter after I slept a few hours but pretended I was asleep. There was talk about having a nightcap and I spied the lover in his nifty clothes putting on a record. Bartók's *Miraculous Mandarin*. Then my friend said, "That bitch finished everything in the house." I closed my eyes as tightly as possible sensing shoes near me. Poor wanderer has drink and suffers abuse. With only cheese and celery in the refrigerator for dinner. Worn out celery at that. They pattered through both sides of the record and I waited to hear something bad said about me whereupon I intended to jump up and tell them to fuck off but they only talked about their dinner host. And what part did the French girl play in their dark pursuits and may I watch. Farm boy molested by three-some, one toothsome. Can't tell what these dirty savages are up to behind my back — maybe she'll look at the pictures and attack my sleeping body. No luck. I slept before the mandarin struck home.

Mumbling in the room, coffee perking and teeth being brushed. I opened my eyes and stared up into the bare ass of the French girl who was leaning over the sink. But then my friend entered from the bedroom and glanced at me and told her that her ass was being started at by a gin pig. She tripped out of the room and I got up, yawned, and asked him why he had to ruin my small pleasures. He only laughed. We had coffee and I said I would replace the gin. He wondered how long I was going to stay and I said I was going home in the afternoon. He told me I would never be an artist if I stayed in the brutal Midwest. We all had a pleasant breakfast together — the lover had gone out to a bakery for croissants. I told the girl she had a beautiful ass but they shrugged in unison and looked at the Tiffany lamp above the table. A conspiracy against me. Cinch I couldn't work into their combination nohow as farmers say. Then I said that oddly enough her ass resembled those owned by American girls and that you couldn't tell by looking at it that she lived on snails and the Marshall Plan. This statement elicited an "Oh lordy" and a shush from my friend. She was embarrassed and I felt that I had forever lost my place in the art world.

I stopped at the fish hatchery again but got out this time and walked around the cement-wall-enclosed ponds and watched the huge trout slide along beneath the surface, gliding slowly, effortlessly with slight strokes of their tails. Someone shouted "hey" at me and I turned—a green-suited man told me officiously that it was six and the hatchery didn't open until eight. I introduced myself and I saw his face brighten up. He told me that he went to grade school with my father; we went into the hatchery building and looked at the tanks of minnows most of which were rainbows. They're a pleasant fish to catch but don't compare with brown trout for intelligence. We went into a back room where there was a coffeepot on a hotplate and a card table with a lunch bucket on it and some chairs. We sat and talked and he said that everyone was sorry about the accident. Fucking cars. The world's not fit to live in. Fucking war and politicians. Seven years since the accident. Yes. What do you do? Not much. Oh. Well back to work, you know.

I drove south again toward Big Rapids and turned east on impulse toward the other farm. May as well say hello to my grandmother who was eighty-three and lived alone now.

An old black-top road with many potholes, a few meager-looking farms to each section. I passed a driveway into the woods where a great-uncle had lived as a hermit for fifty years. Drank a lot. Ate animals freshly run over on the road and trapped some, tilled a large garden and canned his food. He was always very jolly at family gatherings and liked to be teased about a near miss with marriage and responsibility that had taken place in 1922. He ate and drank himself into a giggling somnolence when food and drink were available, and then accused the others of cheating at the pinochle games that always followed dinner. Nelse, Olaf, Gustav, Victor, John, all over here by 1910 to escape the draft in Sweden. Tables turned now. Difference in that they don't chew tobacco any more and some of the Populist spirit is missing. And crazy gaiety about life. No three-day polka parties with tubs of herring and barrels of beer. I turned into the driveway with a terrible pull of homesickness in my chest. A shabby small brown-shingled farmhouse and are the cattle skulls still out there at the edge of the pond? I hope she's up but then she has been getting up at dawn all her life. The barn wasn't there but the granary and the remains of the pigpen and the chicken coop were. I turned and she was looking at me out the kitchen window. I went in and she fixed me breakfast and we talked slowly about the living and the dead. Her ancient blue liquid eyes and Norse accent. The house still the same except in 1956 my father had installed inside plumbing and there was no longer a wood stove in the kitchen. They had later rejected the gift of a TV set—too late in life to start something new. Some relatives had thought them thankless. I went upstairs and looked at some of the

Seton and James Oliver Curwood books and then an entire shelf of Zane Grey novels. I opened a Swedish Bible and wished that I knew the language. Christ in Odin's language. In the attic I looked out at the granary and then at my feet saw the heavy brass spittoon my grandfather used and in the corner there were two steamer trunks that had carried belongings to America seventy years before. Never a cash income over a thousand a year. I went back downstairs and out through the barnyard to the granary. In the corner on a pile of old shelled corn was the harness for the two Belgian horses my grandfather once used, never having raised the price of a tractor. I dragged the harness back and threw it in the car—might bring it back to useless life with saddle soap. I said goodbye to her. We never kissed. Perhaps she had kissed me as a child.